"Do you v
or not, Mr. Jennings?"

"No . . . I didn't mean that . . . I mean do you want me to be your designer?" Jade stammered.

Trask slammed his mug down before answering. "I don't *want* you to work here," he said brusquely. "But it seems I have no other choice. I find myself questioning your motives, Miss Han. Quite frankly, I can't afford you using my company to thumb your nose at a chauvinistic fiancé—or 'intended,' as I think your family called him."

Jade felt the anger start in her toes and claw its way up her cheekbones until she virtually saw red. "This may come as a shock to you, Mr. Jennings," she said through clenched teeth, "but I spent the last four years learning how to design floats, *not* studying to be a wife. And listening to you, I'd say Mikki Chan doesn't have a corner on chauvinism, either. Not that my personal life is any of your business!"

Roz Denny has lived all over the United States, including the Southwest, so vividly described in her first Harlequin Romance, *Red Hot Pepper*. She's currently living in the Seattle area, where her second book, *Romantic Notions*, was set. *The Cinderella Coach* is the result of time spent in California. And Roz has many more story ideas—and locales—to draw on!

Books by Roz Denny

HARLEQUIN ROMANCE
3032—RED HOT PEPPER
3122—ROMANTIC NOTIONS

THE CINDERELLA COACH

Roz Denny

Harlequin Books

TORONTO • NEW YORK • LONDON
AMSTERDAM • PARIS • SYDNEY • HAMBURG
STOCKHOLM • ATHENS • TOKYO • MILAN

ISBN 0-373-03169-6

Harlequin Romance first edition January 1992

My thanks to Rick Chapman and his staff
at Festival Artists for providing crew bios and
background material on float building.
And to The Sons of Italy,
whose float looked better (I hope) as a result of
my first efforts as a volunteer.

CHAPTER ONE

WEDGED INSIDE THE BELLY of a thirty-foot green-and-purple dragon, Jade Han heard the back door of her Beverly Hills home slam. The crash resounded through the patio—the dragon's temporary home—and the screen wheezed in the asthmatic way it only did when her best friend Mei Li Ming came to visit.

Jade chuckled to herself. She'd never understood how a person as demure as Mei Li could wreak such havoc with a door. But she didn't have time to ponder that now, because she needed to determine why this beast she'd engineered for tonight's Chinese New Year festival had suddenly stopped billowing smoke from his colorful nostrils.

"Jade?" Her friend's hesitant query filtered through the layers of papier-mâché blocking her from Jade's sight.

"In here!" Jade cringed as her words echoed loudly along the inside of the dragon's tail. "Aha," she muttered, "a bad chip in the circuit board." She raised her voice again to call out, "Give me a minute, Mei Li. I just need to replace this computer piece that controls the smoke."

"No rush," came the reply. "My father is inside talking with your grandparents. I'll sit out here and play with Wrinks."

Jade could hear the excited yip of her Shar-Pei pup—whom she'd christened Wrinkles, because of the folds upon folds of loose short-haired skin.

Each sound was magnified inside the dragon. Jade heard Mei Li plunk herself down in a patio chair and chatter to the pup. "You are the homeliest dog. You're so homely, you're cute," she crooned.

Jade wriggled out of the confining space, her long golden legs emerging first. Encased in ragged cutoffs, they dangled almost a foot off the ground.

Mei Li, in a delicately feminine dress as usual, expressed dismay. "Jade, I can't believe you're running around like this at ten in the morning! Look at you—you're only half-dressed. No wonder your grandparents call you a hoyden."

Jade dropped to the ground, landing gracefully on her feet. She stooped to give the puppy a quick pat before she set down her circuit tester and case full of tools. Straightening, she made a face at her friend. "It's seventy-seven degrees out here and hotter inside that framework. You try wearing a dress." She loosened the clasp at the back of her head and shook out her long dark hair, then caught it up again into a neat figure eight. "Let's not argue, Mei Li. If your father's here to haul this beast away, I'd better check out the thing's electronics one more time."

Opening a side panel, she reached in and flipped a switch. The dragon came instantly, impressively to life. His head swung slowly back and forth, his tail rose, and one large, long-lashed eye winked. Smoke spewed from each nostril.

Mei Li clapped her hands with glee and giggled like a child. But Wrinkles let out a yelp and headed for his doggie door as fast as his stubby little legs would take him.

"It works," Jade said. She turned off the animated dragon and closed the panel. "I just hope he lasts through tonight's parade."

"You're so clever, Jade." The younger woman's words reflected honest admiration. "All these computerized gizmos just boggle my mind." She shrugged comically, then lowered her voice to ask, "Are your grandparents any happier about your plans to make a career of designing floats now that you've graduated?"

"No." Jade's brows drew together in a frown. But before she could expand on that, the back door opened and Mei Li's father stepped out, along with Jade's elderly grandparents.

"The mailman said this letter is for you, Jade." Her grandmother's precisely enunciated Chinese didn't hide her anxiety. Her hands shook as she passed Jade an official-looking envelope.

Jade smiled lovingly, wanting to ease the old woman's fears. She knew her grandmother remembered a time in mainland China when official documents meant trouble.

Recognizing the logo in the left-hand corner, Jade almost choked on her smile. If the envelope contained what she hoped, her grandparents probably *would* consider it trouble.

Mei Li touched her arm. "What is it Jade? Bad news?"

As if to delay the moment of truth, Jade held the letter gingerly, staring at it with worried eyes. "It's from a special committee for the Tournament of Roses," she whispered. "I entered a contest they sponsored—to design a float—a conveyance for the next Rose Queen."

"Well, open it," Mei Li squealed.

Catching some of her friend's excitement, Jade tore into the envelope. She scanned the enclosed pages quickly, then let out an unladylike whoop. Grabbing Mei Li's hands, she twirled and whirled around the patio. "I won! I won!" The letter held the answer she'd prayed for every night since she'd sent off her entry. Longer even, if one counted the ten years she'd dreamed of designing real tournament floats. A dream shared by her parents and one that since their deaths, had given her life purpose and focus. Still, when Jade caught sight of her grandparents' stern faces, she tempered her excitement; Mei Li did the same.

"Grandmother...Grandfather..." Jade approached them almost shyly. "Winning this means so much to me. Professor Duval, from college, urged me to enter. Please try to see this from my perspective. I've worked hard, and winning is a great honor. It means my design will be used in the next Rose Parade. And I'm guaranteed an apprenticeship under a master float-builder. According to this, Fantasy Floats has been selected to construct my design. I remember Professor Duval saying they're one of the best. This may be the chance of a lifetime!" She hugged the letter to her breast and did another little pirouette. Not even for the sake of her grandparents could she suppress her delight.

Mei Li's father pursed his lips. "Perhaps your grandparents question the suitability of such a vocation for a young woman, Jade."

"Hmph," grumbled Jade's grandmother. Her grandfather added his admonitions in Wu, a Cantonese dialect, and the language he used when he was displeased. "You will forget this nonsense, child, now that I have made other plans for you. Plans I had intended to reveal tonight at the festival. Good news befitting the beginning of a new lunar year." He paced the length of the patio, carefully skirting the cheerfully whimsical dragon. "Telling you now will give you time to let the committee down gently."

"Tell me what, Grandfather?" Jade demanded impatiently. Her Cantonese wasn't nearly as proficient as his. She had long preferred drawing to studying language. Jade recognized that part of her impatience came as a result of a constant inner turmoil—the turmoil of having one foot in each of two cultures. It wasn't easy to contain the bubbling exuberance of her American half around her late father's parents. Because she loved them, she held her tongue and waited for a blending of her two hearts into the more sedate framework of her Chinese self.

"I have selected you a husband, my Jade."

Silence stretched. A muscle in Jade's jaw jumped. This was by far the most outrageous announcement Grandfather Han had ever made.

Mei Li sucked in a quick breath and Mr. Ming began a discreet inspection of the dragon. The letter from the committee fluttered from Jade's hand. Wrinks, who'd waddled back onto the patio, sniffed it suspiciously, keeping a wary eye on his mistress.

"The young man comes from an honorable Chinese family—the grandson of my good friend Wo Chan." Grandfather spoke matter-of-factly, apparently unaware that his declaration had shocked her. "It is fortuitous, Jade, that young Chan arrived in California on business only this week. He has come to Hollywood from Hong Kong to perform the ancient martial art of wing chun for television." The old man beamed like one complacent with the importance of his news.

"Mikki Chan!" Mei Li shook Jade's arm. Her voice rose excitedly. "It has to be *the* Mikki Chan," she exclaimed.

Jade blinked away her shock and focused on Mei Li. Pulling out of her friend's grip, she slumped against the dragon. "I can't—not me! I'm not nearly ready to think of marriage. Tell them I'm not, Mei Li . . ." Her words trailed off as she remembered that her friend had been promised to Roger Cho since birth. When Mei Li continued to babble, Jade hissed in her ear, "Who is he, this Mikki Chan?"

Grandmother Han returned, having slipped away unnoticed. She handed Jade a postcard showing a handsome young man wearing a snow-white tunic bound by a wide black belt. His straight black hair was pushed off his forehead, secured by a narrow band. There was a certain arrogance in his stance, and the name Mikki Chan had been slashed across his legs in the sort of bold scrawl a Hollywood star might use to sign an autograph. Jade's heart sank. Everyone on the patio calmly awaited her approval. Yet for one of the few times in her life, she was speechless.

"It's him," whispered Mei Li in awe. "He's famous! For goodness' sake, Jade, don't you know? He's the idol of the Far East. I've read in magazines that he has a legion of beautiful women in Hong Kong—a different one every week." Raptly, the younger woman stared at the photo, carefully outlining the man's chin with the tip of one manicured finger.

"Bully for him!" Jade snapped, falling into her preferred English slang. "Am I suppose to be overjoyed at the prospect of becoming one of a legion?" Looking up, she chanced to catch her grandmother's look of worry. Jade passed the picture back, and smiled weakly at the tiny woman. Not for the world would she intentionally hurt her grandparents. They were the only family she had left. Rather than refuse outright, she ventured diplomatically in her best Chinese, "This Mikki Chan probably won't want me, either, Grandmother. You remember how Harold Yee refused to escort me to the senior prom, because I was taller."

Grandmother Han scanned the photo. "This union between you and Mikki Chan will do much toward reversing imperfections brought on by Han men having a penchant for foreign women. Maybe your children won't be so tall or have such strange-colored eyes."

Shaken, Jade took her time retrieving the fallen letter. She rather liked some of her unusual features. Her gray eyes, for instance. Secretly she'd always wanted blue, the color of her golden-haired mother's eyes. But gray suited her darker coloring; both her parents had agreed. And she'd never considered her father's love for her mother a "penchant."

Grandfather Han stepped forward. "In a few months you will be twenty-three, Jade, and you will come into a considerable fortune set aside in trust by my son. Many young men will seek you out. For some, their only interest will be your money. It is better to have your future arranged before that happens.''

Sadly, Jade recalled some who'd fawned over her when her parents had died. A few hangers-on thought she had inherited money then. Understandably, perhaps, because her mother was Alyssa Moore, a noted actress, and her father was David Han, a world-renowned cityscape artist.

The rose logo on the letterhead dimmed as tears stung her eyes. She felt pressured—compelled to please her grandparents. They'd been her comfort through some painful years. Yet the idea of marrying a stranger left her despairing and heavyhearted. Her father would have teased that her yin and yang were at odds. Jade brightened. It helped to recall the easy way her father had bridged both cultures.

"Grandfather, I see no reason to rush into marriage. I mean, I've only just finished college. This apprenticeship is just for one season. Think how much it would have pleased my father.'' If there was any way around her grandfather, it was to mention his beloved son.

The old man's lined and weathered features softened. "You have truly been blessed with his artistic talent, my child,'' he agreed, "but consider this good-luck dragon your last contribution. Now Mr. Ming needs our help transporting it to tonight's festival.'' As he opened the side gate with a gnarled hand, he casually added one final bit of wisdom. "Mere mortals cannot hurry *shujing,* my granddaughter. What is to be will be, when the time is right.''

Jade shot Mei Li a worried frown. *Shujing*—a time for living in perfect harmony. She nibbled her lower lip and pondered the Chinese logic behind the term. Her traditional grandparents' idea of harmony was quite different from that of her liberal parents. Nothing in her life had been truly harmonious since their deaths.

Jade stole a moment to reread her letter. Fantasy Floats was a power in the industry. So, if her professor was correct, was the company's owner, Master Builder T. Stratton Jennings. The very thought of working with him for a season brought her a feeling of harmony that Mikki Chan's picture had not. Maybe in this one instance Grandfather was mistaken. Maybe for Jade harmony required boldly reaching out to take this challenge.

WHILE JADE HAN debated the essence of harmony, a few miles away in Pasadena the owner of Fantasy Floats was out behind his company warehouse playing a vigorous game of basketball with his crew. Trask Stratton Jennings, or T.J. as he was known to friends, had just returned from an unsatisfactory meeting with his bankers. And if that wasn't bad enough, in his office sat a letter stating his company had been awarded a bid for a Tournament of Roses special project. A bid he didn't even know Hank had placed. Under normal circumstances he might have welcomed the honor—if his designer hadn't wiped out skiing Mammoth and been benched, so to speak, for the entire season. Poor old Hank had suffered not only fractured ribs and a broken wrist but also severely torn tendons in both knees. Hospitalization, followed by months of therapy, could put him out from now, mid-February, to September, maybe October. Or, worst-case scenario, this time next year.

As it was, Trask's call to the committee chairman had been downright galling. The chair, a man with some highfalutin name, said it was too late to withdraw his bid because the winner had already been notified.

Driving the ball hard toward the basket, Trask grunted, reflecting grimly that bankers and heads of committees bearing lofty names and lofty titles didn't give a damn about his sudden run of bad luck. Not that titles or names impressed him, anyway. His own was a combination of surnames—Trask, Stratton and Jennings—bestowed upon him by three overworked yet empathetic nurses at the children's home where he'd been left abandoned.

For the third time in as many minutes Trask missed the basket and the ball was easily picked off the backboard by an opponent, a full-time crew member who sent it whispering through the net above his head.

"Nice shot, buddy." Dan Jones, the company's floral and technical director swiped a congratulatory punch at the rival. "Did you see that shot, T.J.? That's called basketball. You know, the game I thought we were playing."

Trask scowled, scooped up the ball and gave two quick bounces with his right hand. Then he feinted left before tossing the ball in the opposite direction to where red-haired Greg Sanders, his bean-pole structural engineer, should have been waiting to receive it. Again his shot was neatly intercepted.

"Damn it, T.J., I've never known you to just hand them a game." Sanders hooked the ball into his thin waist, looping his elbow over the curve. "What's wrong with you?"

Chest heaving, Trask stalked to the edge of the court and picked up a dark blue T-shirt from the top of a pile. He mopped his brow, then his neck and casually rubbed his sweating chest, ruffling the golden hair. He scanned the players, who were like brothers to him, and arched an eyebrow at the hint of challenge in Greg's voice. A challenge quickly dropped as Trask glared at him, one strong hand resting loosely on his lean hip above low-riding jeans.

"What's the matter, boss?" Dan Jones took a concerned step closer, shading his eyes with one hand. "You worried about Hank's accident or about losing a couple of our old sponsors? I know we're in a temporary bind, but this year's theme, 'Castles, Kings and Legendary Queens,' is a cinch. We've got eight solid contracts going in and all of us have seen worse starts. How about we loosen up and play ball?"

"We should *all* be worried about Hank." Trask squinted into the sun and closed one eye as he said it. "The doc says he won't be back for months—maybe the whole season."

One of the men behind him uttered an oath. "If only it was Hank's leg instead of his right wrist, then he'd still be able to sketch once he got out of the hospital. Have you thought of hiring someone for the season, boss?"

With an offhand shrug, Trask hid his frustration.

"While we're on the subject of problems," Greg Sanders broke in, "Nell mentioned our cash flow. She said the price for flowers doubled since last year and now you're having trouble getting a loan to tide us over. Won't that rich banker's widow—Cynthia what's-her-name—won't she spot you a loan?"

Trask threw a punch toward Greg, which he neatly avoided. "Cynthia's an old friend, Greg. She's not really a banker. Definitely not *my* banker."

"Yeah," piped up Dan, "maybe her interest rates are too high. She probably wants T.J.'s body."

Greg Sanders clutched his heart and groaned. "I should need a loan so badly. Tell her mine's available."

The crew began poking fun at their youngest member. Trask's grin faded. He could have told them he wasn't half as concerned about anyone wanting his body as he was over having a new apprentice dumped in his lap when money was already tight. But he hadn't worked two jobs all those years in order to buy the company from Max only to lose it now. Even if he had to put in twenty-four hours a day, he wasn't giving up.

Without knowing it, Dan Jones cut right to the heart of T.J.'s irritation. "Say, boss, I heard through the grapevine that the Queen's Committee awarded their pet project this week. Hank told me he'd bid on it. Do you know who got the contract for that fancy chariot they want for the Rose Queen? Grapevine says the money's sweet. The way Hank sounded, all they want is a Cinderella coach."

Trask kicked the toe of a well-worn sneaker along a pock-marked ridge of asphalt. "Seems like Hank should have told me he bid on that damned project. And you're forgetting we're shorthanded. How can we take on something new with our designer down for the count? Did you approve this, Joe?" He asked his general foreman.

Joe Forrester nodded. "Hank wanted to surprise you. If that baby was signed, sealed and delivered to us, I'd personally go out and hire Cinderella's fairy godmother to help build the darned thing."

Greg Sanders snatched the shirt away from Trask, tossed it back on the heap and offered his opinion. "Piece of cake, dude. Joe might need a fairy godmother, but the rest of us could build a thing like that blindfolded. Obviously we didn't get the project, so whaddaya say we quit flappin' our gums and play ball?"

Trask caved in at Greg's antics. "We did get it, you goof-offs," he shouted. "Though I can't say much for your grape-vine. The catch is...the contract isn't all we're getting." He snorted in disgust. "The committee's great project comes complete with its own Beverly Hills designer."

"Well, there you go, T.J. A designer. Our problem's solved."

Trask scowled at his foreman. "You can bet that some lamebrained executive attached to PR handed out the prize in the interests of good old publicity—not designer talent. The kid we're getting has a box-office name. Any of you guys old enough to remember an actress from a few years back by the name of Alyssa Moore?"

Several crew members nodded.

"What's that got to do with anything, T.J.?" Dan Jones asked. "Alyssa Moore was married to a famous artist and they both died in South America. A plane crash, wasn't it?"

"Then it's even worse," Trask groaned. "The press is going to turn this into a damn sideshow. Not to mention that they've probably stuck us with a spoiled Hollywood brat whose only claim to design is wearing Calvin jeans."

"Maybe we should talk to Hank about the kid's winning entry before you count him out," cautioned their foreman. "We may just be getting an ace."

T.J. threw up his hands. "If you want to stick your necks out, go right ahead. I'll even kick in a bonus for the man who ends up high points today—provided he doesn't let this stuck-up brat get any closer to me than a country mile. Deal?"

"Oh, sure," his crew chorused in unison as Trask grabbed the ball and cut in under the basket.

"You always turn in high points, Jennings," Joe Forrester complained. "We might as well quit now. And close as we all work together, just how do you suggest we keep a designer out of your hair?"

Dan Jones muttered, "Maybe easier than you think, guys. The big T's not up to par today. Judging by some of those baskets he missed, his eyesight must be going."

Everyone laughed, and for a time play resumed hot and heavy. Now and again someone speculated on the bonus.

"Throw in a night on the town with Cynthia," Sanders joked, "and I'll try harder."

"No dice, Greg." T.J. missed another shot as he ribbed the younger man. "She's too advanced for a youngster like you. But I'll be happy to let you baby-sit our new design engineer."

"Oh, ho! You didn't say our designer was a woman." Greg smirked. "Surely the great Trask Jennings isn't too old to appreciate one." He stole the ball. "Or maybe you're afraid I'll show you up. Here, watch a *youngster* sink this one!"

Sanders lofted the ball too high and too wide, and Trask lunged for it as it came off the backboard.

At that precise moment, a gleaming black sports car wheeled around the corner of the building, heading much too fast toward court and players.

Crew members were quick to scatter—all except Trask. Already off balance, he flew headlong in the wake of the bouncing basketball—and in a direct collision course with the speeding car.

From behind the wheel of her sporty Mustang coupe, Jade Han glimpsed first a ball, then a man hurtling toward her at breakneck speed. Suddenly a flash of sunlight blinded her and she lost sight of both. Panicked, she slammed a foot on the brake and yanked the wheel hard to the left.

As her car went into a skid, Jade wrinkled her nose against the smell of burning rubber and clamped her teeth, almost standing on the brakes as her car swayed and squealed. With her heart hammering in her throat, she closed her eyes and waited for a thump that never came. In what seemed an eternity, the car slid to a grinding halt.

Swallowing back her dread, Jade opened the door a crack and peeked around it. She could see the man now, blond hair, tanned skin and blue jeans, moving as though in slow motion. Suddenly not more than three feet from her car door, he collapsed facedown and lay still.

Had she hit him? Jade felt the color drain from her face. Easing out a long breath, she braved another look and was greatly relieved to see a group of men converging around him.

Intent on offering help, Jade pushed her door open wider and swung both legs outside the car, only to discover her knees were knocking and her heart wouldn't slow its galloping pace. She didn't dare stand for fear the spiky heels she had on wouldn't support her. What if she *had* bumped him? Until this moment, she hadn't truly believed her car had struck the man. Shuddering, she willed him to stand and checked again. This time, several shades of denim jeans ranging from navy to almost white blocked her view of the victim. Her hand froze on the wheel and her voice lodged in her throat.

Trask, who was hidden behind the wall of denim and dazed from flinging himself flat to the ground, slowly began testing his ability to move. Gingerly, he touched a painful lump forming above his right ear where he'd hit the asphalt. He gave thanks to whatever divine power had intervened to save his life, for in the few short seconds he'd stared at the grill of the oncoming car, his whole life had passed before him. Not all pleasant, either. The sweat ran in rivulets down his neck, from the thick curling hair growing low on his nape. Hair he knew needed cutting. Trask was profoundly grateful he'd still have an opportunity to carry out that simple task.

Scrambling into a half crouch, he felt his knees wobble like unjelled pudding. The crew hovered over him, hands outstretched to help him up, but he waved them away, wanting to stand on his own.

Through a wave of dizziness, Trask noticed legs dangling beneath a polished sports-car door. Very feminine legs, unless he'd died and gone to heaven. Likely he hadn't, though, because the strappy black heels were much too sexy for heaven— at least the heaven they'd taught him about years ago in Sunday school.

Trask lifted a forearm and swept it across his damp brow. Staring at those disembodied legs made him woozier still. Groaning, he struggled to take a deep breath.

"You all right, T.J.?" Greg's voice drifted over him, floating down from somewhere above.

Trask closed his eyes for a moment, hedging his answer. He didn't remember ever feeling this way about ankles before. Cleavage, yes, especially during his lustier youth. Ankles, never! And just how long *had* his crew been clustered around him? Surely no more than a heartbeat. Although from the sounds of it, enough time had passed for them to feel reassured of his well-being.

Brushing aside their helping hands, Trask mustered the strength to stand. "I'm fine," he insisted, although he still swayed unsteadily. What wasn't fine, he decided, was that his crew was now closing off his view of those tantalizing legs.

Nudging Dan aside, Trask made it three full steps toward the sports car. Once there, he grasped the door handle with both hands. Slightly unfocused, his gaze picked up the driver's arrow-slim skirt riding high on thighs that were every bit as enticing as the rest of her legs. Inch by inch his gaze moved higher of its own accord, pausing on an electric-blue blouse opened low enough to show a creamy vee. Another day, the vee might have claimed more of his attention, but at this moment, Trask felt an obsessive need to see a face that would connect these tempting parts and make a whole woman.

Jade Han wrapped and unwrapped nervous fingers around the steering wheel. Though it was a colossal relief to see the man standing, not for one minute did she like him making such a thorough and leisurely assessment of her body. From the moment he loomed over her car door, blocking out the bright sunlight, she'd begun recoiling from a broad expanse of tanned and naked chest. She tried scooting back in the bucket seat, but plush velour just wasn't meant for scooting.

Blinking rapidly, Trask made every effort to keep the woman's almost ethereal image in focus. The fragile oval face framed by a thick fall of midnight hair reminded him of the lovely angel in a De Grazia print hanging above the director's desk at the orphanage. The Arizona artist's work transcended cultures, and his angels weren't the standard pink and white.

Trask Jennings knew that angel intimately. He'd spent untold hours studying her while waiting for the director of the home to hand down punishments following any number of youthful indiscretions. This was the first time he'd successfully conjured her up, though, no matter how desperate his summons. As his eyelids drooped, Trask fought hard to hold the outline of his angel's face in focus.

"Are you all right?" the image suddenly asked him in a smoky voice. "I didn't hit you with my car, did I?"

Those gray eyes, tilted up at the outer corners and looking both exotic and mysterious, made Trask feel that the trouble he was in today must be very bad indeed. Especially if she had, at long last, answered his prayer and come to his rescue.

Behind and all around him, Trask made out whispered voices. Frowning, he tried to block out the noise, but the slightest movement of his eyebrows made his head spin.

Suddenly a heavy hand descended on his shoulder, breaking his concentration. Helplessly he watched her raise her beautiful eyes to look at a man standing behind him. Trask was shaken by a stab of jealousy. He didn't want her looking at another man—not when she belonged to him.

"Angels should fly, not drive," he insisted thickly, once more drawing her attention. "Where are your wings, my angel?" But even as he spoke, his grasp on the car door was slipping. He dropped to his knees, pitched forward and landed, unconscious, with his head in her lap.

Shocked, Jade felt the jolt as he fell. He'd been talking crazy and... Who was he, anyway? Did he work for Fantasy Floats? Was he a future colleague? She frowned. When she'd called to accept the apprenticeship, the secretary had sounded vague, mentioning that Mr. Jennings wasn't certain he'd be able to honor his commitment. Jade knew she could convince him. Except now, there was this... this accident. Feeling the man's body slide, Jade automatically reached out to steady him. Her fingers encountered a trickle of blood. Horrified, she lifted her gaze to the circle of silent faces ringing her car. "Help!" she implored. "Someone! Anyone! He's bleeding."

Tense faces stared back—seeming to blame her. But heavens, didn't she already feel responsible enough? And touching his damp flesh was causing strange though not exactly unpleasant sensations. Sensations she'd never experienced before. It was unsettling to discover them now.

Dan Jones elbowed aside a teammate and dropped down on one knee. "T.J., what in the devil is wrong with you? A few seconds ago you said you were fine. Quit clowning, okay?"

Jade met the speaker eye to eye. "Please, couldn't you just help this poor man? I've come to see Mr. Jennings, owner of Fantasy Floats. Please," she said again.

Finally a husky man, one of the few wearing a shirt, separated himself from the group. "I'm Joe Forrester, foreman for Fantasy Floats." Reaching down, he heaved the man's deadweight from her lap. "At least we can be sure you didn't run the boss down on purpose. This *is* Trask Jennings, lady. Now if you'd follow me to the office, I'll be interested in hearing who in blazes you are."

Jade choked on the lump forming in her throat. Where was her harmony of spirit now? Her first meeting with the owner of Fantasy Floats was not happening at all the way she'd envisioned.

CHAPTER TWO

JADE SMOOTHED A HAND over the creases in her linen skirt—creases made by a man's head. She'd never held a man's head in her lap before. Her grandparents monitored her social life more closely than they did her money, and Jade cringed as she pictured their reaction. Of course, over the years she and Mei Li had managed their fair share of speculation. And though her own fantasies were far bolder than Mei Li's, they'd never discussed men with hairy chests. Or men with eyes the color of golden sherry. Strange how this man's eyes deepened to the shade of tawny port even as he looked her over. Unconsciously, Jade shivered at the memory.

Giving herself a mental shake, she cast a glance after the group and was surprised to see they'd gotten so far ahead of her. Shoulders squared, she took a determined breath and hurried after them.

Once outside the office door, she hesitated. There she heard what sounded like a disagreement, and she could see at a glance that the injured man had regained consciousness. In a loud voice, he was making his recovery known.

"No ambulance, Joe! No doctor! No emergency room, either. I tell you, the car didn't hit me."

Her victim and his foreman were faced off jaw to jaw. Jade could almost see the air between them crackle.

Suddenly a plump, gray-haired woman came into the room, and Fantasy Floats' alleged owner used a more civil tone.

"Oh, thanks, Nell." Accepting a cold pack from her, he flattened it, then settled it above his right ear. Jade winced with him as the icy compress touched his raw wound. She watched the protesting muscles bunch along his suntanned back and felt her own muscles tighten in sympathy. Bracing herself against the doorjamb, Jade realized how unsteady the entire incident had left her.

The woman, Nell, scolded the man with the pack. "You won't get any consolation from me, T.J. You sneak off to play ball like a kid, expecting to get sympathy when you're hurt. Not from me, you don't."

He glared at her. "Tell her, guys! I was going for the ball when this car barreled out of nowhere and I made an all-points landing on the asphalt. After that, even I have to admit my story breaks down."

Jade listened as all the other men tried explaining at once. The noise level inside the small room rose dramatically.

"Whoa!" Grimacing, the injured man held up a hand. "Can't anyone give me the bottom line? Did we get a name for the driver of the Mustang, or find out what she was doing whipping around on my property like it's some kind of race-track?"

Jade shifted uncomfortably as one of the men gestured toward the door, saying he thought she was right behind them. Trask Jennings's low growl did something funny to her insides. The deep timbre of his voice made her stomach tighten like a rope pulled taut.

Fortifying herself with yet another deep breath, Jade prepared her defense. It wouldn't do to let her prospective boss catch her eavesdropping. Though it was a shame, she mused, that she couldn't take a moment more to study him. T. Stratton Jennings had a body any artist could appreciate. He had wide shoulders, with ridges of bronzed muscles coiled tightly beneath, narrowing more tightly still to a finely honed belly. A man of many strengths and few weaknesses, Jade thought, suddenly beleaguered by mounting reservations.

She moved while she still could, casting a long shadow across the room. The men in the circle shifted, opening a direct path between her and the man she'd been observing.

Trask dropped his cold pack in the middle of an open ledger, shooting the older woman an I-told-you-so look. "Well, hello!" Smiling, he levered his body away from the desk. "So you weren't some illusion I conjured up?" Once again Trask felt the pull of the woman's exotic beauty.

Nell sank down into the chair behind her desk and swept the dripping pack from her open ledger. "If the lady came here on business, T.J., I'm surprised she stuck around this long. Unless maybe she's really scouting you fellows for the Lakers."

Trask was used to Nell's needling him about basketball. Playing didn't mix with her idea of the work ethic. Normally he laughed it off, but this time her barb came as a jolt of reality. The woman in the suit wasn't De Grazia's angel and his company was already fraught with problems. He rubbed a thumb distractedly between his brows. "Nell is absolutely right," he said. "If you're looking for someone to build a float, you're wasting your time. We're overbooked as it is."

"Oh?" Jade stepped completely out of the shadows. "That's good news." She smiled. "Business must be booming if you're turning customers away."

Trask sensed a ripple of apprehension running through the room, but his crew remained silent. Stealing a moment, he savored the stranger's subtle scent. Something light and floral wafted toward him on the breeze of the lazily churning office fan. He found it intoxicating and far from cooling.

Indeed, he found her intriguing enough to make him consider adding one more float—if that was what the lady wanted. In any event, he wasn't willing to send her down the street to one of his rivals. "Look," he offered finally, unconsciously rubbing his palm over his bare chest. "You deserve to state your business and I'm not dressed for it. How about letting Nell set you up with an appointment sometime when I'm not so...casual? Perhaps we *could* build one more float." He noticed that his men were now murmuring in low tones behind his back.

Jade lifted her chin. She'd come here with every intention of eating humble pie, but there was something about T. Stratton Jennings that made it impossible to be humble. "I think perhaps you're confused about my reasons for being here, Mr. Jennings." She drew herself up to her full five-foot-eight height. "I'm Jade Han, your new apprentice." *There, how much more confident could she sound?*

For one entire revolution of the fan, no one in the room moved. Jade saw a cool mask drop over Trask Jennings's face, replacing the interest in his eyes with distaste. Now she was the one who felt confused.

Trask put a hand to his head. He was disappointed. He'd imagined himself slaying dragons for this woman. Instead, if past experience was anything to go by, and he thought it was, she was just another rich, spoiled socialite who wasn't worth his effort. "I'm sorry you made the trip... Miss Han, is it? My company's situation has changed since we bid on the Rose Queen project. We need a real designer now—not a trainee."

Jade's temper flared. The man had the venom of a snake and the intelligence of an ox. Pity. He probably had the hide of a rhinoceros, too. To think she'd wasted time worrying that she'd bumped him with her car. Her chin rose a notch higher. "I have recommendations and a portfolio at home," she managed in a civil tone. "Some consider me a *real* designer."

Trask felt more than saw his crew shift uncomfortably, felt their tension—or was it his own? Time to call a halt to this. They'd all be stretched like rubber bands if this haughty woman who looked like a runway model rubbed elbows with them on a daily basis. His lips thinned. "We're not hiring, Miss Han. Period."

"I'm not asking for a job," she said stiffly, "just an apprenticeship as the contest rules promised." She looked to the others as she explained, "I won the contest sponsored by the Queen's Committee."

Nell jumped up and eased her plump body between two of the crew members. "Personally I'd be delighted to see another professional woman on this staff, T.J." She shoved the cold pack into his hand and grinned at Jade. "All too frequently these goons tend to forget that for the better part of a year, I'm a lonely little petunia in an onion patch."

The circle of men guffawed loudly and a couple of the group pretended to play violins. Trask's scowl put a stop to their kidding.

Jade saw her chances slipping. This apprenticeship was her best chance to break into the world of float-building. And without it, she'd have no legitimate reason to put off marriage to Mikki Chan, at least as far as her grandparents were concerned. "Please," she said, remembering Professor Duval had told the class to ask for what they wanted. But then she paused and nibbled at her lower lip. The professor hadn't said beg. And she wouldn't! Not to this man. Not ever. "Fine," she said coldly. "I'll let the committee know of your decision, Mr. Jennings. Perhaps they'll award the contract to another builder." Turning, she swept out, determined he'd never know what it cost her.

Trask felt pain explode behind his eyes. Damn her for looking like a wounded princess and for making him feel like a heel. And damn circumstances for making him need her lousy design. He rubbed two fingers across his forehead and down the bridge of his nose, gritting his teeth to keep from swearing.

"Don't you think you should get her address, boss?" Dan Jones ventured as he casually stuffed his tank top into his beltless jeans. "I mean, in case this temporary insanity you seem to be suffering *is* due to her running you over with her car."

Trask did swear then, before he turned and snatched up his navy T-shirt from Nell's desk. Looping it around his neck, he limped toward the stairwell that led to his private office on the floor above. Did Jade Han's work show the same impossible mix of cool elegance and spontaneous combustion as the artist herself? he wondered. "You want to run the show around here, Jones, let's see the color of your money. Until then, back off!"

At the top of the stairs, Trask thrust open the office door and kicked it shut behind him. Something about Jade Han left him feeling edgy. Like the time he'd been sandwiched bumper to bumper on the Pomona freeway in rush-hour traffic and discovered he'd forgotten to fill the gas tank.

He heard a light tap on the door, and his foreman, Joe Forrester, eased quietly inside without invitation.

Trask yanked off one shoe then the other, and tossed them in a heap in front of a scarred mahogany desk. "I assume you're about to unload on me, too." Resting his hands on his hips, Trask gave his friend a measured look.

Joe spread his hands. "With Hank laid up, we need a design engineer. No one knows that better than you, T.J." The foreman's sandy brows rose fractionally. "So level with me. Since when can't we afford to train someone?"

Trask slid the T-shirt from around his neck, wadded it into an untidy ball and threw it hard against the curved back of a swivel chair. It uncurled and slithered into the seat. "The company's too lean, Joe. I can't take a chance on an unknown designer."

"How lean?" Joe's tone softened.

Turning to stare out the window, Trask massaged his temples. "Without a loan, I won't meet my next payroll."

Joe whistled through his teeth. "How in hell did that happen? Why didn't you say so before? Is it because you endowed that boys' camp for the youth center? Or because you gave all of us a healthy bonus? Damn it, man, if you need help, ask. We'll all tighten our belts for a season."

"Yeah? Well, you guys didn't opt to fund the camp. I did. And it shouldn't cost the crew because those projections ran way over budget. Anyway, that's probably an oversimplification."

"Oh?"

"The reports are just in. We took a beating on flowers this past year. Costs were up two-thirds. It's widespread. Growers aren't giving anyone credit. I called around..." Trask shook his head. "All the foliage people are saying the same. Hell, the thing is ... it's my fault. I should have seen the hike coming. They've had a couple of bad winters in a row."

"Don't be so hard on yourself, T.J. Everyone's stuck with the same deal as far as the flowers go. And we know you're pushing to get the camp completed by Max's birthday. We're behind you one hundred percent in dedicating it to him. Looks to me like we could use the easy money from the coach, though. Now tell me why you just threw it away?"

Trask leaned his forehead against the cool surface of the window and visualized the delicate beauty of Jade Han. "It'd be a rough beginning for a rookie, Joe. You saw her. Did she look to you like she'd make it over the long haul? Pampered rich kid. No stamina, I'd say."

Joe smiled. "She might surprise you. Hillary's the strong one in our family."

A distant look crept into Trask's eyes for a moment when Joe mentioned his family. It wasn't any secret that he envied his friend. He braced his arm against the window ledge, his muscles tight and rigid. Suddenly he relaxed and turned with a rueful grin. "Your wife just might be an exception. She spoils you rotten, you big lummox. But don't you dare tell her I paid her a compliment. I'd lose what little edge I have next time she's begging for my Y chromosomes to even out her dinner parties. By the way," he said dryly, "she still owes me."

"She remembers. You drove such a hard bargain, she refers to you as the Robber Baron." Joe laughed, then glanced at his watch. "Omigosh! Speaking of Hillary, I gotta run. Tonight is her gourmet cooking club and I promised to be home early to baby-sit. You wanna come play uncle? It'd give you a taste of what life is like settling down with a good woman."

"Your ploy won't work, Joe. I'm not hiring the Hollywood kid. She's not in Hillary's category, anyway. Once burned, twice shy, my friend. Women born to money aren't looking to settle down."

"Cynthia has money."

"It's not that way with us. We know too much about each other. Matter of fact, after I shower, I'm heading over there. She mixes a mean martini and knows just how to relax a man."

Joe yanked the door open. "So make it a double, buddy. I predict you're gonna need one to tide you over. I'd say you have a better chance at finding a nudist colony living on an iceberg in the middle of L.A. than you'll have finding another qualified float-design engineer at this late date. But it's your company and your headache...boss!"

Trask felt the reverberations—all of them—as Joe slammed the door. Grabbing a clean shirt, he stalked into the small bathroom adjoining his office. He'd had a bath installed because, more often than not, he spent his nights here once float-building went into full swing. Rubbing a hand over the lump above his ear, Trask also felt the rasp of his five-o'clock shadow and automatically reached for his razor. Cynthia preferred her men neat and tidy. How did Jade Han like hers? he wondered.

Disgusted by the turn of his thoughts, Trask cranked on both faucets. He welcomed the lukewarm spray, letting the water sluice his cares away. He started thinking about all he owed Max Woodard. The man had pulled him off the streets and believed in him when no one else had. Only last week Max's daughter said she was worried about his condition. Trask couldn't delay the camp project much longer—it should be finished by the summer. And if Max's health was failing...
Sometime between the time he began his shower and the time

he toweled dry, he decided to forgo drinks with Cynthia Osborn in favor of taking a drive to Beverly Hills.

Not that he liked the taste of crow, he told himself grudgingly as he buttoned his shirt and headed for his Wagoneer. But he didn't expect one meal of it would kill him, if indeed the lady had talent. What made it palatable was doing it for Max. He wouldn't take a risk like this—on an untried designer—for anyone else. But if he wanted some time and money freed up for the boys' camp, he'd have to accept the coach, Cinderella and all.

In less than an hour, Trask's dusty rig was cruising through the high-rent district of Bel Air. He was genuinely put off by the size of the palatial estates. The opulence seemed almost unforgivable when one considered kids who didn't even have a decent roof over their heads. Trask had all but talked himself into giving up this fool's quest, when he suddenly found himself staring down a long, well-lit drive leading to the Han place.

A low whistle escaped through his teeth. For just a moment, he tried imagining what life might have been like growing up in a mansion like this. Then he caught himself up short. Money didn't guarantee good character or even good manners.

He set the brake, pocketed the keys and slowly climbed from his rig, taking time to study the planes and angles of Jade Han's house. Nowhere did the structure intrude on the California setting, yet one had only to see its stark outline to conjure up images of sampans, rickshaws and majestic pagodas. Places he hadn't known existed until Max helped curb his wild ways and convinced him to work hard and go to college.

With hands thrust loosely in his back pockets, Trask was leisurely surveying twin bronzed lions set to guard carved teak doors, when the left-hand door flew inward and a snarling torpedo of fur catapulted toward his shins.

"Wrinks . . . Wrinkles! What do you think you're doing?"

Even as Trask jumped aside to avoid the animal's sharp teeth, a ripple of pleasure at hearing the woman's sultry, smoky tone curled his toes into the soles of his sneakers. Jade Han's voice sounded exactly as he remembered.

"You! What are you doing lurking around out here?" Though icy at the outset, her words lost some of their chilliness as she grappled with the pup. A pup with a determined grip on Trask's pant leg. "Now, there's a good doggie," she crooned to the animal, after managing to disengage his teeth from the denim. Suddenly she paused, staring up at her uninvited guest. "You weren't hurt, after all, were you?"

"Dog?" Trask's gaze slid from Jade's pale face down to what resembled a carelessly dropped fur stole. "A dog," he repeated tonelessly, a little bemused. "Are you sure of that? You could've fooled me." He flashed a quick grin. "No, I'm not hurt. Better check your pooch, though."

His attempt at humor, silly though it was, relaxed the stiff set of her shoulders. And whether she wanted to or not, Jade laughed. "He's a troublesome pup who fancies himself a guard dog. A Chinese Shar-pei. A friend gave him to me for graduation after learning that during the Han reign in China they were considered war dogs. This one's bark is far worse than his bite. But I meant…were you hurt before? Back at your parking lot. Is that why you've come, Mr. Jennings?"

Trask smiled crookedly, bringing a fleeting dimple to one cheek. "Will you accept that my bark may be worse than my bite, too?" He shrugged as she stared at him coolly. "No? Well, then—" he cleared his throat and raised his fingers in the Boy Scout pledge "—what if I say I've come to see a sample of your work? Provided you're still interested in an apprenticeship, of course. And you can skip the 'mister' and call me Trask or T.J. Everyone does."

Oh, wow! Was she ever interested! Jade bit back a relieved smile. Then she remembered how rude he'd been before. It wouldn't hurt to let him cool his heels a little, now that he'd obviously had a change of heart. She stalled. "I was just on my way out, as you can see. Perhaps I'd better call your office for an appointment, as you suggested earlier."

He let his eyes skim the length of her. Vibrant in red silk brocade, Jade Han combined the unfamiliar beauty of the Orient with a very American elegance. Uncertainty stole his bravado. "Let me guess. A date?" Trask settled one shoulder against the doorjamb and tested his theory in a confident male tone. "Wouldn't want to keep the lucky fellow waiting."

Jade moved back to avoid touching him. "Perhaps you'd like to take my portfolio with you."

"Ah! A woman of mystery, I see." He was slightly miffed that she hadn't risen to his bait. Straightening, he got back to business. "I'd prefer you explain your work, if you want the job. But if you're too busy with a social life, I suppose we could talk tomorrow." *Now why have I offered to waste another of my free days?* Trask frowned down at the pup who'd plopped at his feet and begun chewing contentedly on one of his shoe-laces.

"Bad dog." Jade scolded Wrinks, at the same time training a wary eye on the man. "Shame on you." Bending, she pulled the shoelace away, hoping she looked more at ease than she felt. Jennings had a knack for disarming her. "You don't want to wait while I get my drawings, then?"

"Yes. Get them. I've got all night. You're the one with the date. I'll just make friends with . . . Fu-dog, here."

"Shar-Pei," she corrected sharply. "There is no such thing as a Fu-dog. And I don't have a date."

"Oh?" Trask grinned without knowing why. He knelt quickly, pretending to inspect the soft rolls of fur. Turning the mutt over on his back, Trask tickled his stomach. Wrinks wiggled ecstatically. "Must have been my mistake," Trask murmured, keeping his tone even. "I could've sworn you said you were going out."

"This is the festival of the Lunar New Year," she informed him, not liking his smug smile. "I'm meeting my grandparents and some friends in Chinatown. You know—for the parade, food and fireworks."

"I don't know." He glanced up. "What kind of a parade is it? Do they have floats?"

Jade chuckled at how fast the mention of floats got his interest. Tossing her head, she tangled one hand in the dark hair that tumbled freely about her shoulders. "Not floats on a grand scale as you know them. This parade is all very lighthearted and full of fantasy. Symbolic for the adults and terribly exciting and scary for the children. When I was little, my parents purposely waited here at the house until after dark. They'd let the suspense build in me until I was ready to pop. My father would string out the magic as long as he could. He'd park blocks away and make us walk clear to the end of the parade route." She paused, shrugging. "But I'm boring you." The reminiscence faded from her eyes. "You know how parents are about family customs and traditions."

Something tensed inside him. After almost thirty years, he supposed he should have gone through all the phases of acceptance. But even now it hurt when someone brought up fond childhood memories and he had none to compare. Even in his many foster homes, he'd always felt like an outsider during family celebrations. "You were going to give me your portfolio," he said curtly. "And I believe you were in a hurry."

His sudden reversal puzzled Jade. "Oh, that's all right." She waved his concern away. "My float is at the tail end of the parade. Step inside, won't you, while I dig out my designs? Maybe you'd like to see the mock-up I've done of the coach that won the contest."

"You have a float in tonight's parade?"

She nodded, leading the way into a room filled with lacquered black furniture splashed here and there with the bright red of cushions—her grandparents' choice of decor and not a room where she normally brought her friends. Jade preferred the sun room or other airy spaces with less-ornate furnishings. Her mock-up was in this room because Grandfather had wanted to see for himself what all the fuss was about. What he really wanted to do was judge this thing that was upsetting his plans.

Before she could direct him, Trask caught sight of the replica. "Perfect," he murmured, lightly running a finger over the intricate framework. Forgotten were Jade's remarks about her family and his own uncomfortable response. He was Trask Jennings, float-builder, now. "It's truly a Cinderella coach. Exactly what one of my crew said we needed." He met her eyes. "Cinderella, as in fairy tale. Do you know fairy tales?" He lifted a brow and smiled.

Jade cleared her throat and toyed with the triple strand of pearls circling her neck. "I know fairy tales. My mother read them in English and my father paraphrased them in Chinese." She smiled for a moment, remembering. "But here," she mumbled, abruptly thrusting a thick folder at him. "You wanted to see my other designs. None are quite as elegant as the coach, I'm afraid."

Accepting the folder, Trask quickly scanned her many sketches. Each showed promise. Excellent for a young designer. As he sorted through them, a clock in another part of the house chimed the hour.

"Omigosh," Jade exclaimed. "I didn't realize it was so late. Take the folder if you'd like. I really must run. I don't want my grandparents to worry—they deserve to enjoy the festivities to the fullest. For them," she added softly, "the Chinese New Year is a time when old scores are settled and everything is put right with friends and relatives. I don't follow tradition much myself, except when it makes them happy."

Trask followed her to the front door. "I just realized who your father was when I saw the pictures of the L.A. skyline hanging on your walls. These drawings show you have much of your father's eye for sharp lines and striking contrasts. I studied David Han's work in design class in college, yet the committee chairman only mentioned your mother."

Jade couldn't find her voice. She hadn't expected him to know *anything* about her personal life. Most people were beginning to forget her connection with both the artist and the actress. Somehow it left her feeling exposed, vulnerable. In the end, she stammered out something unintelligible and there was a moment's awkward silence. "I'm sorry to rush off this way," she said, digging through her purse for car keys. "Oh, no," she yelped as Wrinks appeared from nowhere and dashed between them. "Don't let him out."

Lunging, Trask grabbed the wriggling ball of fur. "I wouldn't dream of turning that war dog loose near my truck tires, the way he chews things." He laughed as he handed her the dog and stepped outside. "Go now. We'll talk soon," he promised. She shut and locked the door and hurried to her car.

Trask stood and watched her. He tried to fit Jade Han back into his initial assessment—a spoiled rich kid. She turned and waved then, and treated him to a high-voltage smile that set fires along his nerve endings. But one smile didn't change facts. She was born to a life of privilege and wealth. Much like a woman from his past—a woman he wanted to forget.

He revved up the Wagoneer with every intention of heading home. Instead, he followed Jade to Chinatown, remaining a discreet distance behind her car. His excuse, when he questioned his own action, was that he needed to get a firsthand look at her engineering techniques. Except there was no denying his disappointment when he lost her in heavy traffic. Her small car melted into the darkness, leaving emptiness where anticipation had crept in. But he could still check out her float—the last one in the parade, she'd said.

The first thing to catch Trask's eye when he neared the celebration was the color. Lanterns, clothing, balloons and neon lights, all warm and bright. A city within a city, radiating a rainbow of color. And he was drawn to the great number of extended families whose members ranged from wrinkled octogenarians to smooth-skinned babes in the arms of young parents. Everyone seemed happy—laughing, smiling and talking all at once, the way Trask imagined a big family reunion might be....

Shrugging off a twinge of sadness, he quickly scanned the area for Jade. When he didn't find her, he felt a distinct hollowness in his midsection. But then, he'd skipped eating lunch and dinner, he remembered, as he skirted the cordoned-off street and blended with the throng of merrymakers.

After that, he had no time to speculate. The parade had begun wending slowly past. Thoroughly caught up in a display of graceful dancers, he felt his tension begin to fade. As spellbound as the children, Trask marveled at the young dancers' abilities to dip and sway. Each twirled two multicolored fans forming elaborate pinwheels against the night sky. Musicians followed, using tiny cymbals to play a melody both haunting and delicate. For a moment Trask longed for someone to share his evening with. But as always, he refused to acknowledge the longing.

Entry after entry passed, and Trask was drawn deeper into the magic of the parade. Funny floats and gifted performers beckoned to the child in him more than to the professional float-builder. A mouse in a teacup rolled by and he found himself laughing with a young family standing next to him, though they spoke no English and he understood not a word of Chinese. Long before he was ready to see the parade end, the last float, a whimsical dragon, rumbled past. Suddenly it hit him. This was the float he'd come to inspect.

He quickly threaded his way through the crowd, trying for another look at the cleverly animated dragon. Quite by chance, he saw the great beast's creator standing directly across the street. Fascinated by her expressive face, he watched Jade Han worry her lower lip. Forgetting why he'd come, Trask studied her and let the float go by. How could she possibly be concerned? Didn't she hear the delighted laughter of the children?

Darting around a motorcycle policeman, Trask hurried to Jade's side. Bending, he whispered in her ear, "Forget the adults. Watch the kids. Look. They love him."

"Yes, they do, don't they?" She gave a dreamy sigh. "Parades are so much more exciting when you have children around, don't you think?"

"I do," he answered with feeling, realizing—not for the first time—that he'd like one or two of his own. But what did he know about parenting? Only what he'd learned through his volunteer work with troubled boys.

Jade turned with a start. "What are you doing here, Mr. Jennings?" Then before she could make out what he said, loud bursts of fireworks exploded overhead. Mei Li slipped in beside her, grabbed her arm and pointed skyward. A starburst of red broke above them, then green and blue in rapid succession, each seeming to hover near the moon before falling back to earth in a shower of brilliance. The crowd stopped milling long enough to watch.

Jade, Mei Li and Trask were hemmed in together by revelers for the duration of the display, though the noise and the smoke precluded any introductions.

Funny, Jade thought as she stood shoulder to shoulder beside T. Stratton Jennings—he almost had the feel of a comfortable old friend. But perhaps it was only this situation, where neither had anything to prove. She enjoyed watching an unexpected glimpse of the boy in him.

Then, as rapidly as it had begun, the noise died away. Several seconds of silence passed before the crowd broke, scattering in all directions. Mei Li nudged Jade and quirked one delicate brow toward the tall stranger.

"Oh! Sorry, Mei Li." Jade flushed. "I'd like you to meet the owner of Fantasy Floats, T. Stratton Jennings."

"Call me Trask," he invited, folding Mei Li's small hand into his larger one. Though for some reason, he rather fancied hearing Jade call him T. Stratton. Unless she thought it made him sound more grandiloquent.

Jade barely had time to register his scowl. Her grandparents and Mei Li's parents arrived, accompanied by newcomer Mikki Chan. After receiving her own rather effusive introduction to Mikki in Chinese, Jade did her duty in return, using a mix of English and Cantonese to introduce Trask. "He came to see my dragon float, Grandfather." She was careful to explain his presence to her curious family. "Mr. Jennings's company is the one selected to construct my design."

Trask smiled warmly. He had learned over the years to be comfortable in almost any situation. Therefore, he was jolted when five sets of eyes dismantled him down to the last button on his shirt.

When at last Mr. Han spoke it was in formal, almost stilted English and with something of a bite to his tone. "Does he play mah-jongg?"

Jade arched a brow and turned to Trask. He shrugged and shook his head. "Sorry, but no," he told her.

"Bah!" The old man's one-word response sounded like an expletive.

"Grandfather is always looking for new mah-jongg players," Jade explained patiently. "He rarely loses," she added with pride, "yet he always claims winning is pure luck."

Trask sidestepped a crush of young women who appeared out of nowhere. They giggled and tittered behind their hands, in general disrupting everyone. "Uh...I've heard the name mah-jongg. Is it a game?"

"Ancient," supplied Jade. "The men play with painted tiles, rather like dominos. Do you know dominos?"

By now, another group of girls had arrived. They were bolder in their approach, flirting outright with Mikki. Trask stepped aside to give them room as he answered Jade. "I know dominos." His smile widened. "And I recognize other games when I see them, too." He nodded toward the girls. "I don't think I caught who the popular young man is. A relative of yours?"

Jade hesitated. It was Mei Li who answered for her. "He's Mikki Chan, grand master of wing chun." There was a certain reverence in her voice.

"Which translated is?" Trask asked, still amused by the girls.

"The oldest, most disciplined of all martial arts," Jade murmured.

"Oh." Trask's tone was accepting but not necessarily impressed. "I'm familiar with kung fu." He studied Mikki's muscled frame for only a moment. "Well, I won't intrude on your evening any longer. I really came to tell you that I like what I've seen of your work so far. In fact, I may be able to honor that apprenticeship, after all."

Jade made an effort to contain her glee. Even so, Trask could tell she was pleased. By the same token, he realized the elders in her group were not. "So, what do you say?" he prompted, handing her his business card. "When can we meet to discuss this further?"

Mikki Chan broke free of his admirers. Striding over, he looked Trask up and down. Then he turned to Jade's grandfather and said something rapidly in Chinese.

Grandfather Han responded in kind. The others looked discreetly away.

Jade chewed on her lower lip. It was a habit Trask noticed she had when she was anxious. "Is there some problem?" He matched the men's grave expressions. Did they think he would take advantage—maybe steal her work? "If it's a matter of money, I assure you she'll receive a fair amount for her designs."

Mei Li laughed. "Jade does not need money, Mr. Jennings."

"No, I suppose not," he said tightly. "So what is the trouble?"

Jade's family refused to look at him and remained silent. It was Mei Li's father who finally gave him a clue. "Neither Jade's grandparents nor her intended wish her to accept your offer, Mr. Jennings."

"Her intended?" Trask repeated the term bluntly. "Her intended what?"

Mikki stepped forward and placed a hand on Jade's shoulder. Though he was shorter than Trask by almost a foot, his presence was commanding. "Jade's grandparents and my parents have made a match. We are betrothed." His English was flawless.

Trask's stomach took a nosedive. Maybe that earlier knock on the head had done more damage than he'd thought. Normally he wasn't quite so obtuse. He was out of his depth here—involved in something that was obviously a family matter. If anything could make him uncomfortable, it was family dealings. Still, it had never been his style to back away from something he wanted, and at the moment this young woman was his only hope for a designer. Sidestepping Mikki, Trask confronted Jade directly. "I've yet to hear what the lady wants," he murmured.

Jade's face fell. It was customary for her grandfather to handle the bargaining, and her rebellion on that issue was a constant source of conflict. And though she might want this job more than anything she'd ever wanted, her sense of duty to her family was stronger. Honoring her elders, especially in public, had been instilled in her since birth.

For a long moment Jade met and matched T. Stratton's arrogant stare. He *knew* he was putting her on the spot; she was sure of it. Slowly and deliberately, she tore his business card in half. The American part of her might have flung it at him, too, the way she was feeling. Except that the instant she made the first tear, the owner of Fantasy Floats turned on one heel and walked away. "If that means no, Miss Han, you'd better tell the committee." He tossed the words carelessly over one shoulder.

Apparently Mikki was satisfied. He returned calmly to signing autographs and accepting adulation from his adoring fans. Mei Li, too, abandoned Jade. She joined the line waiting for Mikki's attention.

Sighing, Jade decided against littering the street with T. Stratton's business card. Instead she stuffed the pieces deep into her jacket pocket. If the Chinese New Year was indeed a time for clearing debts, she thought dejectedly, how was it that in the space of a few minutes she'd managed to collect a whole slate of new ones?

CHAPTER THREE

JADE CRUSHED the torn business card into a shapeless wad inside her pocket and stared after the broad-shouldered owner of Fantasy Floats. His wasn't the only float firm in Pasadena, she reminded herself, thrusting out her jaw. So what if the committee had selected him to build her design?

Grandmother Han lingered after Mei Li's parents and Grandfather Han had returned to the festivities. Looking somber, the old woman approached Jade. "The tall American upsets your harmony of spirit, my granddaughter. You would be foolish to relent and accept his offer."

Jade wrinkled her nose. "I have no intention of working for anyone who orders rather than asks."

"Good!" Grandmother Han nodded. "Your time will be better spent staying home learning patience and other womanly traits. Mikki Chan is charming, but quite used to adulation, I see."

"Yes..." Jade murmured, half under her breath, as she turned to watch him with a group of lingering fans. She missed her grandmother's intent—that she consider no job at all. Instead, she was studying Mikki Chan's swagger.

As if sensing he was the topic of discussion, Mikki ushered Mei Li toward Jade once he'd signed the last program. "Well, now!" He rubbed his palms together. "I'm starved. Come, Jade, we'll get better acquainted on the way to the food tables."

Jade opened her mouth to protest his high-handedness. Grandmother Han interrupted, addressing Mikki in Chinese.

"The men are expecting you at the mah-jongg tables. I'm sure Jade will be happy to fix a plate and deliver it to you there."

Laughing, Mei Li gave her friend a good-natured poke in the ribs. "Close your mouth, Jade. You'll catch flies."

Jade's teeth closed with a snap. "If Mikki is hungry, let him fill his own plate. I did not go to college to become a waitress."

Mikki threw back his head and laughed. "In Hong Kong I was warned of sharp-tongued Western women. I did not expect it of you, my lotus flower."

"Isn't he romantic, Jade?" Behind her hand, Mei Li giggled. "Ancient lore says the lotus blossom represents purity and perfection, and he's using it as an endearment."

Jade frowned at the sudden change in Mei Li. "That thinking is so conventional."

"Well, convention has its place." Mikki glanced at his watch. "Right now, however, a test of skill awaits me. Perhaps another time, Jade, you and I will discuss husband-wife roles."

Jade took a step forward. "I'd remind you that you are not yet my husband." *Not ever, if I can help it,* she promised herself.

"Next week, my Jade," Mikki stated firmly as though she'd never spoken, "you will come to Hollywood to watch me work. In the evening, we'll go for dinner. I have reservations at a place one of the actors tells me is the 'in' place right now."

Jade felt her back teeth grind together. *So Mikki didn't believe in asking, either. Were there no gentlemen left?*

Grandmother Han broke in. "Have you also arranged for a proper chaperon?"

The question more or less stopped her younger audience cold. Few of Jade's contemporaries followed such stringent courtship rules. Except maybe Mei Li, who had been allowed to see her betrothed only in the presence of others.

Jade almost smiled. Women raised to be obedient, like Grandmother Han, were not in the habit of questioning any man's decision.

"Jade, you wouldn't really consider going out with him alone, anyway, would you?" Mei Li sounded shocked. "I mean, he does have a fearful reputation with women," she stammered, seeing Jade's arched brow.

Mikki puffed out his chest and preened. "I find it exceedingly interesting that it is the shy one who apparently reads the tabloids. Therefore, I say, let her chaperon. Perhaps she'll consent to tell me just how fearful I'm expected to be." Undaunted, he turned to face Jade's grandmother, executing a low, courtly bow. "I trust Miss Ming is proper enough for you?"

"In my day," Grandmother Han said with a snort, "one so young would never have been considered proper. In this uncivilized country of my son's wife, it is difficult to keep any standards." She waved a wrinkled hand. "This is really for Jade's grandfather to decide. I believe he will approve of Mei Li. She is born under the sign of the ram and is therefore wise beyond her years."

Jade rolled her eyes heavenward and threw her hands up in exasperation. "Has anyone thought of asking Mei Li? Do you mind being a party to this insanity?" she whispered. "Remember, I know how you really feel about your forced engagement to Roger."

"The question is, do you mind, Jade?" Mei Li asked anxiously. "I mean, you were born under the sign of the horse, and everyone knows horse people are short-tempered."

Laughing, Jade enfolded the smaller woman in a hug. "Mei Li, you're too much. Consider me duly reprimanded for my wickedly Western tongue. Until I figure a way out of this whole mess, I'd love you for a chaperon."

"Jade Han, you should be counting your blessings at having such a handsome, outgoing suitor." Mei Li took care to keep her voice low as she lauded Mikki.

Jade knew Mei Li was thinking of how difficult she found making small talk with the brilliant but painfully shy Roger Cho.

"So it's agreed then," Mikki said as he urged the small group toward the food tables. "You ladies will be ready when I send a car promptly at two o'clock next Friday? You'll be in for a treat, I promise."

"Modest, too, isn't he?" Jade drawled near Mei Li's ear.

Ignoring Jade, Mei Li clapped her hands and twittered, "Don't worry, Mikki, we'll be ready. We'll be thrilled to watch you."

Mikki left them near the concessions with Mei Li's mother, where talk ran to children, fashion and local gossip. Mei Li joined in enthusiastically, but Jade, finding little of interest, did as she'd always done during traditional family outings. She designed floats in her head.

Throughout the long evening, the men never once looked up from their game of mah-jongg. It was as if, for them, the women had ceased to exist.

Toying with the halves of T. Stratton Jennings's business card, Jade pulled them out, smoothed the crumpled bits and stared at them with a troubled gaze. Tonight, her career dream had been within arm's reach and she had, out of family loyalty, turned that chance down.

Strange, she thought as she dropped the pieces into the trash, that she'd made her choice and should be content. Yet, once again, her yin and yang were poles apart.

FOLLOWING A RESTLESS week of daydreams and discussions—and no word from Trask Jennings—Jade reached a compromise of sorts with her grandparents. She would accept an apprenticeship position for the season—if she could find one. And if Mikki agreed, something Jade wasn't inclined to worry about. She spent Friday morning making calls to several of her résumés' recipients, but all the float-builders already had designers. She considered buying her own company, since her trust fund would soon mature, giving her the means. Although she expected her grandfather to object, she fully intended to handle the investments her father had left. Ever one to be realistic, Jade soon admitted she lacked the management skills to make buying a float company a viable option.

One of the nicer art directors suggested she send résumés to Miami and New Orleans, homes of the Orange Bowl and Mardi Gras parades, respectively. But Jade couldn't bear the thought of leaving California. This was her home.

It didn't help to have Mei Li calling every half hour asking what she planned to wear for the dinner with Mikki Chan. Thoroughly annoyed with Mei Li's childish exuberance, she finally grew cross and said, "I'd go in blue jeans, if it was just me." Now she was feeling guilty because Mei Li had acted crushed and hadn't called since. Jade knew it was unfair to take her bad mood out on Mei Li, who certainly wasn't to blame for this betrothal that had been thrust upon her. If anything, Mei

Li seemed to envy Jade. But of course that wasn't surprising; Mei Li exemplified tradition.

By the time the limo arrived, Jade's spirits were restored and her apology ready. Mei Li had already forgiven her and was also in a jovial mood.

When they arrived at the studio and Mikki had proudly introduced them, Jade set aside her troubles long enough to enjoy his workout. He executed the intricate moves with precision and speed. The young men he was training for the series also seemed impressed. "Wing chun is fascinating, don't you think, Mei Li?" Sinking deeper into one of the director's chairs, Jade whispered behind her hand, "I wonder if Mikki would consent to teach me."

"I should think not!" Mei Li bolted upright and forgot to whisper.

This prim tone of Mei Li's was another thing that sometimes irked her. Although, like Jade, she had been born into the American culture, Mei Li had a stubborn, old-world naïveté concerning anything adventurous. Especially when it concerned proper conduct for a lady. This was not the first disagreement they'd had on the subject. Nor would it be the last, Jade thought resignedly. "Why not?" she persisted, knowing she should let well enough alone. "I read up on it. According to the book I read, wing chun is the perfect martial art for women. It relies on technique more than power, and its strategy is to conceal strength in weakness and weakness in strength. It sounds suitable for women to me. And think of the terrific body you'd have."

"Well, there's nothing wrong with either of our bodies as is and...and it's simply not feminine," stated Mei Li, refusing to budge. "You, Jade Han, should take up something that'd get you out of blue jeans."

Jade tossed her long hair back over one shoulder. "I can look and dress feminine when it's called for, Mei Li. But I'm talking equality between the sexes. Do you want to walk in some man's shadow for the rest of your life?"

"Of course not. But what's wrong with staying home and letting a man take care of you? Sometimes I don't understand you, Jade. You certainly don't need to work. Why press so hard for a career? What about the value of being a wife and mother? Don't you want that?''

Jade made a steeple with her fingers. "I suppose someday I do, Mei Li. With the right man. But I guess I'd like more from marriage than the passivity my grandmother has. I want an equal say in everything, a partnership. Like my parents. And that means choosing my own partner.''

"Your father wasn't typical, Jade. As for me, I'd like a man to take charge. Roger could learn from Mikki, too," she said, pointing to the stage. "Does that look like a man who'll consider a woman his equal?''

Glancing up, Jade saw Mikki Chan, his thoroughly male features set and implacable. She recognized the look as one that said Mikki would master any opponent, man or woman. Strangely depressed, she fell silent and didn't speak again until it was time to meet Mikki and go for dinner.

Mikki's "in" place was on the ocean side of a very exclusive beach town. The minute they entered, Jade knew the people who made it trendy were the phony, ritzy Hollywood crowd. She found it too noisy and smoky.

Twice while they waited, Jade caught herself grimacing at the music—a hard rock beat so loud she could feel the bass through the soles of her shoes. She loved music, but preferred it more subdued. Before she could suggest finding a quieter spot, Mikki gave his name to the hostess and palmed her a bill.

"Nice," Mikki shouted his approval near the ear of the harried woman seating them. Leaning close to Jade, he confided, "I slipped her fifty to get us a place near the band. It's perfect, don't you agree?''

Jade gave a halfhearted smile. She really wanted to enjoy the evening. Her grandparents would be full of questions, and she owed it to them at least to try to hit it off with Mikki. Still, she was awfully glad Mei Li answered him with enthusiasm, so her lack of response wouldn't be missed.

"It's more than nice, Mikki," Mei Li gushed, scanning the room as she accepted the seat he offered. "It's the greatest. As a celebrity, I imagine you get to do this sort of thing all the time.''

Mikki grinned and nodded. "Once or twice a week.''

Jade buried her face behind a menu while trying to imagine what marriage to Mikki Chan would be like on a day-to-day basis. But the screen of her mind went totally blank. She jumped when Mei Li reached behind Mikki and poked her. "What, Mei Li? Sorry, I was daydreaming."

"I didn't say anything yet. I just wanted to ask if that man over there is your friend from the parade."

Jade lowered the menu and squinted, looking past the lights into the shadows. Her heart stepped up a beat for no reason at all and she could feel the heat rising in her cheeks. How, she wondered in dismay, with all the restaurants in Southern California, could T. Stratton Jennings possibly end up at this one?

He wasn't alone, either. Not that a man like him would be, Jade thought contemptuously, as she studied the pretty woman at his side. She wasn't even tall enough to reach his shoulder and when he bent to listen, his sun-bleached hair looked dark next to the woman's sleek, platinum chignon.

"Well," Jade sniffed. She couldn't fault T. Stratton's taste in women. Too bad she couldn't say the same for his companion's taste in men. She raised her menu just high enough to see and not be seen.

"How about a dance?" Mikki nudged Jade. He was drumming his fingers on the table and swaying in time to the beat.

"Not now, Mikki." She brushed his pleas aside. "Could we order? The way they're packing people in here, it may be quite a wait and I'm starved."

"But you do dance?" He paused in the middle of a drum beat, his expression dubious. Reaching over, he moved her menu aside so he could look her in the eye.

Mei Li piped up in a dreamy voice, "I love dancing. Don't you think this sound just sizzles? I mean, that band is the greatest."

Mikki rocked back in his chair, taking another long look at Mei Li. "Well, you're full of surprises, little sparrow. If Jade prefers to read the menu, why don't you and I dance?"

A guilty expression crossed Mei Li's face.

"Please, you two go," insisted Jade. "I'll watch. You know I've never really liked fast dancing, Mei Li." Her voice trailed, as her gaze followed Trask Jennings and his date, who were being shown to a table directly across the dance floor. *Couldn't they have taken him to a cozy dark corner?* Jade groaned aloud in her growing distress.

"Ah, yes. I see who you are watching," Mikki said. "The man who offered you the job. But of course you're not considering it."

Jade found Mikki's remark disturbing and presumptuous. "Whether I accept Mr. Jennings's offer or wait for another, I *will* design floats, Mikki."

"Not after we're married," Mikki's retort was equally firm as he guided the petite Mei Li onto the crowded dance floor. The smile he gave Jade over Mei Li's shoulder was supremely confident.

Forgetting that she was using the menu as a shield, Jade let it fall to the table. Mikki Chan didn't know her well at all if he thought she'd give up her plans. Designing floats was what she'd had her heart set on since she was ten. Her father had arranged with a floral director for her Girl Scout troop to glue foliage on a marvelous monarch butterfly during the frenzied week before the parade, and that was the beginning of her love affair with floats. Jade shot another guarded look across the room. She'd show them all—Grandfather, Mikki, Mei Li and the supercilious T. Stratton Jennings. She *would* design floats, or her name wasn't Jade Han.

Oblivious of the darts Jade aimed his way, Trask was lamenting his error in letting Cynthia talk him into coming to this hellish night spot. Hellish was his description; Cynthia's was something like "charming," if he recalled correctly.

But when she'd telephoned, he'd been at loose ends. He never liked spending Friday nights alone. Now, with his head feeling as though a solo drummer was trapped inside, Trask wished he'd insisted on one of their old haunts. When he discovered the amplifier for the electric guitar nearly touching his chair, he decided it was worth one more try. "How about if we finish our drinks here, then find some place quieter for dinner, hmm? Take pity on me, Cyn. I've had a rough week."

"Nonsense." Cynthia shook her head firmly. "Nathalie Bell has been raving about this place for a month. One drink is hardly enough time to be noticed by the right people. You should thank me for looking after your professional image.

Goodness knows, *you* never give it a thought. People who show up here are featured in all the papers.''

Groaning, Trask let his gaze travel quickly around the smoke-filled room. To notice anyone here, a person would have to have X-ray vision. He hated it when Cynthia tried to hone his rough edges. He understood her need to climb the social ladder, but he'd been cured of the desire long ago.

Leaning into the curve of the chair, Trask contemplated his boredom. Once he'd thought bright lights and late nights symbolized success. But somehow, when he wasn't paying attention, the fast life had lost its appeal. Maybe it wasn't boredom, after all, he mused. Maybe he'd finally quit trying to make up for a lost childhood and was beginning to look for more substance in a relationship. He doubted that Cynthia, who'd married her late husband for money, gave a thought to having sacrificed happiness.

"Look over there, will you!'' Cynthia grabbed Trask's arm and steered his attention to a well-dressed couple at a table opposite them.

"It's the Baroness Sheffield,'' she hissed. "That man she's with is Vale Ross, a big-shot producer. I heard he's made some bad investments lately. She's one of our accounts. Well, well,'' Cynthia murmured, more to herself than to Trask. "I wonder if it's business or pleasure. I hear his rich Italian wife has a temper.''

Not interested in gossip, Trask tuned Cynthia out. His gaze skipped past the couple she was discussing to a dark-haired woman seated alone at the next table. He closed his eyes, then opened them quickly. For a moment, Trask could have sworn the woman resembled Jade Han. But the flash of light had been fleeting and on second glance the table was once again nestled in darkness.

The strobes crisscrossed high overhead. It must have been a fluke, he thought, relaxing. Or more likely a breakdown in his subconscious. After all, she'd been on his mind a lot this past week. He'd visited Hank in the hospital, taking Jade's portfolio. His injured designer had been impressed, more than Trask had wanted. But even with Hank's stamp of approval, he had reservations. Too many times he'd pictured her in the warehouse—and once, fleetingly, in his bed. He scowled. Not only was Jade Han not his type, she was already taken.

Another light flashed over the room, and this time Trask got a clear view. That *was* Jade Han seated at the far table. And the couple just coming off the dance floor was the man and woman who'd been with her at the festivities in Chinatown. Trask struggled to come up with their names. Mickey and Minnie. No, those were mice. The man was Jade's fiancé. Not a mouse at all, but "grand master" of something.

"Trask!" Cynthia exhaled his name in exasperation. "I don't think you've heard one word I've said." She ran a finger over his furrowed brow and down his cheek in a manner designed to bring her his full attention. "Order me a martini, dry, will you, sweetie? I want a word with the baroness. I know it's tacky, but that man who just sat down with them is a rival of our bank's, and I'd like her to know I'm aware of their little meeting."

"I know that guy." Trask squinted. "Ed Davis. He's the banker who turned me down for a loan."

"You didn't tell me you needed a loan!"

Trask shrugged. "You're not my banker, that's why."

"Is it a personal loan or business?" she pressed, ignoring the off-limits tone of his voice.

"Forget it, Cyn. I don't mix business and friendship."

She gave a sultry laugh. "Don't you mean business and pleasure?" She pouted. "At least come with me to meet the baroness. I'll let Davis know you have Fidelity First's vote of confidence. Maybe he'll reconsider your request."

"No!" The word sliced through her laugh and drew a hurt frown. "I've decided I don't need a loan," he fibbed.

Because Cynthia wasn't really a banker, except insofar as her late husband had indulged her desire to dabble, she accepted his explanation and urged him to join the baroness.

"You don't really want to barge in, do you?" Trask's attempt at persuasion failed. "Tell you what," he offered. "See the group at the table next to your baroness?" He indicated Jade.

Cynthia nodded.

"We'll crash their party and you can eavesdrop all you want."

"How do you know them?" she asked suspiciously, straining to see.

"Business." Standing, Trask motioned for the waitress. "We've discovered friends across the room and we'll be joining them. Would you bring the lady a dry martini? I'll take a beer. Whatever you have that's light." Catching Cynthia's hand, he weaved his way through narrow aisles.

"A beer!" Cynthia tugged at his shirtsleeve. "You can't order beer. This place is classy."

"I just did, Cyn." Trask considered the machinations people went through to make an impression wasted effort. Tonight, her airs annoyed him, even though he knew growing up without a family had been even harder on her than on him.

He stopped abruptly. Cynthia ran into his back. Behind him, she sputtered as he calmly greeted the trio at the table. "Miss Han and company. So we meet again."

Jade whirled and her startled movement knocked a fork from the table. Flustered, she bent to retrieve it. Trask did the same. Their fingers met. She pulled back and he smiled silkily.

"My friend knows Baroness Sheffield over there." He indicated the next table. "Sheer coincidence that I noticed you sitting here. I hope you don't mind if we join you." Having raised his voice to be heard above the loud music, Trask suddenly found himself shouting as the song ended.

Cynthia elbowed him sharply. Without Jade's invitation, Trask sat and pulled Cynthia down beside him. "Good of you to agree." He got right to the introductions. "Cynthia Osborn, meet Jade Han and vice versa. Do you mind finishing? I'm afraid I clean forgot your intended's name," he said, training an owlish gaze on Jade's male companion.

Jade felt the sleek blonde take her measure. She wanted to say she did mind. She minded very much. But good manners precluded her sinking to his level. "Mikki Chan and Mei Li Ming." She kept it simple.

The men shook hands. Neither smiled. From where Jade sat, it looked as if each man was testing the mettle of the other with a firm, combative grip. She hoped it hurt both of them. But if the arrogant T. Stratton suffered any pain, Jade noted that Cynthia quickly soothed it. No doubt about it, the blonde was a toucher.

A waitress came to deliver Trask's and Cynthia's drinks. Without consulting Jade or Mei Li, Mikki ordered iced tea for his table.

Jade protested. "Mikki, you didn't ask our preference. I would have liked a glass of white wine."

"Spirits simply confuse the harmony of mind and body, Jade. You, I think, are confused enough already." Mikki spoke to Jade, but his gaze lingered on Trask.

Jade flushed. For some reason, Mikki viewed Jennings as a rival. If that wasn't farfetched, she didn't know what was. Realizing each man hoped to provoke a reaction, she carefully blanked all sign of emotion from her face. "On second thought, I'll just have water," she said, thwarting them both.

Cynthia immediately excused herself from the group. "I see the baroness has gone to the powder room and I'd like a word with her. Don't go away, sweetie. I'll be right back." She patted Trask's arm.

The moment Cynthia left the table, Jade relaxed. Strange that she'd feel threatened by someone she'd just met.

"Is that woman really a baroness?" Mikki asked bluntly.

Shrugging noncommittally, Trask made patterns of rings on the glass-topped table with the bottom of his frosty bottle, then wiped them away with his napkin. "Beats me. Ask Cynthia. Judging from the rock she's wearing, I'd say she has money. In Hollywood, if you have money, you can call yourself anything."

"I see," Mikki said dryly. "You sound irreverent about money, Jennings. Do you have any?"

"Mikki!" Jade gasped, choking on a swallow of water. "You can't ask such personal questions."

Trask laughed and raised his beer in salute. Tilting the chair backward, he decided to satisfy Mikki's blatant curiosity. "I own my business. Some years I eat steak. Some years, hamburger. I get by. How about you, Chan? Does breaking boards with your hands pay well?" He'd remembered what it was Mikki did.

Mikki straightened and looked down his nose. "Wing chun is an art," he said, leaning forward. "And I am a master craftsman. An artiste. I do not 'break boards,' as you say, though it is well within my power."

Trask ran a hand through a shock of hair falling over one eye. Jade's friend was hanging on Mikki's every word like a star-struck teen. Trask shot a glance at Jade, expecting to see the same adoration. He was surprised to find her cheeks flushed and her lashes lowered. Her submission nettled him. In fact, it provoked him enough to say, "Tell me, Mr. Chan, how does an *artiste* like yourself support a wife? Unless, of course, the artiste's wife works."

Glowering, Mikki snapped his fingers and requested a refill of tea. "My wife will have no need to work. Jade's grandparents settled a generous sum on her. A dowry. It is something like insurance. In our culture a handsome dowry guarantees a better match. More pure bloodlines for the Hans' prospective great-grandchildren."

Jade sat up abruptly. "Grandfather didn't mention a dowry."

"We have a similar practice for racehorses," Trask parried.

Jade shot him a dirty look. "Mikki, you must be mistaken," she insisted.

"Not to worry your head, lotus blossom." Mikki patted her hand and Jade gritted her teeth.

"It's not like Mikki needs the money," Mei Li broke in, defending her idol. "In Hong Kong, Mikki is revered as a master of wing chun. Anyway, your grandfather would never discuss a matter like this with you," she chided Jade. "It's just between men."

Mikki leaned complacently back in his chair. "The sparrow is wise. Listen to her, Jade. Dowries are quite simply a matter of tradition."

Jade refused to look at him, staring instead at her hands, held tightly clenched in her lap.

Mei Li smiled. "I'm glad I have a dowry. My mother calls it an investment in my future. An ample dowry is the key to a long and happy marriage."

Trask snorted contemptuously just as Cynthia returned and slid into her chair. Smiling at her absently, he addressed Mei Li's last remark. "Money with high-priced interest, I'd say. Someone always loses—like in a corporate merger."

Cynthia raised her martini glass. "This conversation seems to have picked up since I left." Reaching over, she straightened Trask's collar. "Should I burst their little bubble, sweetie, and tell them it's what happens in the bedroom, not the boardroom, that insures a happy marriage?"

Trask scowled and brushed her hand away. Mei Li's gasp of offended innocence dictated he should apologize for Cynthia. Jade appeared unmoved. Her hands were now calmly folded on the table and her lashes lowered.

"So what's the going rate for good bloodlines?" Trask probed. Granted, the dowry appeared to be news, but Jade's easy acceptance of the whole arranged-marriage philosophy sent an icy chill spiraling down his spine. Were all women with money so cold-blooded? he wondered. How clearly he was reminded of his first real love affair. He'd been in college, and the girl, a snazzy blonde by the name of Kitty Ferris, had a way of making him feel like a king. At least until her daddy discovered he wasn't an offspring of the Eaton Park Jennings. After that, little Kitty cut him cold without a backward glance. And he'd spent years proving himself ever since....

Not long ago he'd run into Kitty at a charity ball. She'd come on strong, fawning over his success since those years he'd lived in foster homes. In truth, he had matured quite enough to find Kitty Ferris-Pilkington-Betts sadly lacking in finesse—even if the old slight still rankled.

Trask stood up sharply and pulled Cynthia into the circle of one arm. She responded by nuzzling against his side like a sleek kitten. Trask caught Jade's look of unconcealed indignation. What right did she have to pass judgment? In her smug world of arranged marriages and family dowries, what did she know of his and Cynthia's struggles as abandoned kids? His lip curled. "We'll leave you three to your stimulating discussion of genealogy. When we dropped by, it wasn't to compare solid-gold diaper pins."

"Oh? Why did you come?" Jade asked bluntly. The part of her that was Chinese disapproved of public displays. But then, she shouldn't be surprised that he'd stage a scene like this. Hadn't he shown himself to be a man of no modesty and large ego?

"Why do I have the feeling you're about to tell me?" Trask muttered.

"I thought maybe you wanted to discuss my apprenticeship," she said, a hopefulness creeping into her voice despite her annoyance with the man.

"It was my impression that you were no longer interested in . . . discussing your apprenticeship." His voice was cold and Jade knew he recalled the decisive—and humiliating?—way she'd torn up his business card.

"I'd like you to reconsider. Please."

There was a pleading in her gray eyes, and Trask felt his edginess return. Something warned him to forget her as a designer once and for all. "I need someone with more experience," he hedged. "I'd like to honor a commitment Hank made, but—" he shrugged and spread his hands "—I have clients to think about. I'm in no position to take a chance on a rookie. No hard feelings, I hope." He put out a hand, which she ignored.

It was Mikki who clasped Trask's hand, grinning broadly. "Then it's settled! Goodbye, Jennings."

"No, it is not settled!" Jade got to her feet. She shook off the warning hand Mei Li laid on her arm. "The committee guaranteed my design would be built. You, Mr. Jennings, accepted their contract."

His lips thinned and his eyes narrowed. "I'll build your damn coach, Miss Han, and you'll get full credit for the design. What I won't do is employ you as an apprentice."

"The contest promised me a season working with a master builder *and* my design in next year's parade. The two came as a package."

Mikki left his chair and gripped Jade's upper arm. "Jade will stay home and learn the duties of a proper wife from her grandmother," he said smoothly.

"Really?" Trask's gaze flicked over Jade. "Are you sure her dowry is big enough to cover so many lessons? I hear some horses never take to a saddle."

"Stop it!" Jade's hands balled into fists. "Do either of you think you could leave off strutting? You're like a couple of peacocks. People are beginning to stare."

"Yes—at you, Jade," Mikki shot back. "Sit down and I'll order. All this fuss over building fanciful toys is disgraceful. If you feel you must have a hobby, take up embroidery. When we return to Hong Kong, I'll have my grandmother teach you.''

Jade flushed, furious with both men. She wasn't a bone to be fought over or a prize to be displayed. She would see the master builder honor his word and she'd see the wing chun master eat his, if it was the last thing she ever did. Snatching up her purse, Jade gave each man an imperious flash of her eyes. "I'll be at your office Monday morning at eight o'clock sharp, Mr. Jennings. If you're building my design, you'll get the designer as promised. And Mikki, designing floats is *not* a hobby. Now if you'll excuse me, I'm going home." Spinning on her heel, she marched away, her head held high.

Trask let his gaze follow her progress to the door. Lord, did Jade Han ever have that queenly air down to a science, he thought appreciatively. But of course she wouldn't show on Monday. Her family would see to that.

"Did I miss something?" Cynthia blinked and looked up at her companion. "I thought you said you weren't hiring her."

Trask gave a hearty chuckle and gently nudged her in the direction Jade had taken. "I guess what it means," he said, loud enough for Mikki to hear, "is that the lady doesn't like embroidery."

CHAPTER FOUR

JADE HAD ALL WEEKEND to regret her impulsive words. Not
only that, she'd committed an unpardonable sin by leaving Mei
Li at the restaurant unchaperoned. Her grandparents commu-
nicated their disapproval by their silence. Their acceptance of
her decision to pursue a float-designing career had been reluctant at best, and now, in the face of Mikki's objections, they
withdrew even that tentative support. They seemed to blame
everything—from her neglect of Mei Li on Friday night to her
stubborn coolness toward Mikki—on winning the Fantasy
Floats apprenticeship. Then, to make matters worse, Mikki
canceled joining them for Sunday dinner, insinuating that it was
to give Jade time to recognize the error of her ways. From the
master builder himself, she heard nothing. Wrinks remained her
only solace.

By Monday morning, Jade's nerves were coiled as tight as a
hairspring. Yet never once, since Friday, had she considered not
showing up at Fantasy Floats. Unless you counted the sinking
feeling that seeped into the pit of her stomach whenever she
thought about her grandparents' unhappiness, about their in-
ability to understand why she needed to do this.

Wrinks followed her to the car and whined, begging to go.
"Oh, Wrinks, you can't go with me, fella. Come on, I'll take
you back inside. I don't want you trying to chase my car. You
might get hurt."

She scooped him up and returned him to the house, only to
be met by both grandparents, who stood silently just inside the
door, watching her with dark, somber eyes.

Duty made Jade try one last stab at changing their minds.
"Grandmother...Grandfather," she pleaded, handing them
the dog, "please wish me well. For me, designing floats is like

combining my father's gift of art with my mother's love of fantasy. Please try to see how much it means to me.''

The old couple accepted the dog and her plea with the same unblinking silence. But in the end, her determination won out over her sense of guilt.

Traffic, at least, was in her favor. Because it moved smoothly, with no accidents or tie-ups, Jade arrived at Fantasy Floats a full half hour before eight o'clock. The door to the warehouse was securely locked and the front parking lot empty. Jade's resolve faltered. She wondered how T. Stratton would receive her if and when he arrived.

She had a hand on her car door and was pondering whether to climb back in and go for coffee or forget the whole thing, when Trask's bookkeeper, Nell, arrived. The woman's old Volkswagen looked as battered as Jade felt.

''Well, hello!'' Nell's greeting was both warm and effusive as she scrambled from her car. ''I assume your being here so bright and early means T.J. came to his senses. Welcome, Miss Han. Come on in and we'll get the coffee brewing. Or do you drink tea?''

''Coffee,'' Jade said distractedly, trailing the older woman. ''I only drink tea when there's nothing else. If you promise not to tell a soul, I'll confess that I really don't even like the stuff. Oh, and please, call me Jade.'' She paused. ''I can't exactly say Mr. Jennings has come to his senses—yet.''

Nell chuckled at Jade's story as the coffee brewed. Waving away Jade's hesitation, she used the time to give her a quick tour.

Jade was impressed with the operation and felt at home with the smell of paint and solvents. She might have learned much more from Nell if the older woman hadn't opened the back door and exclaimed, ''Well, I'll be! T.J.'s rig is parked out back. He must be upstairs in his office poring over ledgers. I'm surprised he didn't have coffee on. Maybe he's too worried.''

''Excuse me,'' Jade said, ''but is Fantasy Floats in financial straits?''

Nell chuckled. ''Honey, all businesses that depend on selling a once-a-year product have cash-flow problems. T.J.'s a much better manager than the former owner, though. Max Woodard was a darling, always feeding stray cats, dogs and kids, but he supported so many charities that sometimes his own crew took potluck. T.J. is the same when it comes to helping the community, only he pays his staff first. He'll get it together. Always has. If you're going up, take him coffee. Tends to growl until he's had his first cup." She winked. "Can't refuse to let you stay if he's in your debt."

Jade shrugged and watched Nell fill three cups. "How long has Mr. Jennings owned Fantasy Floats?"

"Let me think. He's been around here since he was about sixteen. You should start by calling him T.J. like the rest of us. The permanent crew is like family." She smiled at Jade and ripped open a packet of powdered cream. "I guess it's been, oh, maybe six years since he bought Max out. It was all T.J.'s doing that Max was reunited with his daughter. Years ago, Max's wife took their only child back to her parents' home in the East. Then she quite literally dropped out of sight—but that's another story. At any rate, to make it short, T.J. helped Max locate the girl—woman really, 'cause she had a family. Anyway, Max went to live near his daughter and T.J. worked three jobs to buy the company. Say, this coffee is going to get cold if you don't get a move on. Top of the stairs, door on the right. That's T.J.'s office."

Obediently Jade let Nell hand her two cups and, being careful not to spill, made her way up the stairs. As she balanced both cups and struggled with the office door, she remembered what she'd said to Mikki about not being a waitress. But maybe this was different—more like a favor to Nell. She got the door open and stepped inside. "Oops!" Jade sucked in her breath as the door swished shut behind her and she was smothered in darkness. She stopped to steady the mugs and gradually began to distinguish varying shades of gray. For some reason, her heart slammed erratically. Nell must have been mistaken; T. Stratton wasn't here.

Then, in the pale light filtering in around the shades drawn over two large windows, Jade was able to make out the shapes of furniture. A desk, three chairs and, in the corner, a cot. She gasped. On the cot, apparently sound asleep, sprawled the owner of Fantasy Floats.

Jade backed up until she felt the solid bulk of the door behind her. The coffee cups wobbled dangerously. She'd never seen a man in bed before except on television. And the ones she'd seen always wore manly-looking pajamas. If T. Stratton Jennings wore anything but a precariously draped sheet it wasn't in evidence. Arms flung over his head, he was bared to the waist and his feet and ankles hung out over the mattress.

Goodness, Jade thought, she couldn't awaken him. She shouldn't even be here! But the door seemed to have latched firmly behind her. Jade had no choice but to place the cups on the desk before retreating. A good plan, except that in her nervous haste, she misjudged the height of the desk and slammed the cups down with a force loud enough to bring the man on the cot shooting upward.

Jade jumped and crashed against the desk. Her gaze, having adjusted to the dim light, never left the ghostly sheet sliding ever lower on his hips.

"Lord!" he exclaimed around a yawn, seeming not to notice the sheet. "What time is it? Is that you, Nell? Joe?" he asked, rubbing the sleep from his eyes.

Truly caught, Jade cleared her throat and grabbed one of the mugs. Stepping around the desk, she offered it to him, handle first. "Here. Your morning coffee. It's 8:05, T. Stratton, and you're late for our meeting."

Trask's fingers froze en route to massage his neck. Blindly, he reached out for the cup. He hadn't expected her, even though she hadn't been out of his thoughts all weekend. He forced himself to take a long swallow of coffee while he examined her through half-closed eyes. She sounded ready for battle and it was barely the crack of dawn. Was she always this irritable in the morning? He could definitely think of better things to do with her at 8:05 on a Monday morning than bicker about the time! He took a second swig of coffee.

"I spent Saturday calling designers," he snapped, then found he was totally unprepared for the flash of disappointment that darkened her eyes.

"Oh," she said in a small voice, her fingers toying restlessly with the other mug.

"Yes, damn it," he growled, sliding around until his bare feet hit the floor and his back rested against the wall, with the sheet all but lying on the floor now. She was relieved to note he at least wore a pair of briefs. "I didn't have any luck." He scowled down at his cup.

She gripped her mug tightly in both hands, knowing that to let go would leave them trembling. "I have other drawings I can show you."

"This isn't about your designs."

"What then?" she asked, lifting her head.

Trask ran a hand through his tousled hair. "Could you just throw open one of those curtains?" His tone was sharp.

Jade hurried to oblige, wishing she'd thought of it first. She felt decidedly better as daylight flooded in. At lease she did until she turned and caught the full impact of T. Stratton's sleep-rumpled, half-naked anatomy. "Do you want me or not?" she blurted. "No...I don't mean..." she stammered. "I mean, do you want me to be your designer? Nell said you're a month behind already. What if I go downstairs and give you a chance to..." Her rush of words trailed off at the flash of something like annoyance that drove the blue from his eyes.

Trask slammed his mug down on the floor before answering. "I don't *want* you to work here," he said brusquely. "But it seems I have no other choice. I don't happen to think you have what it takes to stick out this job, Miss Han. I find myself questioning your motives. I've never had an employee listed in Dun and Bradstreet before. Quite frankly, I can't afford you using my company to thumb your nose at a chauvinistic boy-friend—until it suits you to become a wife." He leaned aggressively forward, a hand on one knee. "This isn't child's play, Miss Han. I run a business here. People's jobs are at stake."

Jade felt the anger start in her toes and claw its way up to her cheekbones until she virtually saw red. She marched across the room, stopping only when her well-worn jogging shoe came up tight against T. Stratton Jennings's bare foot. With arms stiff at her sides, hands clenched, she matched him glare for glare. "Nell was mistaken. She said you growl *before* you've had coffee. This may come as a shock to you, Mr. Jennings, but I did not spend four years at the California Polytechnical Institute studying to be a wife. And I'd say Mikki Chan doesn't have a corner on chauvinism, either. I have no intention of *playing* at my profession. And I don't think my personal life is any of your business!"

Trask absorbed the sting of her words. The dark cloud of Jade's hair, rising and falling with the fury of her accusations, mesmerized him. He fought off engulfing waves of her elusively erotic perfume. And although her self-righteous anger was no more bothersome to him than the annoying buzz of a fly, the indignant pout of her full bottom lip was more provocation than he could handle on a Monday morning.

Uncurling from the cot, he stood and in one fluid motion wrapped a large hand around each of her slender shoulders, yanking her into an impatient kiss that cut cleanly through her censure. It soothed an ache deep inside him, one that had begun that fateful first day when he'd been bewitched by her elegant ankles.

His action plunged the room into silence, except for the combined raggedness of their breathing. It was at least a full second before Jade's brain caught up with her involuntary response. In the beginning, her hands had risen defensively to push him away. Failing that, her fingers tangled helplessly in the wiry golden curls covering his chest.

Jade had rarely been kissed before. Her grandparents didn't believe in such intimacies and she realized now that her one experiment with Harvey Yee out behind the school gymnasium lacked quality. But no sooner had she decided to relax and enjoy this heady new experience than it was over and he was thrusting her away.

Trask was disgusted with himself. He wasn't in the habit of forcing his kisses on any woman. Especially one this naive— even though she had an uncanny habit of provoking him.

"Sashay into Mikki's bedroom with all the innocence of Little Red Riding Hood if you like, Miss Han, but stay out of mine unless you want to be gobbled up by the big bad wolf. If it's floats you want to design, go tell Nell to put you on the payroll."

Jade had already begun retreating. Her knees were knocking and her lips felt bruised. She wasn't sure her heart would ever stop somersaulting in her chest. She fumbled with the knob and tugged the door open. "Don't underestimate Little Red Riding Hood, T. Stratton. She isn't so easily fooled these days. The way my father told the story, Little Red had a black belt in kung fu...." She backed out and let the door slam, suddenly horrified by her own temerity.

Halfway down the stairs, she remembered the coffee cups. But not for anything would she go back. Grandmother had been right—T. Stratton Jennings did upset her harmony of spirit. And Grandmother hadn't seen him wearing nothing but a sheet and a pair of tiger-striped briefs, either. She touched her lips and felt her throat constrict.

Because Jade took extra time to compose herself on the way downstairs, she arrived in Nell's office as the last of the crew straggled in. They seemed delighted to hear she was to become part of their team. Among them, they generated enough enthusiasm to make forgetting T. Stratton's kiss almost possible.

Wiry, dark-haired Dan Jones jumped in with an offer to show her the ropes. "You and I will be working together like salt and pepper." He flung a companionable arm around her shoulders and hustled her toward the warehouse. "These floats start with your bright ideas on paper, but I'm the one who gives them life and dimension." He waved a hand, indicating a row of giant grids painted on the concrete floors, beckoning Jade to look. "Joe will take your designs and transfer them to scale proportions right here."

"Then I take over," boasted the freckle-faced Greg Sanders from behind her. He thrust out a hand, shaking Jade's in a warm greeting. "I'm the team's structural engineer. We'll bring in a flatbed of wheels, park her next to Joe's graphs and I'll begin fleshing out your design. Usually I start off with a welded steel frame, then add chicken wire that eventually gets sprayed with polyvinyl chloride to give it strength." He grinned. "It's a dirty job, but somebody has to do it."

"Hey, you warehouse Romeos," a jean-clad and still-unshaven Trask yelled from the doorway, "impress the lady on your own time. If you don't let her get started designing, you jokers won't have anything to build." Impatiently he tucked both hands in his back pockets.

Jade decided he was no less impressive fully clothed. Unconsciously she licked her lips and lowered her lashes, blocking him out.

"Have you designed floats for the Rose Parade before, Jade?" Dan asked. "I mean, can we assume you know this is the most famous parade in America and that everything we do is first-class?"

Jade shot a nervous glance toward the door where Trask hovered. "Well, I've worked on Cal Poly's float four years running. Last year they selected my design to build and enter. Other than that, I've designed and constructed a couple of smaller floats for various local parades."

Dan nodded, accepting her credentials. "Okay, we'll talk some more later. Right now I think the boss wants to see you."

Jade thanked the two men for their advice. She took her time crossing to where Trask had begun a conversation with his general foreman, Joe Forrester.

Joe flashed her a smile. Trask acknowledged her with a curt nod. Jade still couldn't believe her earlier brazenness. Maybe she had more of her mother's flair for drama than she realized. In the aftermath of his kiss, her heart thudded wildly and she was sure someone would notice the heat in her cheeks. She breathed easier when the chief of Fantasy Floats abruptly left and Joe took over. And yet, Jade hated to think he regretted hiring her. Or worse, that he thought she made kissing a man she barely knew a habit.

"What exactly do you do here, Joe?" Jade asked quietly as he escorted her into a well-lit cubicle set up with four drafting boards, the high-tech kind with attached stools.

He chuckled. "My wife often asks the same question. When we start building, the entire crew eats, sleeps and breathes floats. I guess you could say I try to keep the two main departments, the art department and the structural department, working smoothly together."

"I see." She picked up a T square and a slide rule and inspected both before she asked casually, "And T. Stratton—what's his function?"

Joe studied her thoughtfully for a moment, then shrugged. "Are you kidding? T.J. *is* Fantasy Floats. You name it and he does it. He finds sponsors and charms them into signing a contract. He does cost estimates and deals with vendors—soothes ruffled feathers all the way around. Plus, he puts in ten- to fifteen-hour days once construction begins. Outside of the company, he works with disadvantaged kids. I can't tell you how many he's helped. He's not always an easy man, Jade, but he never asks more of his crew than he's willing to give himself. As a result, we're near the top of the heap in the industry. Any particular reason for asking?''

Jade looked up from fingering a supply of mechanical pencils. "No special reason, unless it's wondering why he resents me. I get the impression T. Stratton thinks I'm an albatross." She paused long enough to adjust the height of one of the stools. When she found it satisfactory, she spun it around and asked point-blank, "If you're at the top of the heap, why is there a cash-flow problem?"

Joe crossed his arms, leaned against the door casing and pursed his lips. "I won't lie. We've had better years. But T.J.'s come through leaner ones. He'd pay his crew even if it meant not taking a salary for himself. This business is dependent on tons of foliage, as you know. After two hard winters in a row, the flower growers have stopped extending credit. The new policy is that flowers have to be ordered in April with half the payment up front and the remainder paid on delivery." He sighed. "Float-building isn't for the fainthearted."

"I'm beginning to see that," Jade said, climbing onto the stool. She smoothed a blank sheet of paper on the surface of the table. "I believe you could trim costs by making smaller, more animated floats. It's something that's come up year after year at Cal Poly. Last season we elected to give patrons intricate rather than large. Have you ever considered that option here?"

"Not that I'm aware of. Sounds like a worthy suggestion. Let me round up Greg and Dan. They manage all our hydraulics and animation. Maybe Dan has already run it by T.J. He's been going to school nights for the past year to learn computerized animatronics."

Jade worked while he called the others. She made hand-lettered signs with the parade theme, Castles, Kings and Legendary Queens, and posted one above each drafting unit. By the time the foreman returned with the others she was already dreaming up designs. Because kissing was very much on her mind, she envisioned Sleeping Beauty awakening through animation, following a glorious kiss from a handsome blond prince. She blushed when she realized her vision of the prince looked very much like T. Stratton Jennings. That was all right in the privacy of her mind, but she'd have to be careful that it didn't show up on paper.

The youthful Greg Sanders was the first to give her suggestion his stamp of approval. "I don't know why we didn't think of this before," he said, congratulating Jade. "More intricate animation could be the way of the future, especially as costs go up. We'll be getting the jump on everyone else." He let his exuberance take charge. "We could program computer boards to do the electrohydraulics and install a manual backup panel near the driver for emergencies. I'll bet we could cut our costs in half." Gazing at Jade adoringly, he added, "T.J. will love you for this. He's been sweating profit margins for weeks. I wonder why this didn't occur to him. Too busy, I suppose. If you need anything to get going on these ideas, just sing out. T.J. wants us to start laying out your coach, but we'll come running if you need us."

"Thanks, Greg." Unable to resist his charm, she gave him a warm smile as she reached into the upper cupboard to retrieve a can of colored pencils.

Greg leapt to her aid at once. "Here, let me get that. Hey, what did I just tell you? You shouldn't be lifting these heavy cans," he scolded, almost spilling them in his haste to help out.

"But it's not heavy," she protested, feeling her cheeks flame as she looked up and saw Trask glowering at them through the doorway of Nell's office. When she checked again, he was gone. Still, after she'd thanked Greg for his concern, Jade urged him to get back to his own work. It wouldn't do to upset the boss any more than she already had on her first day.

Putting everything except the theme out of her mind, Jade organized the space that was beginning to feel like her own. The morning soon slipped away. Even though Greg and Dan used every excuse they could invent to interrupt her, she answered their questions patiently and continued to arrange supplies, all the while turning ideas over in her mind.

Trask bustled about with a clipboard, apparently forgetting her, which suited Jade perfectly. Soon she was relaxed enough to hum while she worked, but she made a mental note to bring a radio. Professor Duval used to tease her about chewing gum and working to music. He said the faster the music, the faster she chewed. She smiled in remembrance. Perhaps she'd bring a cassette player, instead. Her favorite work music was the tranquil "New Age" sort.

"Hey, Jade! Can we interest you in going to lunch?" Dan poked his head around the corner and grinned. "Nell usually brown-bags it, but the rest of us go out to the local greasy spoon when we have time."

She hesitated. "I hadn't considered lunch. I'm not really very hungry. Perhaps I'll stay and work."

"Oh, come on," he wheedled. "There'll be plenty of days when you won't eat. This will be a good chance to get to know the crew."

"I think she's had ample opportunity to get to know the crew, Daniel." Trask stepped up behind his floral director, filling the doorway with his broad shoulders. His tone was frosty and accusing and seemed to be aimed at Jade rather than Dan. "The way you've been wearing a path in the concrete outside her door, I'd say she owes me a lunch hour in exchange for all the wasted time."

Jade flushed. She knew the men probably hadn't been too productive, thanks to their frequent visits. But T. Stratton's manner didn't have to be so condescending.

If it bothered Dan, he didn't show it. Laughing, he jammed an elbow into Trask's ribs. "You get up on the wrong side of the bed, boss? You've been like a bear with a sore head all morning. Nell just said you're having lunch with Cynthia. I sure hope she sweetens you up for the afternoon."

Trask glowered at him. "I might be sweeter if my crew did something besides gossip and make cow eyes at my new designer."

His grin fading, Dan shrugged and backed out the door.

Jade picked up her pencil and her T square. She'd felt her stomach twist at hearing that Trask was meeting the elegant blonde for lunch. Though why it should come as any big surprise after seeing them acting so cozy on Friday night, she couldn't say. Unless it was that mind-boggling kiss. The kiss that meant nothing to him but had awakened a rush of unfamiliar emotions in her. Did Cynthia know his skin had the subtle scent of sun and salt and sea, even after a night of sleep? Probably she did, Jade thought with a little pang. And she probably knew other, more intimate details, too.

Greg Sanders called her name, shaking her out of her reverie, for which she was grateful. She couldn't help smiling at the freckle-faced youth who made funny faces behind his boss's back.

"Is Jade telling you about her great idea, T.J.?" Greg dragged a reluctant Dan in behind him and leaned over Jade's drafting table with a proprietary air. "Come take a look at this creation. She talked to us about building smaller floats with more movable parts. More animation. That should make you smile, T.J. It'll save money. Just give the lady a gold star and let us treat her to lunch."

"What do you mean, smaller floats?" Trask sounded suspicious. Two strides took him to Greg's side, where he reached down and snatched up Jade's drawing without asking permission.

"Of course, that one's still pretty rough," she said quickly, sliding her stool back to get out of his way. "I've done a series of sketches over here on another board—just some bare-bones ideas depicting the theme." She indicated a lighted board behind Dan.

"I've seen enough," Trask said, throwing the drawing down on the table with a flip of his wrist. "We don't do cute and clever at Fantasy Floats, Miss Han. We build trophy winners. Grand. Beautiful. Sensational. Crowd pleasers. Understand? Most of all, we build to please our sponsors—astute businessmen who shell out big bucks for our expertise." He waved a hand at the sketch he'd just tossed back. "This stuff might go well in some kiddie parade, but in the Rose Parade it'd leave us looking like rank amateurs." Suddenly he rounded on his men. "I can't imagine how she hoodwinked you into touting these peewee contraptions." He scowled darkly. "On second thought, maybe I can. Serves me right for hiring a debutante. Need I remind you lovesick swains that this company has a reputation to uphold?"

Dan and Greg looked at each other in dismay. They'd both been with Trask a long time and were used to being treated as equals.

Jade was just one blink away from tears. She didn't mind taking constructive criticism, but she thought calling her work amateurish in front of the other team members was unfair.

"What's all the racket?" Joe Forrester appeared and casually leaned a shoulder against the door frame.

No one spoke. The silence was heavy with tension.

"Cynthia's stalking around Nell's office like some caged lion, T.J.," Joe said evenly. "She wants you to know she doesn't have all day. Can I do something to help out here? You three look like you've just been to a funeral."

"Let these two right-brained Romeos make decisions and we'll be holding a funeral for Fantasy Floats," Trask snapped. "In case it's slipped your minds—and I use the term loosely—we're facing impossible deadlines this season. Fun is fun, but *this* is something else." Shaking his finger at her drawing, he headed out the door. "I'm going to lunch, and I'd like to see a little progress by the time I get back."

Trask heard his crew muttering even as he entered Nell's office. Damn, he hated losing his cool, hated treating his crew that way. He knew it hadn't been just the sketches. He supposed part of it was this lunch with Cynthia. He was going to have to ask her to put in a word for him at the bank, after all, and this didn't sit well with him. Especially since Cynthia didn't know a balance sheet from a balance beam. Her husband had given her an office and a title to spite his directors. But the wily old banker had never taken her seriously. Lately it seemed Cynthia was trying to remake Trask into her ideal executive. That was another part of his bad mood. The rest was Jade Han. Pure and simple. He'd enjoyed kissing her far too much. And as a result, he was making everyone suffer. Guilt washed over him. It had to stop.

After T. Stratton stormed out of Jade's cubicle, no amount of pleading from Dan or Greg could convince her to break for lunch. She was determined not to give him any more fuel to feed his cutting remarks.

The silence, once they'd gone, didn't have the positive effect she'd hoped for; her ability to create seemed to have evaporated. No matter how much she doodled, nothing worthwhile took shape.

Jade toyed with her pencils, arranging them according to length and color. Nor had things improved by the time the jovial crew returned. She felt a combination of relief and depression when they all set about their work and left her to her own devices. She could tell the Queen's Committee a thing or two about their wonderful master builder! Lord and master, she thought scornfully, adding a skull and crossbones to a pirate ship she was scribbling.

It was close to three o'clock before the man himself returned, a fact that only added to Jade's discontent. She couldn't think why it made her so angry, unless it was the unfair way he'd treated the crew for making her feel welcome. Apparently he had no compunction about dallying the afternoon away with his girlfriend—though no one else was supposed to spend even five minutes chatting.

That was it, Jade decided in a brilliant flash, as she covertly watched him head out the door carrying a net bag full of basketballs. Maybe he was hoping to make her life so miserable on the job she would quit voluntarily. Then he could build her coach in good conscience—without fulfilling the obligation of the apprenticeship. Well, his lordship could think again. She wasn't budging.

"Jade, you've got a visitor." Nell stood at the door to her office and shouted across the room.

Jade came to her feet in surprise. Through the glass wall of her cubby, she watched Mikki Chan appear behind Nell's broad frame. He was looking rather dashing, she noticed, wearing an off-white linen suit and a muted-print silk tie.

"I was sight-seeing," Mikki said, when she asked why he'd come. "And you haven't called your grandparents at all today, Jade," he scolded. "They are old and they worry." His tone fell just short of reproachful. "Your grandfather suggested I inspect your workplace. I've sent my driver home. I'll ride with you when you're ready to leave."

"You shouldn't have done that without checking first, Mikki. How can I concentrate on my assignment, knowing you're waiting?"

"Why don't you go ahead and take off, Jade," Nell piped up. She'd been openly studying Mikki. "We don't hold much with regular hours when it's a skeleton crew of regulars. Later, you'll need to bring a bedroll." She winked.

Mikki's brows flew up. "Jade will not be sleeping over."

"Maybe I will go now, Nell," Jade broke in, wanting to prevent the confrontation she could see building. She'd had quite enough of confrontations for one day. "Let me get my things," she told Mikki, darting back into her enclosure. "I can sketch at home just as easily as I can here. Will you explain to Mr. Jennings, Nell?"

Propelling Mikki toward the door, Jade noticed how easily he'd given orders—just like her boss. On the way to the car, she thought about how best to broach the problem of their betrothal. She simply couldn't marry him, and she was so caught up in that fact she almost missed what he was saying.

"Today, the sparrow showed me all around the city."

"Mei Li?" Jade paused with her hand on the car door. "You and Mei Li alone?"

"Yes." He thrust out his chin and loosened his tie. "Last week, her parents invited me for dinner. We've discovered much in common. I find Mei Li...exciting."

"You know she's promised to Roger Cho?" Jade asked carefully.

"I know." Mikki handed her inside, then circled the car, climbing in the passenger side. "And we are promised, you and I."

She tossed her drawing materials into the back seat and refused to comment on his last statement. "Roger is working on his master's at Princeton. Afterward, he'll get a doctorate."

"Mei Li does not love Roger," Mikki stated. "Some arranged marriages are doomed from the start."

"You're telling me?" Jade chewed her fingernail. "Mei Li and Roger were matched from birth. She has too much energy for him, but their parents are best friends and I'm afraid they'll never realize how unhappy she is with this situation."

He smiled. "I think they will, given time. I believe her father likes me. Mei Li begged me to seek your help in this matter."

"Mine?" she queried sharply. "How so? I have problems of my own."

"Would you consider only pretending you and I are happily betrothed? Today, Mei Li and I expressed feelings for one another. We dare trust no one but you with the truth, lest Mei Li's parents foolishly force her to marry Roger before we have time to develop a plan."

Jade reeled from the shock. She was happy for Mei Li, yet she felt overwhelmed by the news.

"I'm sorry, lotus blossom," he said, misreading her distress. "I thought you'd be pleased. Mei Li said you would be."

"Oh, I am. Pleased for Mei Li and for you." *And for me*, she realized at once. She threw her arms around Mikki and felt him shift uncomfortably. "But we must tell my grandparents," she said. "And that will not be easy."

He shook his head. "No, we tell no one. Especially not them."

"What? How long do we have to pretend, Mikki?"

"Ah, you wound me, lotus blossom!" Mikki rarely displayed a sense of humor, and Jade had to smile. "Can you tolerate being my fiancée until Christmas?" he went on. "Roger has work obligations that will keep him from coming here any earlier. Will you help us until then?"

"I suppose," Jade muttered. She knew that Mei Li and Mikki needed time to gradually accustom her parents to the idea. "All right. I promise," she said, starting the car. "But only until Christmas. My grandparents are upset with me already."

"It would be more convincing if you'd quit work," he said offhandedly. "That would make them happier."

Jade let out the clutch and the small car shot forward. "No, Mikki. I promise to keep your secret, but I won't give up this apprenticeship. The two aren't related."

"Oh?" Mikki shrugged. He saw the black looks they received from Jade's boss as she drove out of the lot, though Jade was too involved with the conversation to notice.

Trask sank three baskets in a row with deadly precision as he timed Jade's delay in driving away with Mikki. It was barely three-thirty. So much for the lady's dedication, he thought, snapping off a fourth shot that bounced on the rim, rolled around, then dropped out. So he was right. His debutante designer wanted to play at working. It had been a definite waste of his breath defending her to Cynthia, who would have convinced that vice president to back his loan if he'd given her part interest in Fantasy Floats—and with it, the authority to fire Jade. It was her ultimatum that had irked the hell out of him, and they'd had their first major fight.

His next shot fell short by a good foot and he gave the ball a fierce glare. Maybe he was rid of Jade Han for good. He'd seen the hug she and lover boy had shared. Maybe she was heading home to learn embroidery.

"So just say good riddance, Jennings," he muttered, bouncing the ball six times, then laying it in sweetly, without so much as a nick on the rim. "You sure as the devil don't need another Kitty Ferris in your life."

CHAPTER FIVE

JADE BEGGED OFF meeting Mikki and Mei Li for a celebratory dinner that night, but she did call her friend and assure her she couldn't be happier. She was determined to stay up all night if need be to produce a masterpiece capable of eliciting praise from the arrogant owner of Fantasy Floats. If T. Stratton wanted showy, Jade told Mei Li, she'd darn well give him the showiest. "I'll make all these floats' maximum dimensions. Then we'll see what he has to complain about. We'll go to dinner tomorrow, instead, Mei Li. I promise."

Jade scaled her first creation sixty feet long and thirty feet high. She included Cleopatra, Queen of Egypt, and half the Nile. Swathed in golden chrysanthemums, Cleo would command her troops through hydraulics. Before Jade was finished, palm fronds waved, oars dipped and Cleo nodded and raised her arms. The computer panel would be a veritable maze of circuitry.

Jade much preferred her earlier, more delicate creation of Sleeping Beauty, but after all, she'd signed on to learn from a master builder, and if the master said he could win awards only with gigantic monstrosities, then she'd do her level best to oblige.

It was close to daybreak when she closed the cover of her drawing pad on the final renderings of her second float, a rotund King Cole. With the aid of intricate animatronics, the king alternately called for his pipe and bowl and was entertained by his fiddlers three. She'd made Cole so large, the tie rods needed to move his head and arms would weigh a quarter ton—definitely pushing the limits.

Jade yawned, grimaced, then slid her night's work into the portfolio she'd brought home from the office. Wrinks was already curled at the foot of her bed snoring softly. In the last week or so, he'd given up trying to get her to take him for a run. She set her alarm though she longed to sleep in. Jade could just imagine T. Stratton's censure if she arrived late for work. She'd go without a wink of sleep rather than give him the satisfaction.

Even then, Jade tossed fitfully. In a wild dream she was being chased through Pasadena by gargantuan floats. Every street ended in a blind alley, with her escape blocked by grotesque, disapproving males. Some of the lurking figures took on human characteristics and vaguely resembled Grandfather Han, Mikki Chan and T. Stratton Jennings. At the bleat of the alarm, Jade awakened in a cold sweat. The dream had been so terrifyingly real she slogged through her morning ritual with a lingering sense of doom, a feeling she still hadn't managed to shake when she entered the parking lot at Fantasy Floats.

"Hey, princess, you came back. So the boss didn't scare you away?" a bright-eyed Greg Sanders shouted gleefully as he rushed to carry her portfolio. "I sure hope T.J.'s in a better mood today, don't you?" he joked.

Despite her own doubts, Jade flashed him a thin smile. "I seem to bring out the worst in him," she lamented. "But—" she patted her case "—maybe he'll approve of my drawings today. Honestly, I wasn't trying to walk in and change things yesterday, Greg. I just thought the way everyone was worrying about expenses, smaller floats made sense."

Greg placed an arm companionably around her shoulders and shoved open the front door. His words of reassurance were cut off when he glanced up and noticed the lowered brows of the man they'd been discussing.

Eyes like iced sherry flicked over the two of them. "I hate to break up such a cozy scene," Trask bit out, "but Dan needs you, Greg. And you, Miss Han—I'm surprised to see you here today. If it's not treading on your *personal* life too much, I'd like a word with you. We may as well start out by discussing our conflicting versions of acceptable work hours."

Flushing, Jade remembered telling him to stay out of her personal life yesterday. Too vividly she recalled the culminating kiss.

"Looks like we're in for another day of it," murmured Greg near her ear. He gave her shoulder a quick squeeze and let his arm slide away. "Chin up, princess. Once we get going on your coach, T.J. won't be such a sorehead."

"Don't call me 'princess,'" Jade begged. "Not even in jest. I've already heard quite enough of T. Stratton's mistaken views concerning my station in life."

"I don't have all day," barked Trask.

Greg made a face, excusing himself, and Jade approached T.J. warily.

Nell rushed through the front door just then, her face a mask of distress. "My car decided to die in the middle of La Cienega this morning. Sorry I'm late, T.J. I guess I need a new battery."

"You need a new car, Nell," he chided. "When are you going to listen to me and get one? If your son can't get away to help you look, I'll go."

She smiled. "Thanks, anyway, but I'm kind of attached to my old Rabbit."

"It's time to give that animal a decent burial," he scolded. "We'll talk about your softhearted attachment later—or should I say softheaded?" To show he was kidding, he winked. "Now that you're here to catch the phones, I'll start my briefing."

Although his concern for Nell was commendable, Jade found the contrast with the way he'd treated her quite baffling. He'd unceremoniously rushed Greg off to work, yet now he seemed to be in a playful mood himself. It just so happened that her own mood suffered from lack of sleep. "Did you forget about me?" she reminded tartly. "You said you wanted to discuss my leaving early yesterday. I thought you wanted to see my new designs."

"I said Jade could leave early yesterday," Nell broke in, surprised. "Gosh, T.J., I didn't think you'd mind. I figure she'll be putting in extra hours like the rest of us when things get cracking. If you're gonna yell at someone, yell at me."

Trask frowned. In all honesty, he really hadn't expected to see Jade back today, so he hadn't worked out what to say. Jade Han was turning out to be the most irritating female he'd ever had the misfortune to meet. Irritating. Beautiful. And provocative. Today, dressed in form-fitting blue jeans and a pink sweatshirt, her ebony hair divided into two braids, one looped over each ear and tied with pink satin ribbons, she looked about sixteen and totally innocent. In any event, he was far too old and streetwise for the seductive thoughts he was thinking. Best to remind himself that she was rich enough to buy and sell him ten times over—richer, even, than Kitty Ferris. "So let's look at these new ideas," he snapped, without bothering to say he was sorry for misjudging her.

Tight-lipped, Jade yanked out her sketches and spread them along the counter. She'd drawn front views, side views and a cutaway version of each to better show the precision animations. She'd done so many renderings, it took her several minutes to notice that neither Nell nor Trask was saying a word, though they both studied her work.

Jade chewed at her lower lip and wondered what on earth could be the matter this time. She'd done everything T. Stratton said he wanted—or at least she thought she had. Granted they weren't her style, but...

Trask broke the uneasy silence with a fit of coughing. "Is this some kind of joke, Miss Han?" he thundered when he'd caught his breath. "Yesterday, you showed me impossible, immature, matchbox toys, and now you've done these ludicrous monstrosities of tinsel-town grandeur." He slammed one large fist down on merry old Cole, making the king leap. "Just what's with you? Haven't you ever seen a Rose Parade? Or is it your prescribed mission in life to send me into bankruptcy? Can you produce something between microscopic and monstrous?"

Jade slapped her leather portfolio on the counter only inches from his fist. Her anger flared, equal to his. "If I recall correctly, Mr. Jennings," she said in a tone of icy precision, "you were the one who demanded grandeur. Frankly I don't see *any* way of pleasing you. You don't want small. You don't want big. I don't know what you do want, except maybe a different designer." Even as she spoke, Jade stuffed her drawings haphazardly back into her case. She was exhausted from spending half the night on what she knew was second-rate material to please this jerk. *He* was the impossible one.

Most of the sketches had been stowed away when she happened to look up and see a ring of stony faces all fixed on T. Stratton. The crew had gathered in her defense. She felt a rush of appreciation, and tears pressed at the back of her eyes.

"Don't," she warned with a shake of her head. "Don't get into trouble on my account."

Always the moderator, Joe Forrester stepped forward. "I thought we'd pretty much agreed to go full bore on the Cinderella Coach, T.J. Yesterday you said we'd let Jade meet the sponsors—show her some of Hank's past designs. Wasn't that your game plan?"

Trask's brows drew together in a fierce scowl. "At this rate—" he tapped a finger on Cleopatra "—there won't be any sponsors. If they get a gander at these, they'll pull out and go down the street to our competition."

"You were the one who wanted big," Jade said stubbornly. "I'm doing my best to give you what you want. I realize I don't know the sponsors. Perhaps if I could visit with your injured designer . . ." She left the suggestion open.

Dan Jones and Greg Sanders stepped forward simultaneously, flanking her. "I'll be happy to drive Jade to see old Hank," Greg said. "He could give her a rundown on the sponsors and tell her what designs he had in mind."

"Oh, no, you don't," Dan objected. "You have to get those underpinnings on the coach stabilized. If anyone takes Jade to see Hank, I will."

Trask glanced from one to the other and snorted in disgust. "I knew the first day she walked through the door there'd be calamity in the ranks. I should have stuck to my guns."

"Now, just a darn minute, T.J.," Dan sputtered in his own defense. "When have we ever not given you more than one hundred percent?"

"Stop. Please, all of you stop." Jade put out a hand toward Trask, then pulled it back, clutching her portfolio to her chest. "I'm capable of finding this Hank person on my own. I've seen every Rose Parade since I was five. I'll come up with what you want."

The men began pitching in on her behalf again. Suddenly Nell stuck her head around the door and whistled shrilly. Conversation stopped cold. Jade almost laughed at the shock on the men's faces, T. Stratton's included.

"It just so happens I'm going to visit Hank during my lunch break," the older woman said into the silence. "Jade can ride with me. That way, there won't be anything to squabble about. T.J., you've got a phone call from Perkins Flowers.''

Trask brushed past Jade without a word. "Wish me luck," he murmured to Joe. "Perkins is our last hope for credit." Closing his eyes, he rubbed both temples. "Oh...and Joe. What I wanted to tell everyone in the briefing is that a spokesperson for the Queen's float called. We've been asked to step up the timetable on the Cinderella coach. They want to use it in other parades and for television promotion, starting the end of April. So from now on, every second counts. Pretty soon you'll all be too busy to wait on our new designer.''

Jade resented his high-handed method of sharing such important news, although part of her was thrilled to know that her design was one step closer to reality. A reality that would be viewed and enjoyed by nearly three million parade-lovers, whether they lined up along Pasadena's Colorado Boulevard or saw it on TV in their homes. A shiver traveled up her spine, and Jade found herself wishing she had someone special to share in her excitement. Someone like the master builder...

"What are we waiting for?" Joe whooped with enthusiasm and followed T.J. out the door. He motioned to Jade. "Let's get a move on.''

"All...all right." She took a deep breath, unable to dispel a bubble of apprehension that welled up. If only there was some way to keep T. Stratton on the phone to Perkins Flowers until her float was finished, she thought, her future as a float-designer would be more secure.

Jade was to make that wish repeatedly over the next busy weeks as float-building settled into full swing and her boss inspected her work all too frequently. Hank, already on the mend except for his wrist, had been complimentary and encouraging. But T. Stratton continued to blow hot and cold as he pushed his crew, often beyond what Jade considered normal human endurance. Still, she had to acknowledge that he worked even harder himself.

Although Jade hadn't actually spent an entire night at the warehouse yet, she was there enough hours to draw daily censure from her grandparents. Mikki had just returned from three weeks in Hong Kong, and he and Mei Li weren't happy with her, either. Without her, they had no legitimate excuse to meet.

Jade felt she wasn't managing to please anyone these days, least of all, T. Stratton.

One morning when she arrived early for work after a particularly trying evening of making a round of nightclubs with Mikki and Mei Li, it was to find the other crew members also red-eyed and out of sorts. They'd been in since sunrise, engineering the crucial synchronization needed to turn the wheels on the coach. One of their twenty-foot ladders broke, and Greg Sanders had very nearly plummeted to the concrete floor. He'd been saved only because he'd crashed through the papier-mâché roof of the conveyance. Now, precious hours were needed to repair and reshape the crown at the top. Jade could feel the hostile vibrations as she greeted the men with her usual "Hi, there."

"It's about time you showed up, Jade." Dan's short response was uncharacteristic. "The batteries on my ghetto blaster gave out this morning. Why'd you lock the lower cabinet in your cubby? We never lock anything inside the building, because we all keep such screwy hours. Lord knows no one here would steal your tapes. Nobody'd want that highbrow music. But I could have used your recorder until I have a chance to go out and get batteries."

"My music isn't highbrow," she shot back. "It's soothing—which is something we could all use today."

"Too late for that, I'm afraid," muttered Joe. He was staring balefully at the fracture in the roof of the coach.

"I almost broke my neck on that defective ladder," Greg complained, sliding out on a wooden creeper from beneath the coach. "Ask anybody here if they care. All they're worried about is your design."

"Everyone needs a breather, I think," she suggested gently. "Me included. I didn't take time to do my morning exercises. I'll bet you guys wolfed down breakfast, if you bothered to eat at all." She sent a quick glance around the room, looking for T. Stratton. When she didn't see him, she tossed out an idea she'd been considering for several days. "The Chinese have an exercise form called t'ai chuan to help the body relax and to refresh the mind. There's plenty of room here, and I'd be happy to show you some of the moves if anyone's interested."

Dan looked skeptical, but Greg jumped agilely to his feet and said with enthusiasm, "Hey, I have some friends who take t'ai chi. Is this similar?"

Jade shrugged. "You'll have to tell me."

"So what're we waiting for?" Greg dusted his hands on his jeans. "Bring on the music, Jade. I'm ready for anything guaranteed to loosen me up. Too bad T.J.'s upstairs poring over the books again. If anyone's been uptight lately, it's the boss."

"Tai chuan requires a certain amount of harmony between the body and the spirit," Jade pointed out. "If we disturb T. Stratton and take him away from his ledgers, we could end up more tense."

"She's got a point," Joe said dryly. "I'll admit we need something, so let's give it a try. But it's only fair to warn you that the Queen's Committee called T.J. yesterday and added pressure. They're paying extra to get the coach sooner."

"How much sooner?" asked Dan, rubbing his neck.

Joe shook his head. "T.J. just said sooner. He didn't say when."

"All the more reason to hang loose while we've got the chance," Greg put in, helping Jade set up her cassette player.

She shoved in a tape and listened for a moment to the hollow strains of a muted wind instrument. Then she caught up her long hair in a figure eight and secured it tightly before she slipped off her shoes. After positioning the men and giving them each sufficient room to move freely, Jade stood in front of them. "Now just try to follow me," she instructed. "We'll take a moment or two to loosen up. Then I want you to do as I do. Don't worry about technique. Let the music flow through you."

The men accepted her instructions awkwardly, amid much good-natured joking. She turned up the volume until the music filled the room. Then she executed a series of slow stretching routines, speaking softly, taking care not to interrupt the rich, silvery chords swirling around them. Soon everyone was lost in the ancient, mystical artistry of shadow boxing, and the men stopped joking to concentrate on following her limber kicks.

Trask had finished signing checks and was bringing them back to Nell when he heard the music. "What gives out there?" he asked her, jerking a thumb toward the warehouse.

"Beats me." Nell shrugged. "I've got all I can do keeping up with the supply orders you left here last night. Don't you ever sleep, T.J.?"

"Sleeping is time wasted. I can't afford to waste any time this season. I've set a killer schedule to get everything done. Especially that coach. Frankly, Nell, if we don't finish it by tomorrow and get the last installment, payday won't be a very pretty sight around here. Construction costs on the camp came in twenty percent over budget, which almost wiped out my personal savings. I used the first payment from the coach to purchase what essentials we needed to get started on the next float. This is the tightest year I've seen in a long while. Guess I let those few fat years go to my head."

Nell gave him a confident smile. "You've got enough to keep you awake nights, that's for sure. But worrying isn't going to pay the bills any faster. If you worry yourself to a frazzle, where will the company be? You work too hard, T.J. If you want my opinion, a young fellow like you should be home nights cuddling a wife and bouncing a baby on his knee, instead of curled up with a cold ledger."

T.J. lowered his brows. "I don't recall asking."

Looking sour, Nell slapped a sheaf of pink messages on the counter in front of him. "Better tell Mrs. Osborn how busy you are. She doesn't think I have anything better to do with my time than check to see why her calls aren't getting through to you."

"I know you don't like Cynthia, Nell, but I think you could leave off calling her Mrs. Osborn in a tone that insinuates I'm consorting with a married woman. We're nothing more than friends."

"You're never going to have any babies if you stick with the likes of her," Nell grumbled. "Babies would get sticky fingers all over her expensive dresses and she wouldn't like that one bit. The widow fancies herself more than just your good buddy, boss. Mark my words."

"Is that music getting louder out there, or is it my imagination?" Trask asked abruptly, ignoring Nell's repeated jabs at

Cynthia. "What in thunder?" he ground out, pausing half-way through the door.

Trask's breath caught in his throat, and a swift punch, like a blow from someone's fist, sent his stomach spiraling. Before him, like a Gypsy, Jade Han whirled and leapt in time to the strange music he'd been hearing for the past ten minutes. Her well-washed blue jeans clung to the enticing curves of her der-riere as she kicked out, then nimbly danced away. Totally cap-tivated by her graceful moves, Trask allowed several seconds to slip past before he realized his entire crew was imitating her movements, or at least trying to.

"Well, I never," exclaimed Nell, joining him at the door. "Did you ever see anything like it?" She chuckled, crossing plump arms over ample breasts. "Looks like fun, T.J. Shall we join them?"

Trask did his best to tamp down a sudden surge of desire. It wasn't the first desire he'd felt for Jade Han, and he was get-ting damn tired of feeling like this. She was off limits in more ways than one. Why was it so hard to accept? he wondered. Lately he'd had to search long and hard to find reasons for keeping her at arm's length. But this time she'd gone too far. The anger he needed to cover unwanted feelings of passion bubbled to the surface. It was both real and swift.

In one quick stride, he entered the room and ordered the music shut off. By the time the dancers had all stopped and faced him, Trask had his emotions controlled and firmly locked in place. "I would expect a work slowdown from you, Miss Han," he spat, "but the rest of my crew knows what it takes to bring a finished product in on time. So, what have you fellows got to say for yourselves?"

No one spoke. At last Jade stalked past him and picked up the paintbrushes she needed to complete a task Joe had as-signed her the day before. "Coffee break's over, guys. I hope the exercises eased some of your tension. Although that's a lot to expect even from t'ai chuan."

Joe crossed the room and stepped between T.J. and Jade be-fore his boss could explode. "Looks to me like we'll come close to finishing up today, T.J. If not by tonight, then for sure by morning. Why don't you give me a hand unloading the foliage that just came in? Jade was on her way to paint the last of the mosaics...weren't you, Jade?'' She paused, and without turning to see T. Stratton's anger, nodded.

Trask drew his eyes away from her slender back. "They've asked for an inspection at ten o'clock tomorrow. Can we have the coach ready by then?"

Joe rubbed the bridge of his nose. "Probably, if we come in with the chickens. I can't stay late tonight or Hillary will kill me. She's had tickets to a performance at the Hollywood Bowl for three months now."

"Tonight's my regular poker night," yelled Dan from the far side of the coach. "I'd cancel, but it's at my place."

Greg poked his head out from under the left edge. "Omigosh, T.J., I've got a hot date with Emily Davis. I hope you don't ask me to beg off. She's been telling me no for a year now."

Jade was the only member of the crew who didn't ask to be excused. "I'll stay, if you think I can help," she offered quietly.

Trask's liquid gaze flowed over her. "That just might make up for this morning's nonsense," he said tautly, wheeling away.

Jade stuck out her tongue at his broad back. She heard Greg chuckle. Blushing, she busied herself at the coach before he could tease her unmercifully, as he was prone to do. She knew Mei Li wouldn't like the fact that she was staying. She was scheduled to go to a movie with Mei Li and Mikki, and she knew that the couple held hands in the dark. She couldn't fault them for wanting these rare times together, but if she'd known how hard it would be to listen to her grandparents making wedding plans, she'd never have promised to keep silent. No wonder she was feeling under stress. And T. Stratton didn't help matters, with his snide comments and heated glances that sent such mixed messages and caused her blood pressure to soar.

Trying not to think about him, Jade redoubled her efforts. Everyone skipped lunch and worked. By midafternoon, the entire skeleton for the elegant coach was in place. Six dappled horses pranced—due to precision robotics—and tapered spoked wheels looked as if they were spinning, though they really weren't moving at all. At the normal quitting time, the crew began one by one to drift out. By six o'clock Jade was so tired she didn't think she could raise her arms to finish the crucial color-by-number mosaic; this was the map, painted directly on the coach, that indicated where foliage of different kinds would be glued.

It was only when Nell poked her head into the warehouse and yelled, "Hey, you two, are you going to work all night?" that Jade realized she and T. Stratton were the only ones left.

"We may, Nell," Trask called back, wiping his greasy hands on a towel he picked up from the creeper Greg had abandoned earlier. "I'm ready to start gluing marigolds and eucalyptus bark. I can't speak for Jade, though. She looks ready to drop. Any chance you could go out and grab us something to eat before you take off for the night, Nell? I hate to ask, but . . ."

"Sure you hate to ask." Nell gave him a huge grin. "If I had a dime for every time you and Max asked me to run out and get you something to eat, I'd be a rich woman. Do you want Mexican or Chinese?"

Trask raked a hand through his hair, leaving the sun-blond curls uneven and in further disarray. "Your choice," he said, deferring to Jade.

"Mexican," she replied without hesitation. "I hate Chinese food."

Nell looked genuinely shocked and Trask broke into a belly laugh. "You never cease to amaze me, Miss Han," he said. "Most unpredictable female I've ever met. Mexican it is, Nell." Digging into his pocket, he pulled out a wadded-up twenty-dollar bill and passed it to her.

Jade balanced her clipboard and started to climb down from the ladder. "I'll get my purse, Nell. How much for a burrito and a soft drink?"

T.J. stiffened and threw her a dark look. "I can afford to buy your dinner. It's the least I can do for a crew member who works overtime."

Jade would have argued, but something in the set of his jaw changed her mind. "All right. Thank you for dinner, T. Stratton. I hope you don't object if I take a short break first. I need to call my grandparents."

"What about lover boy?"

She lifted her chin and glared at him. She'd like to tell him how things stood between her and Mikki—just to see his shock. Instead, she answered calmly, "Mikki will spend the evening playing mah-jongg with my grandfather. I doubt he'll miss me." That, at least, was true.

Trask spun on his heel. "If you were my woman, I wouldn't settle for playing mah-jongg with your grandfather."

"I'm my own woman," she murmured, jumping from the last rung.

"Go make your call," he said sharply. "I'll bring in the first case of flowers and a bucket of rubber cement. If they're planning to play until you get home, you might want to suggest Monopoly. I can see this taking us a while."

Jade threw her brushes into a can of solvent and followed Nell into the office. Nothing she did ever met with T. Stratton's approval. Did he know which buttons to push to make her furious? Or was it accidental?

"Don't pay him any attention, honey," Nell consoled her. "He's got a lot on his mind right now—a lot riding on that design of yours. He works too hard, I can tell you." She smoothed out the twenty he'd given her. "What I can't tell you is when he had his last home-cooked meal. It's not good for a man to eat out all the time."

Jade scowled as she picked up the phone and began to dial. "Don't tell *me*. Why isn't Cynthia cooking him meals?"

"Heaven forbid. She might break a nail." Nell shook her head as she thrust the money into her purse and headed toward the door.

Jade's retort was cut off by Grandfather Han answering the telephone. Sometime she'd have to ask Nell what she had against T. Stratton's girlfriend.

Grandfather was not at all understanding, and Jade felt guilty listening to him chastise her for neglecting Mikki, even though she knew the truth.

It was a good thing T. Stratton seemed to turn over a new leaf, going out of his way to be pleasant, or she might have left with Nell. But because he relaxed, Jade felt revived enough after eating to continue work. The master builder, T. Stratton Jennings, could be quite charming when he put his mind to it, she thought, scrambling back up the tall ladder.

Left alone, the two of them worked well together. Jade soaked up everything and anything he cared to teach her. Under his tutelage she learned the proper way to break apart gladioli buds without bruising the petals. Before, whenever she'd volunteered, someone else had separated the flowers. Jade soon found there was an art to peeling the buds down in order to use every available bit of flower. With painstaking thoroughness, Trask showed her how to gild the filigree with dusty miller and how to bring the carriage wheels to life by dipping them in glue, then rolling them in carrot seeds.

She knew the rules stating that the exterior of every float had to be covered in natural foliage, but there was nothing like watching a piece being realized to see the delicate balance between nature and artifice. Entranced, Jade helped her dream bloom into life under T. Stratton's expert guidance. When the last butterscotch mum had finally been pressed into place, they each stepped back and silently admired the finished coach.

Jade clapped her hands together. Ignoring their sticky coating of rubber cement, she marveled, "I can almost see the Queen's gown. Yards and yards of filmy blue draped over hooped skirts. She'll wear puffed short sleeves trimmed with sequins."

"It'll be satin," he murmured, lifting a hand to smooth back a strand of Jade's jet-black hair. A single coil had slipped from the mother-of-pearl clasp holding the heavy mass atop her head. "White satin," he corrected. "Cut heart-shaped over her breasts and nipped tight beneath to show off a tiny waist." Even as he spoke, his fingers slipped down to span her waist.

"But that sounds more like a wedding dress, T. Stratton," she whispered, letting her gaze follow the line of his lean cheek and exquisitely shaped mouth.

"Blue, then . . . Have it your way. Pale blue." Jade hardly realized she'd stopped thinking about the coach as she watched his chest rise and fall with each murmured word.

Somehow she focused on his lips and began to wish he'd kiss her again. Caught in his spell, Jade moved an inch closer and placed both palms flat against his broad chest. "Are you always so bossy, T. Stratton?" Her lashes lowered slowly until his face became a blur.

"Open your eyes and say my name again," he ordered huskily.

Her lashes fluttered upward. Had she spoken his name out loud? Jade didn't remember. "T. Stratton." Her lips moved, sounding his name in the tiniest whisper. She was no more able to deny his simple request than to consider what was happening.

"I like it. Everyone else calls me Trask or T.J."

Then he *was* kissing her. It was a demanding kiss, and Jade felt her stomach churn and her knees go weak. Still, it was a giving kiss that chased her tiredness away until she began feverishly to kiss him back.

Like that first morning in his office, Trask felt his control slipping. Silly thoughts swam in his head. Thoughts about liking the fact that they were almost the same height . . . liking her softness, her willowy strength. Suddenly he didn't want to think at all. Taking the kiss deeper, Trask blanked his mind and lost himself in her generous response—until the moment was shattered by the loud ringing of a telephone. Trask would have ignored it, but Jade struggled out of his embrace.

"The telephone," she gasped, breathless. "We'd better get it. It might be my grandfather or someone—"

She meant someone like Mikki, but Trask cut her off with a sharp "Right!" Then he wheeled around and snatched up the receiver, barking, "Hello!" He didn't care to be reminded of Mikki Chan. It hurt his ego—and maybe more than his ego—to think another man might be on her mind while she was kissing him.

Jade hovered nearby, listening to his conversation and chewing nervously at her bottom lip.

"It's Greg," he growled, hunching his shoulders to keep from yanking her against him again. He made a face and rolled his eyes. "He's got car trouble and no money to call a cab. Emily has a curfew."

Jade wilted, but she smiled her understanding. "You'd better go help him then, T. Stratton." She gave him a little push. "I'll finish picking things up around here. It's been a long day for both of us. You must be pleased knowing the coach is done. And I'm tired."

Trask could have told her his thoughts weren't all connected to the coach. Hadn't been for several minutes. However, because Jade's wide gray eyes seemed shadowed by doubt, he nodded and had the presence of mind to ask Greg for the address where his car had given up the ghost.

He tucked the paper with the address in his shirt pocket and strode quickly to where she'd already begun stacking cartons. Lifting her hands and bringing them to his lips, he placed a light kiss on each row of knuckles. "Your Cinderella coach is beautiful, Jade. You're beautiful . . . and I've been a bear to work with the past months. No wonder you're done in. Why don't you sleep late tomorrow? If you get here by ten, you'll still hear the committee's rave reviews. That's when they'll be picking up the coach." He yawned, grinning sheepishly. "Guess I'm tired, too. Good thing Greg's date doesn't live far from my apartment. I think I'll go home tonight and crash in my own bed for a change. Care to join me?" he teased.

Jade looked embarrassed and pulled her hands away. "You'd better hurry, T. Stratton. Greg will never forgive you if he can't take Emily out again. You'll get blamed if she misses curfew."

He closed his eyes and rubbed the back of his neck. "Will you be okay here? I don't like leaving you alone in this old building at night."

She busied herself with the brushes and cans again. "I'll be fine," she murmured. "I'm a grown-up." Her chin rose defiantly.

"Grown-up enough to know what you want?"

"Of course," she declared.

He touched her lips and felt her shiver. "Good." He smiled. "When you get home, tell lover boy to find someone else's grandfather to play mah-jongg with. Now, leave this mess and go."

Jade frowned. If only she could explain the situation with Mikki and Mei Li. But no—she'd promised and was bound by an oath of silence. And she owed them so much, her grandparents and Mei Li. They'd been there for her during the hardest time in her life. She had to do this for them, had to keep the secret. But at least she could try to explain tradition. "Mikki's grandparents and mine escaped from the mainland when it was dangerous. They grew up with totally different codes from ours. To them, custom is everything."

"No custom is that strong. Surely your grandparents don't expect you to marry someone you don't love?" His brows drew together and he gripped her upper arms tight. "Do you kiss

Mikki the way you kissed me?" he demanded, his eyes growing dark and troubled.

Jade flushed and looked away, shaking loose from his hold. "I don't kiss Mikki at all." That was true. "The Chinese have rules for courtship," she went on. "Physical displays are not encouraged. Please...go," she urged, fearing she'd break the promise. "I'll clean up." Her eyes blurred, but she whisked her doubts away and joked, "It's almost midnight. If I hurry, I'll be home before my fairy godmother turns the coach into a pumpkin."

"I see you're determined to change the subject, Jade. Since Greg's waiting, I guess I don't have any other choice tonight." He smoothed a thumb over a smudge on her cheek. "Poor little Cinderella. You look too tired for dancing at the ball." Turning, he pulled open the door. "Don't forget to set the night lock." On a swift rush of night air, he was gone.

Jade could barely make her fingers stop shaking long enough to clean up. Did he wish she was poor like Cinderella? He always seemed to resent her money, and in just a few weeks, when she came into her trust, she'd have more. Yet, by all reports, he'd been successful before. Anyone could have a run of bad luck. She looked at the coach and brightened. He was definitely good at what he did. Maybe she could find a discreet way to ease his financial stress.

It was after midnight by the time Jade doused the light shining on her Cinderella coach. Before leaving, she carefully double bolted the door, even yanking on it a second time to make certain it was locked tight. Now that she'd put her masterpiece safely to bed, she was free to daydream about the master builder himself on her drive across the city.

Jade was glad Mikki had left and the house was dark when she arrived home. She would have found it difficult to face Grandfather after allowing T. Stratton to kiss her. Tomorrow she would have to talk to Mei Li about breaking the news to Roger sooner. If Mei Li wasn't so burdened by guilt herself, it would be infinitely easier to bring up the subject.

Snuggling under the covers, Jade nudged Wrinks over. Grandfather would come around. He set great store by *shujing,* but he was also practical. T. Stratton needed her. That was fact. Twining her fingers in Wrinks's soft fur, Jade smiled and slept, dreaming of harmony—and T. Stratton's kisses.

TRASK DIDN'T SLEEP. He was worried that committee officials might find some fault with Jade's Cinderella coach. Not to mention how keyed up he was over his precipitous parting from her. By the time he'd delivered Greg's girlfriend to her home and helped the kid get his car started, sleep was out of the question. He hardly had time to grab a quick shower and some clean clothes before the pink streaks of dawn were igniting the San Gabriel Mountains.

Lost in thought, Trask paid little attention to the panoramic view as he headed for the warehouse. Jade was foremost on his mind as he pulled into the empty parking lot. He was getting close to admitting he liked her. Liked her a lot, wealthy debutante or not. He grinned to himself. What would the crew say when they found out he'd come full circle?

Whistling a happy tune somewhat off-key, Trask grasped the doorknob at the back entrance. His thoughts raced ahead to fresh-brewed coffee, followed by a detailed rundown of every last inch of the Cinderella coach before anyone else arrived. Suddenly, what seemed more important to him than his own success was that Jade's design turn out to be perfect so she could achieve the success *she* deserved. The realization came as a shock.

Not as much of a shock, though, as when he felt the door give easily under his hand. *Lord, but I'd only been half kidding when I said I didn't want to leave her alone last night.* Throwing open the door, Trask raced inside, never even considering the possibility that he might encounter danger himself. Dazed, it took him a moment to realize that the spot where the coach had stood last night was now empty.

No, not quite empty. He crossed the room and dropped to one knee. Where last night he'd left the sparkling Cinderella coach, today sat a large golden pumpkin and a cage with six white mice.

Jade's words came back clearly. She'd promised to leave before midnight—before her fairy godmother could turn the coach into a pumpkin.

Bitterness rose like bile in his throat. Did she think he'd find her childish prank amusing? Who had she charmed into helping spirit the coach away? Not Dan, surely. And Joe wouldn't have had any part in it. He'd rescued Greg. That left only Mikki Chan. Oh, how they must have enjoyed themselves at his expense!

He paced the room and smacked a fist into his open palm. Damn it! Jade knew how important the coach was to Fantasy Floats. To him. Not just important, he corrected. Crucial. Had she been laughing and plotting even as he kissed her? That hurt almost more than losing the coach. Kitty's long-ago rejection and the memory of her friends' laughter echoed in his mind.

Well, he'd been hurt before, but now his feelings were tougher. Jade Han could damn well get the coach back. Trask took one last look at the cage and stalked to the door. Jerking it open, he slammed it so hard in his wake that it rattled the windows on either side. If she thought he'd see Fantasy Floats go down the tubes for a lousy kiss, she had another think coming. Wouldn't he enjoy hauling her out of bed this morning to tell her? Jade Han made little Kitty Ferris look like an angel of mercy!

CHAPTER SIX

JADE AWOKE with a smile on her face. She stretched leisurely and contemplated the changes that had occurred between T. Stratton and her in one day. Pleasurable changes. Who would have thought it possible? She sat up and tugged lovingly on one of Wrinks's ears.

The pup opened an eye and wiggled under her hand.

"Like that, do you, fella?" she murmured, reaching for her slippers. "I know how you feel. Come on, lazybones. Today we'll start with a run. If I don't burn off this excess energy, I'll explode."

Securing her hair in one long braid, Jade pulled on sweats and jogging shoes while the dog paced restlessly between the bed and the door. He took the stairs two at a time, almost faster than his short legs would allow.

Laughing at his clumsy antics, Jade was brought up short at the kitchen door by her grandmother's stern reproval.

"Such frivolity from a young woman who left her betrothed waiting the night away? Your grandfather was not pleased, child."

Jade paused with her hand on the door. "I called and explained having to work late." Then Jade gave up trying to contain her excitement. "Oh, Grandmother! I saw my design finished last night. What a joy!"

Wrinks whined as Grandmother Han set the kettle down hard on a front burner and lit the gas beneath it with a hiss. "Last evening, Mikki brought pictures of Hong Kong. When you were not here, he took them over to show Mei Li and the Mings."

Jade absorbed the thinly veiled reprimand. Anger showed in every line of her grandmother's stiff back and in the sharp tone of her voice. Some of Jade's pleasure died. Darn Mikki. She understood his desire to see Mei Li, but why provoke her family? After all, she was doing him a favor.

Not only that, the longer Mikki and Mei Li waited, the more her grandparents would suffer. Granted, she'd agreed to give the couple time, but patience had never been one of her virtues. Jade sighed as she opened the door. Then she took a deep breath. "I'm taking Wrinks for a run, Grandmother. Mr. Jennings said I could go in late today." She turned with a bright smile. "I've got an idea. When I return, we'll have tea—the way we did whenever I had a late class."

Grandmother Han's features relaxed. "Go, then." She smiled indulgently. "I will never understand this appetite you have for running, Jade. You should have babies to occupy your time. Nevertheless, I'll be happy to have your company over breakfast. We'll talk—like old times."

Jade closed the door quietly behind her. Old times. She wondered if that meant old times before her parents died, or old times after. Either way, coming from her grandmother, it meant a serious lecture on etiquette.

Throughout her run, Jade's thoughts kept straying to her grandmother's remark about babies. What color eyes would babies coming of a union between T. Stratton and her have? The mere speculation caused her step to falter and her heart to beat faster.

In anticipation of a real womanly chat—the first in a long while—Jade rushed through her shower. She was skipping lightly down the stairs, buttoning the collar of her new blouse, when she heard the squeal of brakes in the drive and then a loud hammering on the door.

Grandfather Han reached it first and flung it open to reveal a clearly furious Trask Jennings.

"Where's Jade?" he demanded, following a curt dip of his head by way of greeting the elder Han.

"T. Stratton! What's wrong?" Jade's smile fled and her eyes widened as she moved in behind her grandfather and got a good look at her boss's lowered brows and set lips. "You did say...I mean, I...I...I'm not late, am I?" she stammered.

Trask skirted the man and glowered down at Jade. "Who took it?" he asked coldly. "You have one hour to get it back. Not a minute longer."

She looked puzzled. Wrinks loped down the stairs and immediately seized T. Stratton's pant leg.

He bent to disengage the animal's sharp teeth from his jeans, but the pup growled and refused to be dislodged.

"Will you call off this attack dog?" Trask roared, hopping around with Wrinks clamped to one leg.

Jade smothered a laugh and snapped her fingers to call off the rebellious young dog, who ignored her. "I'm sorry, T. Stratton," she said, frowning. "I think he's going through his adolescent stage. Wrinks! Stop that!" She grabbed the pup's collar. "Now what were you saying? Who took what?"

"You know what. Who helped you dream up that charade? Or did you manage it all on your own?" Giving up trying to free his pant leg, Trask reached down and wrapped a hand around her upper arm, pulling her up and onto her tiptoes.

"Stop, you're hurting me," she complained. Wrinks finally let go of the jeans and bared his teeth. She pulled away, massaging her arm. "I can see you're very upset about something," she said, waving away her grandfather's intervention and scooping up the dog. "But for the life of me, I don't know what this is about. I cleaned up last night as we agreed. And I was careful to put everything back in its rightful place. If something's been misplaced, I'm sure I didn't do it."

"The coach is gone." His face contorted at her gasp. "Don't expect me to believe you're innocent," he said scornfully. "Leaving the pumpkin and the white mice was a dead giveaway, Jade. Who else would have left such an ingenious calling card? Your fairy godmother?" He took a step forward and loomed over her. "Well, hear this, Miss Han. This is no fairy tale. It comes under the heading of grand theft."

The color drained from Jade's face. "But I locked the door and tested it before I left. T. Stratton...I never...I wouldn't..." She let her sentence trail off as the full impact of his accusation hit her. Then she felt the storm in her eyes grow to match his. "How could you even think such a thing? It's my design. Why would I take it? What would I do with it? I mean it's not as if floats are in demand on the black market."

"Don't pull that fake innocence on me, lady. There may be any number of reasons you'd like to see me fall on my face. Far be it from me to know what's in that devious mind of yours.

Like a fool, I lost my head last night and played right into your hands. Today I'm smarter. Ten o'clock sharp, princess. If the coach isn't back by then, I swear we'll see how you like quoting fairy tales to the Pasadena police.''

Trask glared at Jade's grandfather, then as if remembering his manners, he bowed deeply from the waist before he slammed out the door. His Wagoneer was spitting gravel by the time Jade came to her senses.

''Of all the no-good, arrogant jerks! Just where does he get off, accusing me?'' She stalked to the door, Wrinks clutched under one arm, and yanked it open to watch Trask's vehicle turn onto the main street, spewing a trail of dust. ''Ha! I think it's more likely this is all *his* doing. Now that he has my coach, maybe he thinks he can find a *real* designer. . . .'' Tears pressed at the back of her eyes. ''I'm the fool,'' she muttered against the dog's soft fur. ''He never wanted me as an apprentice.'' She would have broken completely, but stopped when she saw a smile pass between her grandparents.

''You weren't behind this by any chance, were you, Grandfather?'' she asked suspiciously. ''After all, you've made it clear you think I should quit.''

The old man smiled serenely, closing his eyes and folding his hands. ''I didn't spirit your design away from Mr. Jennings, Granddaughter. I smile because destiny has a way of working itself out. Shall we eat?''

''Eat? I couldn't eat a bite.'' Jade dumped a contented dog into the old man's arms and grabbed her purse. ''Sometimes destiny needs a push in the right direction, Grandfather. And I'm about to help T. Stratton out with a hefty shove.'' Digging for her car keys, she stamped out.

Jade fumed all the way to Fantasy Floats. She slipped in the back door, not wanting to take a chance on meeting T. Stratton. She was so furious she could spit nails. Catching Greg Sanders's eye, she motioned him over.

''Say, princess,'' he said, giving a low whistle. ''Your stock isn't worth much with the boss just now. So where's the coach?''

''I was hoping you or Dan or one of the others would know that,'' she whispered. ''You didn't really think I'd steal it, did you?''

"Nah! I didn't . . . not really. But we don't have a clue." He began to chuckle. "You have to admit it's pretty funny. I'd give a week's pay to have seen T.J.'s face when he got a load of that pumpkin and the white mice. Go see for yourself. They're sitting in Nell's office and she's in a tizzy."

Jade stared at him, unsmiling, until his laugh gave way to a lopsided grin.

"Does anyone have it in for T. Stratton?" she asked, frowning.

"He's one of the most well-liked guys I know," said Dan Jones, stepping up behind her. "Doesn't have an enemy in the world. Does he, Joe?" He turned to their foreman.

"Trask seems positive Jade's at the bottom of this." Joe studied her solemnly. "How about it? We can all appreciate a joke. And you owe him one if anyone does. Truth is, we've been known to pull a few good ones ourselves, but the timing on this is off."

"You too, Joe?" Her tone reflected the sorrow his accusations caused. "I don't see how you can work with me and think I'm a thief. I'll just go gather my personal things." Her lip trembled. "Would you let me know, please, if you get the coach back?" Head bent, she turned away.

"I didn't call you a thief, Jade," Joe protested. "I said *joke.*"

"A thin line between the two in this case, wouldn't you say?"

They all whipped around as Trask strode into their midst. His barely checked anger was almost palpable.

"Now, T.J.," Dan countered, "whatever happened to that good old American belief that you're innocent until proven guilty? You know as well as I do that it would've taken a truck to move that baby. Jade doesn't have a truck."

"Knock, knock. Anybody home?"

Simultaneously the crew turned toward the voice. A brown-haired man stood grinning at them mischievously through the back door. Soon he was joined by a second man, who could have been his twin except for darker eyes and a huskier build.

Trask moved to greet them. "Charlie! Calvin! What brings you two out on a workday? If you're looking to filch some of our designs, think again." Vigorously he shook hands with first one, then the other.

"How's everything going, T.J.? Looks mighty dead around here if you ask me. You got problems?"

Trask shot his team a warning look. "We're doing fine, Calvin. Have all the contracts we can handle. How about you?"

Greg cupped a hand over his mouth and whispered to Jade, "It's the Rasmussen brothers from down the street. Our closest competitors."

"Hey, Charles!" Dan yelled. "You come by to give me the twenty you owe me from last week's poker game? I figured you'd try and welch."

"Got it right here, Jones." The more slender of the two waved a bill. "As a matter of fact, I dropped by last night to leave it. Thought maybe I'd take a gander at that Cinderella coach you've been bragging about. Met Nell in the parking lot on her way out. She said you'd already gone. Said you were out fleecing somebody else."

"My four queens beat your full house, fair and square."

"Okay, okay. Don't get huffy." Charlie darted a glance around the room as he approached, and gave a little Cheshire cat grin. "Cal and I kind of thought you fellows might be needing a fairy godmother." He handed over a crisp twenty-dollar bill and scratched his head, then winked at his brother.

Greg Sanders let out a yelp. "You guys stole our coach. Son of a gun!" He smacked his head with a palm. "We should have guessed. After that number we pulled on you last season—when we sent you the phony cable saying your foliage order was screwed up and you wouldn't be getting any flowers." Bounding over, Greg caught the younger Rasmussen around the neck. "Where is it, clod? Either of you wanna see the light of day again, you better give it back fast."

Trask simply stared from one to the other in dismay as his crew pounced, following Greg's lead.

Jade stood quietly in the background, overwhelmed by relief.

"We give. We give," yelled Charlie in the midst of a tussle. "But darn it all. After all our clever midnight requisitioning, there wasn't a peep out of you...." He threw up his hands in mock despair. "What's this world coming to if you can't even play a decent joke on your friends?" He laughed. "We walked right through your front door. Unlocked the window in Nell's office yesterday afternoon, big as you please. Then we sneaked back later."

"Friends," Trask bellowed, pushing the huskier of the two men toward the door. "Thieves—both of you. Another hour and I'd have been doomed. If that's the mark of a friend, don't give me enemies." He glanced back over one shoulder. "Joe, will you bring the truck? We'll go pick up our merchandise while we have some brawn to help us get it back here. While you're at it, give Charlie back his damn white mice before Nell quits."

Jade chewed at her lip as the men all made a beeline for the door. Not one of them stopped to apologize for suspecting her and that made her furious. If T. Stratton Jennings didn't say he was sorry soon, she'd tell him to find that new designer, with her blessing—if he thought it'd be so easy.

Hours passed and T. Stratton didn't stop by. Then, like magic, when she was gone for lunch, a crystal dish with a delicate white lotus blossom appeared on her desk. There was no card, but Jade knew *he'd* left it. Especially when she heard from Joe that he'd given her full credit with the committee. She told herself that T. Stratton would probably come by later, but he continued to avoid her. Puzzled by his strange behavior, she decided to wait him out. Two could play his game of silence— and after all, the lovely lotus blossom was almost an apology.

SPRING MELTED into summer unnoticed. The crew was well on its way to completing Jade's version of Rapunzel and the workdays were growing longer. She noticed T. Stratton was spending more time closeted with Nell. Adding-machine tape spilled from the bookkeeper's desk to the floor. Was he still in a financial bind even after he'd received the final payment on the coach?

One night Jade was leaving later than usual and paused in the front office to speak with Nell. "I've missed you at lunch lately. Have you stopped brown-bagging it?"

"Heavens no, Jade. I can't afford to do anything but pack my own. You know I had to break down and get a new car." She grimaced.

"I didn't know," Jade answered. "What kind did you end up with?"

"This time I bought American. An economy Ford. T.J. said it would be less expensive if I ever needed any work done. It's not new, but he checked it out thoroughly."

"Oh, is he a mechanic, too?" Jade rested her portfolio on the counter. "Sounds like our boss is quite versatile. How does he find the time to run his business and do all the volunteer work I keep hearing about, too?"

Nell glanced up from her spreadsheet. "Do I detect a note of sarcasm? You know, Jade, it really isn't any of my business, but I wish you wouldn't be so hard on him. The boy has had a rough life."

"Boy?" Jade arched a brow.

Nell flushed. "Well, when you get to be my age, they're all boys."

"What made his life so hard?" Jade asked out of curiosity.

"Well, I guess I wouldn't be telling you anything you couldn't find out from the others if you asked. T.J. was left on the steps of an orphanage as an infant. Growing up, he developed a tough exterior that made him virtually unadoptable. He was in and out of foster homes and kicked from pillar to post." She picked up her pencil and toyed with it. "Underneath is still a piece of that lost little boy. What he needs is a good woman."

Jade bit her lip. "You mean he doesn't know anything about his parents?" She thought about her own heritage, traced back for centuries.

"Not even a name. Is it any wonder he donates his spare time to helping kids nobody wants? I tell him he should get married and have one or two of his own. He could always adopt some, too."

"I imagine it would be hard knowing you weren't wanted," Jade said thoughtfully. "Uh, I haven't seen Cynthia around much in the past few weeks. I assumed they were involved. Is it over?"

Nell gave an unladylike snort. "Wouldn't that be a blessing? But no such luck. Mrs. Osborn is summering in a cooler climate. She says the dry heat is bad for her skin. I just wish she'd stop calling T.J. every day. If I don't have him get back to her within ten minutes, she's on the phone again, accusing me of not giving him the message."

Jade smiled and hefted her portfolio. "Sounds like Mei Li. Either she or Mikki calls and interrupts my work just when I'm busiest."

"Mikki... He's the muscle man in the white suit, right?" Nell grinned as Jade gave an indifferent shrug. "Why don't you just tell him to get lost?"

"She can't," T.J. said sarcastically, coming around the corner. "Mikki is her intended."

Nell's mouth dropped. "As in future husband?" she asked.

"Bingo," drawled Trask. "Give the lady a Kewpie doll. You're quicker than I was, Nell. I asked 'intended what?' "

Jade glared at him. She hadn't confided in anyone else at work. Now she'd either have to tell more lies or break her word to Mei Li. Darn T. Stratton. He hadn't come near her in weeks. Why now? "It's a long story, Nell," she mumbled. "Mikki is my grandparents' choice of a husband for me." That much was true, she reasoned.

The older woman's eyes took on a faraway look. "I chose my Johnny and he chose me. We had some thirty glorious years together and him with a bad heart all along. If I'd listened to my family, I wouldn't have married him and I'd have been alone and miserable those same thirty years. Sometimes people have to make a stand for what they feel is right."

Jade saw that T. Stratton was riffling through a stack of mail. His shoulders seemed tense as if he cared about her answer, though she knew that couldn't be. "It's not as easy as you might think to go against custom, Nell. But listen, I've kept you from your work long enough. I'd better go."

"Don't give up," Nell called out after her. "You just haven't found a man who's worth fighting for yet. All I'm saying, Jade, is you should think about what you want. Don't ever settle for second-best."

Jade did think about it all the way home. In fact, she grew morose brooding about her predicament and had to force herself to go swimming with Mikki and Mei Li. Never had she felt more guilty than she did now, knowing that in the end, her grandparents would still be hurt. What if they never forgave her bringing shame to the family? At times like this, Jade missed her parents more than she could say. But then, if they'd lived, she wouldn't have been in this dilemma.

Summer reached its height, but resolutions on both home and work fronts continued to evade her. There were more facets of the business to be learned than she had ever imagined. After her chat with Nell, Jade went out of her way to be more considerate of T. Stratton's feelings. In the mornings, she treated him to her very best smile and throughout the day, she pitched in without complaint.

At times she caught him watching her, a faint frown creasing his brow. Sometimes she even thought she saw some deeper, more indefinable expression on his strained features, but he rarely entered her cubicle. Neither did he mention the TV campaign spotlighting her coach. From the others, she heard that he praised her later designs, but that was only hearsay.

Observing him, she wondered when he'd had time to praise anything. He pushed himself unmercifully and it was obvious he wasn't sleeping well or eating right. His cheeks were gaunt and he was losing weight. Plus, she noticed, he was spending an inordinate amount of time on the telephone.

One day as Jade passed Nell's office, she happened to see him slam the phone down, then close his eyes and cover his face with his hands as he massaged his forehead with his fingertips. She paused a moment, then continued on her way. Her heart ached for him.

Just outside her cubby, she encountered Joe, their harried foreman, as he wheeled a cart laden with chicken wire toward the latest float beginning to take shape. "Do you have a minute, Joe?" she asked urgently.

He stopped and bowed extravagantly, dropping the handle of the cart. "Your slightest wish is my command, princess."

"No joking, Joe. I'm serious. Is construction going well? Are we having problems with this newest design that you're not telling me?"

He pulled a handkerchief from his back pocket and wiped the sweat from his brow. The end of July was unbearable in the warehouse because the double doors had to be kept open for the many delivery trucks.

"I thought we were looking pretty good." He stuffed the handkerchief into his pocket again. "You knew about the initial problems we had with the circuitry on Snow White's wicked stepmama." Joe winked. "Once Daniel Jones, our resident electrical wizard, got his head out of the clouds and checked his textbook the way you suggested, the old dame's mirror image talked up a storm. I know he still has his nose out of joint because you were right, but did you see something else I should know about?''

She smiled. ''I wasn't thinking about Dan. It's T. Stratton. Lately he looks so stressed.'' She drew her lower lip between her teeth and glanced away. ''Of course, I didn't really expect him to take part in the surprise birthday celebration the crew gave me last week, but he didn't even stop working long enough to taste a piece of Nell's cake.''

''Hey, the boss signed your card, didn't he? Don't take it personally, Jade. It's the foliage thing rearing its ugly head again. The second installment is due and T.J.'s short on cash. Nell says sponsors are slow to pay. We don't have much in the way of collateral, you know. He still owes on this building and we lease the sheds.''

''No, I didn't know. Lately I've been handling some of my father's investments. I'm learning how stocks work, but I've never had to get a loan. And don't you dare call me princess again.'' She glared at him. ''The other day Nell mentioned a second mortgage. Does he own a house?''

Joe rubbed the back of his neck. ''A condo, and he's already mortgaged to the hilt. Last year he secured it to buy land in the Sierra Madres in order to build a camp for disadvantaged boys. Price of lumber shot up and construction on the bunkhouses and the recreation center's been going slow. But, hey, no need for you to concern yourself with the nitty-gritty details. T.J. will figure it out. He always does.''

Her eyes flashed. ''Can't any of you see he's about to drop? Maybe in the past he's always saved the day, but I see him floundering. If someone doesn't make him relax, before long there won't be any Fantasy Floats.''

''Point well taken.'' Joe looked contrite. ''T.J.'s as stubborn as they come and proud to boot. Tell you what, Jade. Over the next couple of days I expect a lull in our workload. It won't last, but if you can think of a way to spirit him out of here for six or eight hours, why not try? The rest of us have about given up. Me included. Now if I don't get this wire over to Greg, we'll be even further behind. I'll wish you luck, Jade.''

Jade was already turning the problem over in her mind. The Chinese celebration of the Eighth Moon was drawing near. This was a time for families to honor their ancestors. But there was nothing somber about it—a joyous, uplifting celebration that involved eating, watching puppetry, playing games and relaxing. Jade decided it was the perfect solution, if only she could convince her family and the Mings to include T. Stratton in their festivities. After much thought, she hit upon a second idea—a way to ease his financial woes.

Her spirits buoyed, Jade made a quick telephone call to Mei Li's parents. They were hosting this year's festival for a group of close friends. Mikki would be back from his latest personal appearance tour in Hong Kong, so Mei Li's mother readily gave her consent. Now, Jade thought, if she could only get T. Stratton to agree, she'd deal with her grandparents later.

"T. Stratton." Jade tapped on the door to Nell's office where she could see him still buried in the books. Without waiting for an invitation, she walked in. Her plan was to enlist the bookkeeper's support, too; however, Trask was alone in the office.

"If you need Nell, she went to the post office." He marked his place in the ledger with a ruler and glanced up. "Your new designs coming along?"

"Mmm . . . yes," she said. Then before she could lose her nerve, she plunged in. "Next Sunday, Mei Li's family is having a celebration. Joe mentioned there'd be a break in the workload."

As she paused for breath, he started to speak, his voice carefully nonchalant. "Ah! Another birthday party, huh?" He leaned back in his chair and let his gaze drift over her. "Well, you don't look any the worse for wear after the last one. It's when you turn thirty that those wild parties have to go." He smiled. "Take a day, Jade. You've earned it. Have fun!"

"It's not for my birthday, T. Stratton," she blurted. "It's a major Chinese celebration. One to which it's customary to invite friends and sometimes even strangers for the day. My friends wish to include you." Because she knew he was about to turn her down, she added, "I'll lose face if you refuse." Crossing her fingers behind her back—something that she'd learned in elementary school to ward off little white lies—she dropped her lashes and stood very still.

Trask's heart thundered a warning in his ears. When Jade
Han lowered her long lashes as she was in the habit of doing,
it was all he could do to keep his hands off her. All these weeks
when he'd forced himself to look elsewhere, to go out of his
way to avoid her, all were lost in that one innocent gesture. Her
quietly submissive posture rammed home the fact that he
should be the one down on his knees begging her forgiveness.
He'd never apologized for accusing her of stealing that blasted
coach. He recognized now that in sending her that flower, he'd
taken the coward's way out. It was time to make amends.

Trask cleared his throat. "Well...we, ah, can't have anyone losing face now, can we? I read something in a magazine
recently about the Eighth Moon ritual. I'll look forward to
joining in. Tell me where and when. I'll be there." He didn't
add that in his spare moments he was reading up on all Chinese customs.

Jade's eyes flew open, meeting his. His easy acceptance had
shocked her. She had to work at hiding her surprise.

"And Jade," he said softly, "I should have suspected the
Rasmussens. I—" Just then the telephone shrilled. Throwing
her a helpless shrug, he grabbed it on the third ring. The conversation plunged him deep in business again, allowing Jade
time to control her rampaging heart. Before he changed his
mind, she sketched a map to the Mings and tucked it beneath
his drumming fingers, then quickly slipped out.

All the way home, Jade prepared logical reasons to give to
her grandparents for including him in this annual event. Much
to her surprise, they accepted her first rationale without qualm.
Caught up in the spirit of the celebration, the elder Hans agreed
that a person having no family of his own should be asked to
share theirs.

At first Jade felt guilty about doubting their compassion. But
as the days sped by, she began to feel more relaxed and lighthearted. She and Mei Li spent the evening baking moon
cakes—the party treats filled with a sweet mixture of ground
lotus, sesame seeds and duck-egg yolk. It felt like old times. As
they fashioned the fragile lanterns that had become significant
for this special day, Jade felt sure she'd done the right thing in
inviting T. Stratton. When Mikki returned, he grumbled and

said it would be awkward, but in the end he gave in, because Mei Li cajoled him.

Sunday came and Jade's stomach seemed to be full of butterflies. She dressed early and paced until it was time to go. Although T. Stratton wouldn't be the only guest, he might very well be the only non-Chinese, and Jade didn't want him to feel out of place.

Again he surprised her, this time by his sensitivity in bringing his hosts a gift, in keeping with Chinese practice. A small porcelain vase. Delicate, yet not outrageously expensive. A proper choice. And he looked wonderful, as Mei Li was quick to point out.

"Psst, Jade! Your Mr. Jennings is very handsome in those cream slacks and black polo. Are you quite certain all your late nights have been confined to building floats?"

Jade blushed. "Shh, Mei Li. Someone might hear you."

"You're right, of course." Mei Li sighed. "I'm not cut out for cloak-and-dagger activities. Sometimes I wish Mikki would just pick up the phone and call Roger."

"Why don't you call him?" Jade asked—not for the first time.

"I couldn't," Mei Li answered. "It's not my place. You forget how it is for me. Look—" she changed the subject "—Mikki seems restless, doesn't he? Do you think we dare walk on the beach alone? Oh, I know, Jade, let's ask your Mr. Jennings to join us."

"Mr. Jennings is not mine, Mei Li," Jade reminded her sharply. "You know that." Then in a more indulgent voice, she added, "A walk would be nice. I have a business proposition I'd like to discuss with T. Stratton. Can you keep Mikki occupied for a time?"

Mei Li smiled her thanks and nodded eagerly.

As they approached the men, Jade couldn't help thinking that each was handsome in his own right. Remembering how solid and strong T. Stratton's chest had felt under her hands brought a new wave of color to her cheeks. She would do well to keep her thoughts on business.

Redondo Beach was filled with Sunday bathers. Walkers, bikers and skateboarders all vied for space. The two couples sauntered along the harder-packed sand near the ocean's edge and made idle talk.

"This reminds me of Ocean Park near Repulse Bay in Hong Kong." Mikki sounded nostalgic. "I've reserved a suite there for our honeymoon."

Because she knew T. Stratton would assume he meant a honeymoon with her, Jade bent swiftly and picked up a smooth clam shell. She was angry with Mikki for bringing up the subject of marriage at all.

Trask stopped beside her. He stared out to sea, shading his eyes. "Will that be soon? I thought you were going to finish out the season with Fantasy Floats. Our busiest days are still to come."

"My family is due here in December," Mikki cut in coldly. "Jade's grandparents want her to show them around."

Jade and Mei Li exchanged a look of dismay. What was Mikki doing?

Trask's jaw tensed. "You'd leave us high and dry in December? That's our most crucial month."

"Look, there's a marvelous house over on the bluff." Determined to change the subject—for now—Jade strode toward a weathered gray structure, all angles, windows and skylights.

Everyone turned automatically.

Mei Li climbed the few steps built into the bank. "It's for sale, Jade," she called, beckoning them to come.

"Can you imagine what a view it'd have at sunset?" Jade leaned forward to touch the low fence. "And that top room. The one jutting out over the porch. I'll bet the lighting would be perfect for my drawing."

Mikki sniffed. "It's too small for proper entertaining. You can see there's no privacy at all." He swept a hand, encompassing the busy beach. "I have a lovely old home on Victoria Peak picked out. As you know, that's one of the most prestigious neighborhoods in Hong Kong. The house I've selected has large rooms, high ceilings, a center courtyard and is walled all around."

"Sounds beautiful, Mikki," Mei Li squealed. "Tell me all about it." Taking him by the arm, she pulled him away, giving Jade a signal to stay behind.

Jade chewed her lip, casting a last wistful look at the beach house before falling silently into step with Trask. "I won't leave you in the lurch, T. Stratton," she promised. "I said I'd stay and I will."

"I'll bet," he growled.

"I will! Slow down. I have a present for you." Jade stopped, reached into the patch pocket of her full skirt and retrieved a folded paper.

He paused in midstride. "A present? Now wait. If someone told you it was my birthday, they didn't tell the truth." He backed away from the paper she extended. "I don't celebrate my birthday."

"All presents aren't for birthdays, T. Stratton. Here, take it. Unlike my pup, this gift won't bite you." She stepped close, laughing up into his eyes.

Mesmerized by her smile, he accepted what looked to be some sort of contract. Scanning it, Trask saw that it authorized him to purchase flowers at cost from a wholesale flower company in Holland. He raised his head so fast he almost dropped the sheet of paper.

"Is this some kind of joke?"

The excitement in her eyes abruptly died. "It's no joke, T. Stratton. It's a present, as I told you. I have controlling stock in this company—part of a trust set up by my father. He chose this for me because he knew I planned to make floats my career." She shrugged. "I thought it would make you happy. You need a flower source, don't you? Why must you make everything so complicated? The Eighth Moon is a time for giving gifts."

"A bottle of wine is a gift. A box of chocolates is a gift. This," he said, "is more like handing over the keys to Fort Knox." Refolding the paper, he shoved it back in her hand. Pointing to Mikki, who was by now far down the beach with Mei Li, he bit out sarcastically, "Lover boy may live off a lady's money, but not me! I make my own way in this world and don't you forget it."

"Why are you so angry? I only meant to help." Her eyes began to fill with tears despite her effort to fight them back.

He ran one hand through his hair in agitation. "Does Mikki know you offered me this gift?"

She looked stricken, knowing he thought Mikki would soon be sharing her bank account and therefore her investments. "N-no, he doesn't," she stammered, telling the truth as far as it went, but bound by honor not to say more. "We—" she started, then stopped. He would never understand.

"Never mind," he said curtly, holding up a hand. "When your family finds out what you've done, they'll squelch it soon enough."

For a minute there, Trask had almost broken his own code— had almost been tempted by her unexpected generosity. Damn, he wanted to believe she was different. Then his eyes lit on the contract she held. Jade Han was no different than Kitty Ferris or a dozen others he'd met. Sooner or later all women with money thought they could buy a man.

T.J. abandoned his emotional struggle and felt his face grow rigid. "Make my excuses to the Mings, please," he requested in a tight voice. Then he walked away and left her standing there, alone.

CHAPTER SEVEN

DURING THE REMAINDER of the Eighth Moon celebration, Jade retreated into her misery. If only she had some idea why her gift had made T. Stratton so angry, she might be able to concentrate on the puppet show. She hadn't meant to insult him. Pride was something she understood.

Sighing, Jade rubbed her temples. He needed affordable flowers. So he needed her... and maybe in other ways, too. Somehow she must find a way to help. Jade frowned, remembering Nell's confidences about her boss. Were all men in need so stubborn?

"What were you and Jennings arguing about before he left, Jade?" Mikki whispered near her ear. "This show is outstanding, yet you've hardly noticed. I saw you rubbing your head. If the man gives you a headache, you should quit." His gaze narrowed on her. "Frown lines cause aging. See how happy and carefree Mei Li is. She will look young much longer."

"Mei Li *is* younger than I am, Mikki," Jade said dryly. "And Mr. Jennings did not give me a headache. He and I were discussing the cost of flowers. But it bothered me that you let him think our marriage was still on."

Mikki compressed his lips. "I owe it to your grandparents, Jade. I'm afraid Jennings is after your fortune."

Jade gasped. "That's ridiculous, Mikki!"

"Well, why would he come to a family gathering?"

"Because I invited him. And you had no right insinuating I'd leave him in a bind. I gave my word."

"I say he's a fortune hunter. And everyone knows a woman's word is quite different from a man's."

For a stunned moment, Jade simply stared at him. Then her voice rose in anger. "T. Stratton's the most unmaterialistic person I know, Mikki Chan. And furthermore, my word is as valuable as yours."

"Shh! Keep your voice down, Jade. Other people are trying to enjoy the performance. You know perfectly well that women are as changeable as the seasons."

She jumped to her feet and shot Mei Li a look of pity. "If women have so little value, Mikki, I can't imagine why you want a wife. Maybe *you* should rethink getting married."

"Maybe you should, Mikki," shouted the male puppet from the stage. Members of the audience cast mildly curious glances toward the young couple and a few hid snickers behind their hands. Public outbursts were not common at Chinese gatherings.

Mikki passed a hand through his hair and nervously popped open the top button of his shirt. "Sit down, Jade," he hissed. "Do you want to ruin everything for Mei Li and me? Why can't you learn to curb your impetuosity?"

Jade would have exploded then and there, blowing the whole sham, had she not chanced to overhear her grandmother whispering to Mrs. Ming. "Things will be better," the older woman confided, "once this marriage is over and we all return to Hong Kong." Shocked, Jade heard her mention counting the days until her granddaughter's contract with the float company ended and they all returned to their beloved Hong Kong.

Ice balled in the pit of Jade's stomach. Now she understood; her marriage was a ticket out of California for the elder Hans. What a mess she was in. Yet she loved them, this gentle couple who had stayed and made a home for her when her world seemed irreparably shattered. Suddenly it became terribly clear what she must do. She must talk with Mikki and Mei Li and arrange for her grandparents to accompany them to Hong Kong.

Jade felt her cheeks go hot, then cold. She struggled with her own pain at the thought of their leaving. "Please excuse me," she mumbled, standing up, knowing she had to get away. "I'm not feeling well. I think I'll go home and lie down."

Guests in the row where she was seated shifted silently to let her pass.

Mei Li jumped as if to follow, but Mikki shook his head and pulled her back. "Let her go, Mei Li. By tomorrow, this will all have blown over. We cannot let your family or hers think she questions my authority. You know I speak the truth, don't you, little sparrow?''

Slumping back in her seat, Mei Li nodded unhappily.

That night, Jade tossed and turned, plagued by visions of being abandoned by her grandparents and her best friend. She grappled with floats having no flowers and T. Stratton losing his company. In the morning, she had circles under her eyes and a queasy stomach. Likewise, her grandmother awakened with a touch of the flu, and her grandfather seemed content just to let Jade brew his wife's favorite herb tea and minister to her needs. Jade gladly played nurse, knowing this might be her last opportunity to show how much she cared. Fortunately Grandfather didn't bring up her argument with Mikki. If he had, Jade wasn't sure what her response would have been.

She left for work feeling unusually low—like an ungrateful granddaughter. It hadn't helped her mood to have Grandmother Han request her photo albums. The old woman chattered on and on about fond memories of Hong Kong as she and Jade shared a pot of tea.

What she had to do, Jade decided as she backed down the long drive, was confront Mikki. This was California. There were no matchmakers. If he loved Mei Li, he should stand up and ask for her hand. It occurred to her that T. Stratton would speak up for someone he loved; a man so direct about his likes and dislikes naturally would.

No, he certainly didn't shy away from dislikes, Jade found as she stepped through the warehouse door and T. Stratton pounced.

"You're late, Miss Han. We've turned your workstation upside down looking for a supply list for the castle and drawbridge on the Henderson float. Haven't you learned the value of keeping accurate records?"

"Missed your morning coffee, did you, T. Stratton?" Jade asked sweetly, sweeping past him with her head held high. So, they were back to Miss Han, were they?

From behind her boss, who paced the office like a tiger, Nell rolled her eyes heavenward. Greg Sanders made a throat-cutting motion with his hand. Joe Forrester shook his head grimly. But Jade simply smiled.

Marching down the hall, she thought how like a parade they must look, with T. Stratton and his crew trailing behind her. She took down a clipboard from a nail in her cubby and handed it over to T.J. with a flourish. "Here you go, sir," she said in the same honey-sweet tone. "Duplicates of all my preliminary supply lists in date order, most recent on top. Just as you taught me," she finished, not without sarcasm. "Is there a problem with our shipment?"

Trask rubbed a hand over his chin and accepted the sheaf of orders. He eyed her acerbically. "They claim they didn't receive *your* last order. I'll have Nell follow up on this right away." He turned back to her after dismissing the others.

"You sound awfully chipper this morning," Trask said, his tone somewhat lighter. "I take it your holiday ended a success?"

She arched a brow. Was he offering a truce? The timbre of his voice was gentler than she remembered. To keep her gaze off his lips, Jade turned and riffled through a stack of drawings. He moved to stand behind her and said how nice it had been of her family to include him. How sorry he was to have missed the rest of the festivities. His apology touched a raw nerve.

But as she whirled, intending to tell him what his action had cost her, she could see that he was genuinely sorry.

"You only missed the puppet show, T. Stratton," she mumbled, suddenly softening. "Puppet shows always have the same predictable characters. A handsome hero, an evil-looking villain and a tragic but beautiful heroine. Normally I love to watch the story unfold, but yesterday..." She didn't finish, afraid that if she told him she'd left early, he would think she blamed him.

Trask turned away, massaging the back of his neck. Damn it, the stricken look he'd seen in her eyes during their argument on the beach had haunted him all night and was largely responsible for his bad mood today. Yet nothing had changed—except that he wished things were different between them.

"Look," he said impatiently, releasing a pent-up breath, "I've known all along you wouldn't last the season. I don't like it, but I understand."

She'd been busy braiding her long hair while he talked. Now she twisted it into a loop at the back of her head and secured it with a large tortoiseshell clasp. "You don't understand anything, T. Stratton. I'm not leaving." She smiled. "Now, if that's all you need from me, I'd better get to work. When I left yesterday, Dan was struggling with a half-raised drawbridge and a moat filled with alligators refusing to snap." Laughing, she practically danced away.

Openmouthed, he watched her leave and wondered what it would be like next year when she was gone. The word "dismal" came to mind.

FOR MUCH OF SEPTEMBER, Trask's company was beset with problems. Shipments were late, the wrong goods delivered, and toward the end of the month, long-haul truckers went on strike. By the beginning of October, his team still had three floats left to construct and bits and pieces of others to complete.

Tempers flared daily, often running out of control. Jade spent so much time at work walking on eggshells that her problems at home paled by comparison.

Mikki had gone on another lengthy PR trip and Mei Li didn't seem to realize that her friend was functioning by rote when she called and cried on Jade's shoulder every night.

"I wish I had half your strength, Jade," she lamented during one of these conversations. "I love Mikki so much, but I hate this pretense. But I'm so afraid that if my parents had any inkling, they'd whisk me off to marry Roger tomorrow. I'd die if that happened, Jade. I really would."

She knew Mei Li spoke the truth about her parents. In the Ming household, her father's word was law. Jade didn't like continuing the deception, either, but she owed Mei Li unwavering friendship. "You *are* strong, Mei Li. I leaned on you when my parents died. Trust me, I won't give away your secret. Just hang in there, okay? When Mikki gets back, we'll go to the opera."

Mei Li's spirits revived immediately, but Jade sighed and wondered at her own softhearted capitulation.

However, considering that she didn't have the energy to confront her own family, she had no right to chastise Mikki and Mei Li. And there was poor innocent Roger to consider, too. But when Mikki finally did return in mid-October, he was so attentive to Mei Li that he no longer bothered playacting around her grandparents. Life fell into a comfortable pattern for Jade, both at home and at work, where she saw very little of her boss—he seemed to be avoiding her these days. Their relationship, such as it was, seemed to be at a standstill.

Like T. Stratton, Mikki could be quite charming and likable when he wasn't being lordly. Deep down, Jade knew it was wrong to keep pretending, but the weeks just seemed to slide past without anyone taking steps to set matters straight. It rarely occurred to Jade anymore that she was simply working herself into a tighter corner. Only when she saw T. Stratton did she realize what she was doing. But she was usually so distracted by his presence that the thought never stayed with her long.

Toward the end of a particularly trying week in late October, things perked up when Joe Forrester announced to the crew that he and his wife, Hillary, were hosting an old-fashioned Halloween party on Saturday night.

"Yahoo!" whooped Greg. "I've been looking for a chance to get Emily alone in a dark corner. Do you think you could arrange to tell some spooky stories so she'll get good and scared?"

"I guess you'll be inviting couples only, then," Dan reflected in a gloomy voice. "Say, Jade," he said, brightening, "I don't suppose you'd like to dump the karate kid and go with me?"

She put down her pen and frowned. "Mikki's art isn't for fighting—like karate." Without realizing she was defending him, she went on, "Wing chun was used centuries ago in China by the Shaolin as a form of spiritual self-discipline."

"So whoop-de-do!" Dan said, placing hands on hips. "Does that mean you won't forgo Mr. Wonderful and be my date?"

"I don't think I'll go at all," she said. Not that she didn't want to, but it would be easier to stay home than explain to her grandparents.

"I'll be your date, Daniel," Nell broke in. "If pairing up with you is the only way to get some of Hillary's gourmet cooking, I'll make the supreme sacrifice." She turned to Jade. "If you don't go, honey, you'll miss the best food of your life. How about bringing Mikki? It's time he met this crazy group."

Jade felt the color drain from her face. She mumbled something about not being able to go without Mei Li as chaperon and hoped that would be the end of the discussion.

"So we'll get your chaperon a date," Nell insisted. "Let Dan be your friend's partner and I'll invite my son. How does that sound?"

"Dan?" Jade looked horrified. "Oh, no. I'm sure he and Mei Li wouldn't—"

"And just why not?" the stocky engineer blustered. "Are you ashamed of your co-workers?"

"Of course not." Jade shook her head.

"Good, then it's settled." Joe rubbed his hands together briskly. "Everyone can come. Now let's get back to work."

"Did you invite T. Stratton, Joe?" Jade asked offhandedly when the others had gone back to their tasks.

"Sure did. I ran it by him first, just in case he expected us to work late on Saturday. In the beginning he wasn't keen on the idea, but Cynthia came in while we were discussing the party and she talked him into it. Lucky thing for us she's so persuasive."

"Huh...yes," Jade muttered. "Very lucky for us." She returned to her drawing board. Her hand shook as she drew her first line and she inadvertently smudged the paper. Ripping the ruined sheet from the tablet, she wadded it up and threw it into the trash. Maybe Mikki and Mei Li would simply refuse to go to the party.

But of course they didn't. At first Mikki grumbled about Jade's pairing Mei Li up with Dan, but he gave in when Mei Li pointed out that they could ride together. Because Mikki had to be on the set that day, they agreed Jade would go to the party directly from work. Mikki arranged for the limo to pick up Mei Li, knowing her family would be appeased. Jade felt the web of lies tighten. But in spite of her personal reservations about the evening, the promised party had the desired effect on the other crew members. Even T. Stratton.

Jade's own spirits lifted as she followed Joe home. Hillary greeted her at the door and joked, "So you're the new woman in my husband's life?" Jade attempted a protest, but Hillary held up a staying hand. "It's good. It's good," she proclaimed, laying her hand over her heart. "Gives Joe something to talk about besides basketball and float-building.'' The sprightly redhead ushered Jade through a homey living room, where a trio of rowdy young boys were sprawled in the middle of the floor tussling over a board game. ''By the way,'' she said, laughing, ''how has the wily fox taken to having you on staff?'' Because Jade looked blank, Hillary prompted, ''I mean T.J. He's so sure women are basically untrustworthy it must have been a rude awakening to have you bail him out of a tight spot.''

Jade was saved from commenting by the ringing of a telephone in the distance.

''That was a message for you, Jade,'' Hillary said on returning. ''Someone named Mikki. He said to tell you he was sorry, but they called a night shoot. He and Mei Li have to cancel tonight.''

''Oh, no!'' Jade bit her lip. ''That will ruin your numbers. I'll go, too.''

''You'll do no such thing,'' Hillary insisted. ''This isn't a couples' party. We can work out teams for the scavenger hunt. Joe said you were planning on Mei Li joining Dan—doesn't that leave him without a partner?''

Jade's stomach settled. Dan was fun. She could handle being teamed with him.

Joe, who'd put his three young sons to bed, joined the women again and quickly squelched that idea. ''Dan rang in on my business line just now. Can you believe it? The yo-yo forgot he had a date tonight. What could I do but tell him to bring her along? He's afraid Jade will have his hide for leaving her friend in the lurch.'' Joe rolled his eyes. ''You'll be gentle, won't you?''

''And of course you believe that two-hundred-pound weakling is afraid of me, right?'' When the others stopped laughing, she shrugged. ''If you think teams will work, I'll stay. I've never been on a scavenger hunt before. I've always thought they sounded fun.''

''Never?'' asked Joe and Hillary in unison.

''No.'' Jade shook her head. ''When my parents were alive, we carved jack-o'-lanterns. But my grandparents only celebrate Chinese holidays.''

"Well, you're in for a treat," Joe exclaimed. "Scavenger hunts are my favorite. With this zany bunch, anything can happen."

Which T.J. proved by arriving just then, also without a date. He stood in the doorway, declining to come in. "Cynthia has a terrible migraine headache, Hillary. I don't want to mess up another one of your dinners by being odd man out."

Hillary threw up her hands in defeat. "There's a lot of that going around, T.J. My table is beginning to look like Swiss cheese. Besides—" she quickly calculated on her fingers "—if I haven't lost count, the numbers are even again. You and Jade can be partners."

Across the room, Jade nearly choked on the apple cider Joe had just poured her. She would die of embarrassment if her boss refused to be paired with her—which he well might. But he agreed without hesitation.

Joe introduced the members of Hillary's gourmet-cooking group. Nell and her son, John Junior, arrived next. Nell's son was a surprise to Jade. He was gray-haired and looked almost as old as his mother. But he was a shy, pleasant man, and Jade found him easy to talk with when they drew each other as partners in an apple-bobbing contest. She would have made a pact with Lucifer to keep from touching noses with T. Stratton Jennings during that event.

Everyone did so poorly Joe broke out the hard cider. Once they all began to mellow and interact comfortably with one another, he announced the scavenger hunt.

Trask was the first to snap up a list. He could barely contain himself long enough to listen while Hillary went over the rules. Without the slightest restraint, he shoved the list at Jade and whispered, "Let's get a jump on this mangy crew."

Jade hung back. "Wait, T. Stratton. I've never been on one of these hunts before."

"Nothing to it," he insisted, grabbing her jacket and holding open the door. "I haven't been on one for years, but it's like riding a bicycle. Once you learn how, you never forget. Come on. I'll drive. You read the list and I'll select a likely house. Together we'll be unbeatable. What's the prize, anyway?"

"A candlelight dinner for two," Jade read from the sheet. "Prepared by Hillary and delivered to the winner's house." She felt her cheeks flame and was glad the porch light had been covered with black crepe paper. For a moment she envisioned what it would be like to share such an intimate dinner with T. Stratton.

"Quite a prize," he murmured. "Do you cook?" he asked curiously.

Jade dipped her head and climbed into his Wagoneer. "No, I don't."

He smiled. "Why did I know that? Well, Hillary's the only lady I know who cooks like a chef, and she's taken."

"We'll never find these things, T. Stratton," Jade burst out, aghast. She'd snapped on the overhead light and was reading through the list. "Just listen to this! One new brown shoelace, a spool of yellow thread, a package of filtered cigarettes, the twist cap from a bottle of light beer, a used pizza carton, a canceled stamp, a label from cream of mushroom soup and five unshelled peanuts." Her eyes met his, reflecting her concern.

"Sounds pretty easy to me," he assured her. "We'll pick a house where it looks like they're having a roaring party. If they're already in the swing of things, you can usually get everything you need from one or two stops. The brown shoelace may be the toughest, because nobody will want to give one up. But basically, they're all simple things. I think speed is the real test here. Look—see that house over there?"

"Oh. They have jack-o'-lanterns! I haven't carved one in years." Jade pressed her nose to the window, trying to take it all in. "Look!" She gripped his arm. "All the houses along this street have them grinning at us. Some are so evil-looking they make me nervous."

"Scaredy-cat," he admonished, whipping the Wagoneer into a clear parking space. "Just hurry, will you? I like eating."

"You like winning," she corrected, as she arrived in front of a stranger's door, hot on his heels and out of breath.

As Trask made his pitch to the host, Jade could see why he was so successful. He could charm a person out of his socks if he set his mind to it. The revelers really got into the spirit of the enterprise and supplied them with all but two items. Hard as they tried, the fun-loving crowd couldn't come up with a pizza carton or a soup label. Giving a hurried thanks to a gruesome pirate who followed them to the door, Trask propelled Jade to his vehicle and drove as fast as he dared until he found a pizza parlor. When he had sweet-talked the cute young teenager at the cash register out of a discarded box, he drove down the street to the nearest convenience market, having decided the easiest approach was just to buy a can of soup.

Trask was digging in his pockets almost before the Wagoneer stopped. An odd expression crossed his face. "Damn! I left my wallet on the bed. Do you have any change, Jade?"

"I didn't bring my purse. Hillary said it would just get in the way."

He snapped his fingers and grinned. "Tell you what. I've done all the work up to now. The soup is all yours."

She gasped. "T. Stratton... I've never done this before."

"So live a little, kid. Go in there and throw yourself on the mercy of that clerk. Make something up. Tell him you—" He laughed when he saw her anguish. "Never mind," he said. "That obviously won't work."

She gave him a weak smile.

"I'll bet you've never told a lie in your life. That's one of the things I admire about you, Jade. I've met damn few honest women, but you're one. Don't change," he said softly, running a gentle finger down her cheek.

Jade shied away. He couldn't have said anything that caused her more pain. She thought of the many lies she'd told lately. She didn't deserve any of the nice things he said. Darn it, she wanted him to win this contest.

He had been rechecking all his pockets and was now rummaging around in the glove compartment.

"Wait," she said, grabbing his arm. "There—under that map. Two quarters." She snatched them up. "Do you think fifty cents will buy a can of soup?"

Trask looked doubtful.

"Stay right here. Don't go away," she said. "I'm going to get that soup. This is my challenge, T. Stratton." Thrusting open the door, she dashed in and quickly found the soup. It cost more than she had by a few cents, but she didn't give up. She explained her dilemma to the clerk.

The man took pity on her and accepted the two quarters. Jade promised to come back with the remainder, but he waved her away, telling her he hoped she won.

Back inside the Wagoneer, she tossed the can into the sack and recounted her success. Trask laughed and hugged her. "Remind me to send you to deal with all my vendors, sweetheart."

The hug happened so fast, Jade's pulse leapt. After that, each time their gazes accidentally met, conspiratorial laughter erupted between them—enough to send her pulse skyrocketing.

"Aha!" Trask shouted, pulling up in front of the Forrester home. "We're the first ones back. Didn't I tell you?" He tweaked her nose. "I can almost taste that gourmet meal. We'll share it. Wonder if the winners get to choose the main course."

Jade enjoyed seeing his exuberance. "You'd better quit tasting and run," she warned. "Dan and his date are pulling in right behind us."

Trask grabbed her hand and charged up the steps. Within minutes, all the other scavenger hunters arrived back on the scene. Each group had some funny tale to tell. T.J. listened, taking in their stories with a smug smile. He reminded everyone that he was first to check in and crowed over Jade's bartering skills until she turned crimson with embarrassment.

"Okay, everyone!" Hillary clapped her hands. "Joe and I will go through the sacks and announce the winner."

Trask hooted. "Save yourself the effort. Hand over that certificate for my dinner, Hillary."

Joe opened up T.J.'s and Jade's sack first. The resigned smile on his face tapered to a look of surprise. "T.J.," he castigated mildly, "you didn't win. Look, the list says cream of mushroom soup label. What you have here is cream of chicken."

Trask rushed to the table and snatched up the can. The look on his face was one of total dismay.

Jade's spirits plummeted. "This is all my fault," she wailed, remembering how much he'd wanted to win.

"It's okay," he promised, hugging her tight. "It's only a game."

"But you did everything right. You deserved to win."

Dan slapped Trask on the shoulder. "The way he was bragging? Serves him right."

Dan's ribbing was only the first he took, yet he received it in good humor. As it turned out, Nell and her son were the winners, even though they'd checked in dead last.

Jade thought Trask sounded genuinely happy when he congratulated them. She knew she'd had her first real glimpse of the Trask Jennings everyone loved when he smiled at her and winked, saying, "So now you see the way of scavenger hunts, princess—and how pride goeth before a fall."

She realized the extent of their loss when Hillary served gourmet hors d'oeuvres and heartier fare—a feast that disappeared with truly astonishing speed.

Soon after, Joe put on music for dancing and Trask pulled Jade aside, suggesting they leave.

"Fine," she agreed, almost hating to see the evening end. Around a yawn, she admitted, "I'm tired, anyhow."

"I didn't mean we'd go home. But we can dance any time. I'm in the Halloween spirit now. You mentioned not having carved a jack-o'-lantern in a while. It gave me an idea. Do you know I've never carved one?"

"Because you were always out tricking, no doubt," Jade teased.

He pulled a wry face. "No doubt! But I still never had the pleasure. What do you say? You can follow me in your car and we'll stop at an all-night market, pick up two pumpkins and go back to my place and carve our own."

Jade's first inclination was to refuse. But when she saw the wistful expression in his tawny eyes, she conceded. "Sounds like fun. Lead on."

Later, trailing him into the parking area behind a row of dark condominiums, she remembered Mikki's warning about her impulsiveness and had second thoughts. Going home with a man as worldly as T. Stratton was totally out of character for her. Going home with *any* man was out of character for her. Panic rose at the last minute, but when he opened her car door like a gentleman and grinned at her like a happy little boy, Jade knew she'd done the right thing. She even enjoyed helping him lug the heavy pumpkins up three flights of stairs.

Jade found it touching that when they got inside, T. Stratton seemed nervous, too. Somehow, his nervousness gave her the advantage and allowed her to take charge of the carving, almost as if she'd been the one to suggest it.

"If we practice on paper, T. Stratton, we won't mess up. That way it won't matter if our first try isn't perfect."

"I never thought of that," he said, searching through his cabinets for pencils and paper. "You being an artist, you'd know stuff like that."

"You don't have to be an artist to carve a good pumpkin. If anything, I think it might make me too critical. I warn you, I'm a perfectionist."

He turned and looked at her squarely for the first time all evening. It took his breath away. Her hair had fallen from its clasp and she looked so at home sorting through his knife drawer that it made his stomach tighten with need. He made a big production out of clearing a space and cutting the tops off each pumpkin as she directed. So what if he needed an extra-tall glass of wine to take his mind off kissing her? If he accidentally cut his wrist through this folly, he'd go a happy man, Trask decided—until she slapped a spoon in his hand and showed him how to dig out seeds and the slimy project drove all lustful thoughts right out of his mind.

Before long they were acting like a couple of kids. Jade taught him about roasting the pumpkin seeds in butter and salt to a crisp golden brown. He found them tasty.

She remembered warmly that this was something her parents had always done. Work and other related topics that normally caused dissension between Trask and her didn't come up. Jade relaxed and time slipped away.

"Don't look," he said, not wanting her to see his jack-o'-lantern until it was completed.

"Why so secretive, T. Stratton?" she teased. "This isn't a contest."

Still, after that, he noticed she guarded her creation, too. When at last they'd finished, he made Jade hide her eyes while he dimmed the lights and placed a candle into each golden sphere.

"Okay, you can look now," he announced. But the jack-o'-lanterns no longer claimed his attention; instead, he couldn't take his eyes off Jade. He took pleasure in her childish delight as she exclaimed over the eerie way they glowed.

"Your carving is a masterpiece!" she exclaimed. "A ferocious monster. Mine looks more like a big smiley-face pin." She
crossed her arms and studied the pumpkins again. "Yours
would win in a contest," she admitted.

For no reason at all, he felt a surge of pride. They fell together, laughing, much the same way as they had on another
night—the night they'd completed the Cinderella coach.
Awareness spiraled in them simultaneously.

Trask held her at arm's length, tenderly wiping the tears of
laughter from her eyes with the rough pads of his thumbs. Before she could utter a protest, he drew her close again and ran
both hands fiercely down her back. "You feel so damn good in
my arms," he groaned. "I had a great time tonight, Jade. A
wonderful time. Tell me you did, too."

She caught him around the waist, tilted back her head and
met his anxious gaze. "I had the greatest evening, T. Stratton.
In fact, I don't know when I've had better. Why is it that at
work we always seem to be at each other's throats? Especially
when we've, ah...ah..." Her voice failed as he bent toward
her and trailed tiny kisses along her jawline.

"I've noticed." He nipped her ear. "But I have a solution."

"What is it?" she murmured, feeling her knees give way as
he continued to kiss a path from her ear down the sensitive cord
in her neck to the point where the collar of her blouse formed
a barrier.

"Let's make love. Not war. Sex has a way of healing rifts.
Don't you agree?"

Jade let a shocked breath escape. "T. Stratton. I...we..."
She slipped out of his arms and walked away, steepling her
fingers in front of her lips as she struggled to come up with the
right words.

For what seemed an excruciating length of time, he watched
her study the flicker of the candles. "What's the matter, Jade?
We're both adults. You said you weren't traditional."

Jade stood wondering how, with her life in such shambles,
she could engage in more deceit. Yet for all Trask knew, she was
still promised to Mikki. And on this subject, she discovered, she
was traditional. Loyalty to her grandparents and Mei Li, family honor, the sanctity of a promise—these things all meant so
much. Swallowing a sob, Jade pleaded, "Let me go, T. Strat-

ton. It's getting late.'' Quickly she snatched up her purse and jacket from where she'd tossed them on a kitchen chair.

He took a step toward her.

''Don't touch me again.''

The catch in her voice held him at bay.

''There are reasons why you shouldn't be kissing me... why I shouldn't be kissing you.''

''What reasons?''

''Mikki,'' she lied, catching her lip between her teeth. ''My family...''

''Of course,'' he murmured. ''And don't forget Daddy's money.'' Trask remembered how Kitty's father had cut off her charge cards and called in her Porsche. How could he have forgotten the power wielded by old family money?

She saw his pain. ''Not money,'' she insisted.

His lip curled. ''Oh? What then? Tell me.''

Her face fell. How did she explain the situation—the old-world customs and strict family codes forcing her into a tangle of lies? How did she explain this to a man who looked for honesty in a woman above all else? ''I can't,'' came her strangled reply. And she fled before he could discover the truth. That Jade Han was falling in love with T. Stratton Jennings...

The door slammed behind her, and the flames in the carved pumpkins leapt wildly.

CHAPTER EIGHT

IN SPITE OF THE WAY she and T. Stratton had parted, Jade wouldn't trade what they'd shared that night. The tight lines around his mouth had faded briefly during the pumpkin carving—not to mention during their kiss. Especially during their kiss. Jade ran a finger experimentally over her lips as she came to a stop in her driveway. The memory was pleasant.

After dreamily locking her car, she slowly approached the rear entrance of her home. Only then did she notice that the section her grandparents occupied was still blazing with lights. Strange. Normally Wrinks was the only one up to greet her at this hour.

Not even in her wildest imaginings did Jade suppose Mikki would be waiting inside. Dressed in his white tunic and black belt, he was pacing the length of her living room like a caged panther. Her grandparents sat stiffly together on the couch.

As if sensing her presence, Mikki whirled the moment she walked through the door. "Where have you been? It's nearly midnight," he accused. "Your grandparents have been worried sick. They called me at work. I telephoned the Forresters. They said you'd been gone for hours. Did you have trouble with your car?"

Jade let her shoulder bag slip onto the nearest chair. She shot a guilty glance toward her grandfather. His back was straight, his gaze carefully blank.

"No trouble with my car, Mikki. I...I've been carving jack-o'-lanterns. Ah...at...T. Stratton's house," she stammered.

Mikki's brows furrowed. "Jack-o'-lanterns? You mean those grinning faces cut in vegetables? You spend half the night frittering away time on child's play while your grandparents fret?"

Jade stared at him. "Why do you care, Mikki?" Her voice was sharper than she'd intended.

He stepped in front of her with a warning look. "Why would I not be worried about my fiancée?"

Jade's lashes dropped suddenly, concealing the anger and despair. "Your nose is going to be a foot long, Mikki," she muttered half under her breath.

He frowned and felt his nose.

A laugh bubbled up in Jade's throat and refused to be contained. "Pinocchio," she chuckled. "I guess you aren't familiar with the story. His nose grew long from lying."

"Stop it, Jade," Mikki hissed close to her ear. "Does your word mean nothing?" In a louder voice he demanded, "What is wrong with you?"

Grandfather Han stood and pulled his wife to her feet. "It's California, Mikki. I wanted to raise her in Hong Kong, but my son's will made it impossible. Jade will gain wisdom when you take her home. You will see."

Jade tamped down a rush of anger. "Grandfather, I'm not leaving California. This is my home."

"Soon your home will be with Mikki," the old man replied, ignoring her. "The choice is his."

"No," Jade said stubbornly. "Tell them, Mikki. The truth."

He puffed out his chest and blustered a bit, then hustled the old couple toward the hall. "A lovers' quarrel," he assured them in a low tone. "Leave us, please. I promise to be a gentleman."

Jade saw her grandmother hesitate and felt a moment's contrition. Because the whole purpose of this charade was to spare them pain and dishonor, she sighed and let them go.

"Now," Mikki said, closing the door firmly, "what is all this about? Mei Li and I planned our wedding tonight, but for now, everyone must believe the vows spoken will be yours and mine. You have Mei Li's happiness and mine in your hands."

Jade chewed on her lip. When he put it that way, she couldn't help feeling petty. Picking up Wrinks, she rubbed her face against the dog's soft fur. "I don't like all the lies. They have a way of getting bigger as time goes on. Like a snowball rolling downhill."

"Ah," he said, nodding his head. "You have fallen in love, my little lotus blossom. Tell me it's not with the insufferably arrogant Mr. Jennings."

"Love." Jade squeezed Wrinks so tight, he yelped. She loosened her hold, staring at Mikki. Was it that obvious? And who was Mikki to call T. Stratton arrogant? "I'm not in love, Mikki," she said patiently, letting the pup go. "It's...it's...part of it is my grandparents' wanting to return to Hong Kong."

"So," he said. "Let them. They have many friends there. My parents are coming for the wedding. They can travel back together."

"Your wedding, Mikki—and mine. My grandparents are counting on that. Only it's not mine. Doesn't that bother you?"

He shrugged. "My family will love Mei Li. Your grandparents will go home as they wish, and you will stay and build floats."

"Why does it sound so simple when you rationalize it, Mikki? It feels much more complicated in here." She put a hand over her heart.

"Two months is all that's left, Jade." He gave her a broad smile. "Sleep on it, won't you? I'll have Mei Li call you tomorrow."

"Why do you want to live in Hong Kong? So many people are leaving. Doesn't it disturb you knowing the Chinese will soon have control?"

Mikki observed her solemnly. "We are Chinese, Jade. And you said it earlier, I think. It is home." He bowed, then squared his shoulders and left.

Jade pondered the problem most of the night. Before this, she hadn't thought much about life without her grandparents. They had come for a visit when she was a teen. Through much cajoling, her parents had convinced them to stay a year. However, even during that time, her father had had to maintain a fine balance between the two diverse cultures housed under his roof. She had a new respect for the loving partnership he'd forged with his headstrong liberal wife, and his equally loving manner with aging parents who remained entrenched in the traditions of their homeland.

In those happier days, she'd been free to pick and choose traits from each culture at will. Then came the plane crash killing her parents, and she had been thankful for her grandparents' stoicism. Mei Li, too, was a great salvation. How could one measure such a debt of love? As for loving T. Stratton, she dared not even consider it. Certainly not under the present circumstances . . .

Solutions eluded her throughout the night. Jade rose before her grandparents and hurried from the house. Daybreak had barely splintered the eastern sky in shades of pink and gold when she arrived at work. Having left T. Stratton at his condominium last night, she didn't cast her usual curious glance at the stairs leading up to his office as she made her way down the hall. Even a quick glance always reminded her of that first and only foray into his quarters; her fingers would all turn into thumbs for at least half an hour. Today she had other more pressing problems.

She sipped from a first cup of coffee, critically eyeing a rendering of water fairies she'd been working on for a new client. T. Stratton told her the company, which sold bottled water, had been quite specific about wanting to make a "big splash" in the parade. They'd all laughed over his play on words. But the company was entrusting a large part of its advertising budget to Fantasy Floats. Jade wanted to give them their money's worth. She envisioned a float filled with delicate elflike creatures slipping down waterfalls and dancing over giant flowering lily pads. The problem was, Dan couldn't get the fairies to dance.

Reaching for a favorite tape, Jade popped it into her cassette player and rested her hip against the table as she took another mouthful of coffee. Impatiently she waited for the music to begin.

Out of the corner of one eye, she saw something dark skitter toward her across the table. Her throat closed and the coffee lodged somewhere between her lungs and her larynx. It was a spider. The largest she'd ever seen—and she hated even small ones.

A scream rose in her throat, vying for space with the coffee. The scream won and the cup crashed to the cement floor, shattering into a thousand pieces.

Upstairs, Trask heard the scream. He was jerked upright out of a sound sleep. After Jade had left so abruptly the night before he'd come to the office to think. He'd only just fallen asleep, no closer to knowing where she fit into his life. The noise was decidedly an irritation.

Below, Jade debated how to cope. Groping along the table-top in search of a sturdy weapon, her fingers happened to collide with a can of acrylic spray. Thank goodness! It meant she didn't have to get close to the horrible intruder.

As though he sensed an enemy, the spider halted his march across the table. As Jade plotted her strategy, he ran the other way. She squeezed the plunger. A thick mist fogged the room, choking her.

Apparently stunned by the sticky spray, the spider spun in circles, then fell to the floor. Jade savored a taste of victory. Too soon the spider got his second wind and scrambled toward a safe haven beneath her desk.

She launched a second attack, diving under the table in hot pursuit, upsetting her can of colored pencils. They rained around her like pickup sticks, making a terrible racket.

The last commotion drove Trask from his bed. He tugged on cold jeans and raced barefoot down the stairs, where, still half-asleep, he burst through the double doors into the warehouse. His brain had finally awakened enough for him to remember that more often than not, Jade was the first to arrive. He panicked at the thought of finding her in trouble with a float. He wasn't so sleepy that he didn't remember with chilling clarity the number of tragedies that happened each year in his industry, when heavy floats accidentally slid from moorings.

So when he found her safe and unharmed, he had no idea why the sight of her scrambling around under a table sent a white-hot stab of anger through him.

Taking a deep breath, he glared at the logo on the rear pocket of her jeans and bellowed, "What in the name of almighty heaven are you doing?" The acrid spray filled his lungs and he dissolved in a fit of coughing.

Jade's head came up swiftly enough to smack the underside of the table.

"Ouch!" She rubbed the top of her head and eased out backward, the aerosol can still spewing weakly.

"Are you all right?" he asked, covering his mouth and nose. "What happened here?"

"T. Stratton! You scared me to death." Squinting up, Jade thought her heart was going to stop beating. He was hovering too close for comfort—barefoot and shirtless, his jeans unbuttoned and riding low on his hips. Suddenly faint, Jade closed her eyes and sank back on her heels.

Trask bent down until they were face-to-face. Her eyes were watering from the pungent vapor and he found it hard to sustain his anger. "Did you scream bloody murder a few minutes ago?"

She nodded, trying not to stare at his broad chest with its golden tufts of hair, his flat stomach, his... "Be careful of your bare feet, T. Stratton," she warned in a strangled voice. "I dropped my coffee cup. There's glass all over the floor."

He was overcome by another fit of choking. Grasping her free arm, he hauled her upright and out the door into cleaner air.

"I expected to come down and find you pinned underneath a float. I envisioned aid cars and ambulances screaming to your rescue. Would it be too much to ask what in blue blazes you were doing?"

Jade's lashes dropped. For a moment, she studied the label on the can. "Sound must be really magnified upstairs," she mumbled. "I saw a spider."

His jaw dropped. "A spider," he repeated. "You scared me out of ten years' growth—all over some poor little spider?"

Jade's lids snapped up. "He wasn't little." She shivered. "He was more like a . . . a tarantula."

Then because T. Stratton looked about to explode at any minute, she tried to explain. "A boy in school threw one on me once. I hate spiders. I know it's not rational, but they terrify me." She shuddered. "I think he's under my desk. I'm sorry if I woke you."

She looked so apologetic. So nervous. So damn kissable, chewing on her lip that way. It was all he could do not to take her into his arms. Then he remembered how things had ended last night, and he vowed to keep their relationship on a strictly professional basis.

Raking a hand through his uncombed hair, he counted slowly to ten. Around number eight, the humor of the whole situation struck him and he began to laugh. He laughed until tears rolled down his cheeks. "You are absolutely wicked with an aerosol can," he sputtered. "Please, don't ever come gunning for me." He backed away, palms up.

"If you'd seen the size of that spider, you wouldn't find this so amusing," she said indignantly. "Talk about scaring someone..." Hands on hips, she faced him. "Why aren't you home sleeping in your own bed?"

He stopped laughing. His gaze heated as it slid over her. In the silence that suddenly stretched between them, Trask looked away and passed a hand over his bare chest. "Maybe the prospect of that big bed seemed too lonely after you left last night," he growled, all trace of laughter gone.

Jade dropped the can and turned. On the outside he was granite, yet those eyes were pure quicksand. And at this moment, she was in grave danger of slipping in over her head. Running her sweating palms over denim-clad thighs, Jade told herself she couldn't play any more emotional games. "I'm here to learn float-building from you, T. Stratton, nothing more. Hank's getting stronger every day. He'll be back next year. I'm storing up all I can."

"Ah, yes," Trask drawled bitterly, "but I wonder why, when Mikki is only interested in having you learn embroidery."

Jade's chin jutted. "My father always said if you can't say something nice about a person, T. Stratton, you shouldn't say anything at all."

Trask flinched. In all his life, he couldn't remember a woman ever coming to his defense the way she'd just flown to Mikki's. "You're absolutely right," he said, irrationally angry at Mikki Chan. "Your mind is made up. There's no need to say anything further."

"You talk in riddles," she snapped. "I love building floats. I can't imagine anything bringing me as much happiness."

"Really?" His eyelids dropped, hiding a sudden flare of desire. "Then ol' Mikki better spend some of that dowry money on lessons, too."

"Is this about my money, T. Stratton?" Her brows rose.

His nostrils flared. "You and I will never see eye to eye on money, Miss Han."

"Miss Han?" she repeated, sounding amused. "Whenever we discuss money, you revert to being formal. Is it my money you find intimidating, or am I a scapegoat for something—or someone—out of your past?"

Her words landed like a blow to the stomach. She was right, of course. He was making her pay for Kitty's slight. Had been making her pay ever since she'd waltzed into his life. But he also realized that it had less to do with money or with Kitty than with her being promised to Mikki Chan. It had to do with the family loyalty she exemplified and he didn't understand. But he couldn't admit his shortcomings. "Time is money in this business, Jade. You have work to do and I need a shower."

Jade felt the floor shake as he took the stairs two at a time. Why did T. Stratton always leave her knees weak and her head confused? None of the other crew members—in fact, no other man—had such a powerful effect on her senses.

That was reinforced when moments later, Greg Sanders popped in to greet her. He made her laugh. He even retrieved the spider and carried him outside, joking all the while about his prowess as big-game hunter and rescuer of maidens. But when T. Stratton returned, his hair damp and smelling of herbal shampoo, she suddenly felt clumsy again and nothing seemed to go right.

DURING THE NEXT few weeks, Jade developed a routine of coming early and staying late. She avoided T. Stratton whenever possible, and at home she saw little of her grandparents.

Hank dropped in one day. His therapy was due to finish in December. It reminded Jade that her time with Fantasy Floats was almost over. Thoroughly dispirited, she let Mei Li arrange social outings. The more Jade wasn't home, the less guilt she suffered when she looked at her unsuspecting grandparents.

Caught up in a frantic schedule, both professionally and socially, Jade pushed any thought of the deception from her mind until it ceased to be an issue. She would have pushed T. Stratton from her mind, too, but that was hopeless. She thought of him constantly. She longed for his kisses.

One morning she awakened in a state of exhaustion, wanting only to hide her head under the pillow and forget the day. At work, they'd been having trouble getting her water fairies to dance and fly in the right sequence—in any sequence, for that matter—which meant that the crew had worked half the night to comb the circuitry for errors. By 3:00 a.m. the problem still eluded them, and they'd all given up in a hail of bad tempers.

Jade groaned into her pillow. Wrinks sniffed her ear, begging to be taken for a run. Their daily outings had gone by the wayside lately, she thought with a guilty conscience. "Okay, boy. This morning we're going for a run. I can't ignore you any longer. You may be my best friend in the whole world just now. I can't afford to lose you, too."

It felt good to stretch and to work some of the kinks out of her muscles. On the run, Jade decided to call Mei Li and cancel out of a party that evening. Mikki would be furious, she knew. For the past week, he'd been talking about nothing but this "intimate" affair at the home of one of the more important movie stars in his series. Actually he was feeling smug because he'd wangled invitations for the three of them.

Well, tough, she thought, toweling dry after her shower. They could rope someone else into going as chaperon, or go alone. All she planned to be intimate with tonight was her pillow.

However, once she got to work and resumed her struggles with the water fairies, she forgot about calling Mei Li. It was midafternoon before she remembered. "Rats!" She threw the circuit board down and stood up. Her rotten disposition had worsened when Trask took off at noon with Cynthia—and he hadn't come back yet. Granted, it was a while since they'd been blessed with Cynthia's presence, but now, with her defenses down, Jade was shocked by her feelings of jealousy. And she had no defense against Mei Lei's cajoling.

"Mikki's been on the phone all week trying to set up this night out for us, Jade. It's important for his career and you'll feel better if you go."

"I'm sorry, Mei Li, but I'm exhausted."

"Please," the younger woman wheedled. "I'll cancel tomorrow's plans. I'll cook for us myself over the weekend. Jade, *everyone's* going to be there."

"Look. I'm really sorry." Jade groaned. She was remembering the nightclub where they'd also gone for the sake of Mikki's image. It was the night she'd insisted T. Stratton honor his commitment. "Well..." she vacillated. At least the chances of running into T. Stratton and Cynthia at a private Hollywood party were virtually nonexistent. "All right," she capitulated after a lengthy silence, "but only on the condition that

I don't have to dance. Give me directions. I'll take my car and meet you there, in case I want to leave early."

"I'll tell Mikki. Honestly, Jade, you need a night off. You're losing so much weight you look practically anorexic. You'll never find a wedding dress that fits."

"I'm not looking for a wedding dress, Mei Li."

"No, silly! You'll be looking for me. But you will be trying them on in front of Mikki's mother. We *were* about the same size, but now . . ." She sighed. "I'm so nervous, Jade. What if Mikki's mother doesn't like me?"

A wave of depression rolled over Jade. "Mei Li, do I have to carry this charade through to buying a dress?"

"Please!"

Jade cleared her throat. "I have to go, Mei Li. Don't worry. Mikki's mother will love you." She clutched the receiver even after the click, feeling thoroughly drained.

THE MANSION where the party was being held hung over a cliff in Laguna Hills. Inside, the myriad rooms, dimly lit and stifling with smoke, were packed with sequined starlets and overstuffed men.

"Private! Intimate!" Mei Li gushed, as they worked their way to a patio outside by a pool, where musicians belted out acid rock.

At least outside the glow cast by an almost full moon was spectacular. Entranced by its shimmer, Jade sank into a wicker chair by a small table and accepted a glass of champagne from a passing waiter. She was content to let Mikki talk with their host—a chubby man wearing gold chains and diamond rings on both pinkies. A blonde half his age clung to one arm. Ah, Hollywood, she thought, grimacing.

"Psst! Jade! You're never going to believe this." Mei Li leaned across Mikki's empty chair and shook Jade's arm.

"What?" Startled, Jade drew her gaze away from an eccentric couple dancing some bizarre dance. Mikki had been enticed away by a statuesque redhead and they were deep in conversation. Jade hadn't noticed earlier, but now Mikki held a drink in his hand.

"Your boss and his girlfriend. Just inside the sun room."

"No!" Afraid to look, Jade slid lower in her seat. This couldn't be happening. She opened one eye a sliver and peeped over Mei Li's shoulder. Sure enough. T. Stratton and the coolly beautiful Cynthia Osborn were coming toward them. Each had changed clothes since she'd seen them leave for lunch. Had T. Stratton's big lonely bed been filled for the afternoon? Jade wondered with another stab of jealousy.

The patio was large and angular. It seemed to Jade that fate was playing cruel tricks as she watched Cynthia head for an empty table near the pool. Jade measured her chances of escape and saw none.

"Did you arrange this, Jade?" demanded Mikki in an accusing tone as he returned to his chair.

"I most certainly did not!" Affronted that he should even think such a thing, she pointed out, "I'm not the one who knows the host. I didn't even want to come."

Mikki didn't look convinced. He summoned a waiter and helped himself to another glass of champagne. Jade had never seen Mikki drink, and now he'd taken a second. Without saying a word, he downed the bubbling liquid. He had a third in his hand when T. Stratton drew abreast of their table.

Cynthia stopped midsentence.

Trask blinked, then said, "Well, well! Taking time out to play, Miss Han?" His barb was meant to get a rise out of her and it did.

She spilled her drink and was forced to mop it up. What did he think? That she was following him?

"Come on, T.J." Cynthia tugged on his arm. "I see another table inside. We're not here to hobnob with the help."

Mikki drained his glass, thumped it back on the tray and leaned toward Jade. "You think a career brings respect? Can't you just hear how much?"

"Hold on a minute." T.J. stayed his companion with a hand. "Cynthia, I believe you owe Jade an apology."

She turned away with a sniff. "What for? She *is* your hired help. I'm already getting bored with this party, T.J. Let's leave."

Mikki stood up and swaggered around the table. "Do you always let women tell you what to do, Jennings?"

Trask frowned. He sidestepped Mikki, excused himself and started after Cynthia.

Mikki followed, continuing to press.

Jade exchanged worried glances with Mei Li. "Mikki isn't used to champagne. He rarely drinks. Perhaps you should try to get him to go home."

Mei Li nodded. However, by the time the two women worked their way through the crowd to the entry hall, Mikki was exchanging heated words with a punk rocker.

Trask stood by the door watching. Cynthia had flown off in a huff. And what did he owe Chan? Not one damn thing, he thought—until he caught a glimpse of Jade's pale face. Her eyes, too large and luminous, looked haunted. "Damn." But he moved toward Mikki and suggested evenly, "Why don't you get Jade out of here before that punker takes it upon himself to rearrange your face, Chan?"

Jade heard Mikki's indrawn breath.

"You don't believe my hands are lethal weapons, do you, Jennings?" Mikki goaded. "Well, I'll show you. You, too," he snarled at the young tough with the spiked orange hair. Turning, Mikki yanked a small table out from beneath a hall mirror, slamming it down between himself and Trask.

"I believe you, Mikki," Trask said placatingly. "Come outside. Get some air."

Ignoring a tittering group that was beginning to gather, Mikki threw out a challenge. "If I break this table in one blow, will you release Jade from her work contract immediately?"

Trask's troubled gaze met Jade's.

"No," Jade whispered. "T. Stratton," she begged, "don't let him do this."

"Stay out of it, Jade," Mikki snapped. "This is a wager between men."

"Leave it, Chan." Trask turned his back. Several bystanders dug in their pockets and pulled out large bills. One man added fuel to the growing interest by throwing a hundred-dollar-bill on the floor; a pile of others soon followed.

Mikki bowed low over the wooden table for a moment, then straightened abruptly and gave a fearsome yell.

Trask whirled just as the table exploded under Mikki's hand.

Jade watched in horror. The whack was deafening. The pieces flew into the air and one hit Trask in the face. Then silence reigned.

Suddenly the voice of their host rose hysterically. "Who's responsible for this? Call the police! Fools! That table was a priceless antique."

CHAPTER NINE

"GET IN, T. STRATTON. I'm taking you home." Jade unlocked the passenger door of her small sports car and curtly motioned him in.

"I don't recall asking any favors," he grumbled, climbing in and adjusting an ice pack over his right eye. Leaning back against the headrest, he closed his one good eye and groaned.

"Are you all right?" she asked, suddenly solicitous.

His left eye opened a crack. "Outside of feeling like a complete donkey, you mean?"

"I didn't say that. Mikki was acting abominably. You tried to intervene and you even apologized."

He straightened, easing his long legs to the side. "Yes, for disrupting the party. And I apologized to Chan, because in all honesty, I didn't believe he could do it." His teeth flashed in a grin. "That move was something, wasn't it?" he said, shaking his head. "Of course, I regret that he chose an expensive antique. And I regret standing so close."

Jade threw him an exasperated look. "Here I was giving you credit for trying to stop him."

He tilted his head and studied her with his good eye. "Yeah?" He coughed. "Well, that was for you. You looked so...so..." He shrugged and waved a hand.

"Why, thank you, T. Stratton. I had no idea you were being chivalrous." She paused. "Is that why you insisted on paying for all the damages? I know you can't afford what that table cost."

A streetlight illuminated his rueful smile. "I'll regret that tomorrow, too—and next week when I have to eat beans. Tonight it did something for my ego, knowing Mikki didn't have a cent on him or even a checkbook."

Jade laughed. "I didn't, either. But I'll pay Mikki's share." She stole another peek. "In fact, you shouldn't pay at all. The whole mess was Mikki's doing."

A muscle twitched in Trask's jaw. "Go ahead, take on Mikki's debts, princess."

"I'm not taking on Mikki's debts," Jade corrected. "It's you I'm thinking about. Nell says costs have escalated this year. Why are you so obstinate?"

"I'm not always this hard up, Jade." He rubbed his chin. "I suppose Nell told you about the boys' camp?"

Jade nodded. "Very commendable of you, T. Stratton."

"I don't want commendations," he growled. When he spoke again, his voice had a slight catch. "Just recently I learned that Max, the man to whom we're dedicating the camp, has inoperable cancer. I'm pushing hard to finish the project before he..." His words trailed off. "I guess you could say Max is the closest thing to family I've got, outside of the crew."

"Nell told me about the camp and she told me about Max," Jade murmured, her heart going out to him. It sounded as if he loved Max the way she loved her grandfather. "Let me pay for tonight's damages," she said softly. "You could always consider it my donation to your camp."

"No! Why would you do that? You don't know Max or these kids." Trask dismissed her offer and changed the subject. "I hate your having to drive me across town this way, Jade. My condo isn't exactly in your neighborhood. And what about your...intended?"

"Considering Cynthia left without you, T. Stratton, I thought it better if someone drove you home. Mei Li will give Mikki the proper sympathy tonight." She frowned. "I'll have more patience tomorrow."

Trask gave a snort. "Cynthia was being a brat. And I predict you'll need more than patience tomorrow, princess. Mikki wasn't happy about your taking me. He wants you to quit work."

She pursed her lips, whipping onto a freeway exit. "Whether or not I design floats is not Mikki's concern," she said primly.

Trask braced an arm on the dash to keep from landing in her lap. "Tsk, tsk. Trouble in paradise already. Frankly, I can't see why you two are getting married."

Jade caught the mockery in his tone and worried her lip between her teeth. If only she could tell him the truth. How long until Roger arrived? A month and a half. Unconsciously, she pressed her foot harder on the gas. The small car swayed.

"You've got a lead foot, princess," he chided.

"You've got a one-track mind, Jennings," she shot back.

He threw back his head and laughed.

Fortunately they arrived at his complex before he could bully her further.

"Do you have any problem with the way I design floats, T. Stratton?" she asked, instead of letting well enough alone. "If not, I think we should avoid getting personal."

T. Stratton tossed the melting ice pack on her dashboard. "Your designs are okay." He grinned. "When you first came on board, I had doubts, as you well know. And if you don't want me getting personal, princess, don't call me T. Stratton in that sexy whiskey voice."

Jade curled her fingers tightly around the steering wheel. She avoided his eyes. "But . . . but you sign your name T. Stratton. It was on the letter the committee sent me. I'm sorry if you don't like it." She turned away and stared out the side window.

"Did I say I didn't like it?" He touched her chin and forced her eyes to meet his.

A spotlight mounted on the corner of the building shed enough light for Jade to see that his left eye was almost swollen shut.

"I like it too much," he said softly.

The interior of the car seemed to shrink. Her heart began a mad gallop. There was something new in his voice, something new in his touch, that threatened her promise to Mei Li. "I'll call you T.J." she promised, her voice breathless.

He released her and reached for the door. "Forget it. Call me T. Stratton. The way you say T.J. is worse."

She held out his ice pack. "I'll work on it. Here, you'd better take this or tomorrow your eye will be horribly black and blue."

He shot her a cocky grin and touched a finger to her nose. "Quit mothering. It doesn't go with the image I have of you."

It was news that he had any image of her. She was afraid to think what it might be. Remembering something, she caught his sleeve. "Could I ask a favor?" Without waiting for his response, she rushed on, "Mikki could get into real trouble if word gets back to Hong Kong that he used wing chun the way he did tonight. You won't say anything to the police or the press, will you?"

"What's in it for me?" His lips quirked faintly.

She lifted her chin. "What do you want?"

"Nothing. Skip it. So I was wrong about your marriage. It'll be made in heaven." He threw open the door and unfolded his long body from the cramped interior. "Don't give it another thought. Lover boy's secret is safe with me. Thanks for the lift."

Jade sat motionless while he climbed the stairs to his condo. She waited until he disappeared inside. Why was it she never seemed to say the right thing?

Driving home, Jade blamed her trembling hands on exhaustion. Just yesterday Grandfather had said sleeplessness caused disharmony of spirit. Jade rubbed at the tension building in the back of her neck. Why did she only seem to suffer disharmony of spirit when T. Stratton was around? Idly, she shoved a classical tape in her player and turned it up loud.

She half expected Mei Li and Mikki to be waiting on her doorstep and was relieved when they were not. With barely enough energy to move Wrinks out of the middle of her bed, Jade fell into a troubled sleep the moment her head touched the pillow.

She awakened earlier than usual, dressed quickly, but decided to skip her morning run. It was cowardly, she knew, but she wanted to avoid questions from her grandparents. They'd be sure to show interest in the party. And what could she say? That she was far more concerned about the way she'd left things with T. Stratton than about Mikki's reputation?

Early as she arrived at the warehouse, Dan and Greg were both already hard at work. T. Stratton was nowhere in sight.

"Jade! Come see," Greg yelled before she'd even had time to put her handbag away. "Your water fairies are flying around the frog prince. Watch. They're attached to this clear plastic tubing that shoots right up out of the center of each lily pad. I don't know why we didn't think of it before. This stuff is practically invisible.''

When indeed the captivating fairies danced on cue, Jade clapped her hands, applauding the results. Set on a timed sequence, the colorful creatures popped up intermittently, exactly as she'd envisioned.

''You fellows are veritable geniuses,'' she said, grinning. ''Have you been here all night working on this? If so, I'm impressed.''

Dan shut the unit down and turned to her. ''Actually, you owe T.J. for this one. I think *he* worked all night.'' Dan shook his head. ''He rousted me out in the wee hours with a phone call—said he's decided to visit Max. He mentioned being gone at least a week, maybe two. You won't believe how casually he said he'd fixed our problem. By that time, I was awake and decided to come and see for myself. But he'd already gone.''

A lump rose in Jade's throat. Before she could think of some innocuous comment, Greg bobbed up from the far side of the float. ''You didn't tell me T.J. was going out of town, Dan. Did he solve our delivery crisis? Are you sure he didn't sneak off with Cynthia? Yesterday I overheard her begging him to go to the mountains.''

''What if he did?'' asked Dan. ''He deserves a break.''

''I'm just complaining,'' Greg muttered.

Jade swallowed with difficulty. Did he call Cynthia last night? Did she come to soothe his injuries? Idly, she picked at the gossamer wings of a fairy. If that was what had happened, she didn't want to know.

Dan threw a wet rag at Greg. ''T.J. said he'd call here a couple of times a day to touch base. I guess you can ask if Cynthia's with him then, nosy.''

To Jade's relief, other crew members began arriving. With luck, they'd change the subject. Frankly, she was glad he was going to be away. A week would give her a chance to concentrate on coloring the mosaics on the last two floats.

Joe rushed in late. He was delighted to see the progress on the water-fairy float, then promptly moved it aside and set up for the next one, which Jade considered her best design so far. A Hawaiian sugarcane company had contracted T.J. to do a replica of King Kamehameha. They'd requested that space be left for real Hawaiian dancers—one to depict the ancient folklore of each major island. The challenge for Jade was to create a realistic setting and numerous exotic birds. In addition, she'd added a smoking volcano and a shimmering waterfall. T. Stratton had been skeptical when he'd viewed the plans. More than skeptical, really.

Determined to surprise him with the finished product, Jade threw herself into her work. Time flew by in a whirlwind of activity. T. Stratton called in periodically as promised. He talked with Nell or Joe, and they reported that his visit with Max went well. Now he was at the boys' camp.

Around noon on Monday of his second week away, Nell poked her head into Jade's cubicle and asked her to come to the telephone. "T.J. wants a word with you, Jade. Have you got a minute?"

"Me?" Jade looked up from her painting. "Are you sure he wants to talk to me?"

Nell laughed. "Do you know another Jade who works here?"

"No. But I . . . It's such a surprise."

"He wants to discuss something that came in today's mail. It's the top envelope in my stack. If you don't mind, I'll leave you to finish up with him. I'm going out to lunch with Dan and Greg. And Joe's got an errand to run. You want me to pick you up some lunch?"

"No, thanks. I brought mine today. Enjoy. It's rare for anyone to go out these days." Jade squeezed the older woman's arm as she slipped past her and went into the office. She experienced a slight tremor in her fingers as she picked up the receiver.

"Hello?" Jade suspected her voice was no steadier than her hands.

"Jade." Trask's deep response seemed to put him in the room. "Did Nell tell you about our invitation to the Coronation Ball? Yes? No?" he asked, laughing when Jade didn't answer. "The Queen's Committee has invited us to be guests of honor. This coming Saturday. It includes a buffet and a formal dance after crowning the queen. Plus, we'll be introduced. Can you make it?"

Jade found the gilt-edged invitation just where Nell had said it would be. The envelope had only T. Stratton's name on it, and the note inside said he would be honored as builder of the coach. She ran a finger along the engraved lettering. Such invitations were exclusive. His inclusion of her was special. Touching. Her heart began to flop in her chest like a newly caught fish in a net. Clearing her throat, she struggled to find her voice. "Would it just be the two of us?"

She heard his quick intake of breath and was afraid she'd said the wrong thing.

"For a moment there, I forgot your intended. Forgive me. By all means, invite Mikki. My eye is almost back to normal." His sarcasm reached across the wire.

"I was just asking," she murmured. "My name isn't on the invitation. Perhaps I shouldn't go. I . . . ah . . . and there's Mei Li." Oh, how she wanted to go.

"Give me your friend's telephone number," Trask growled. "Cynthia's gone to Mexico scuba diving for a couple of weeks. I'll take the sparrow, as Mikki calls her, as my date."

Stunned, Jade almost dropped the phone. "I don't know if she'll go." She supposed it would depend on whether Mikki gave his approval.

"Why not? I assure you, I can be civilized when the need arises. And speaking of civilized, tuxedos are in order that night. Be sure lover boy knows."

"I don't want to go at all if you and Mikki are going to needle one another." A little wistfully, she added, "I would like to see the royal party. . . ."

"It's settled then. We'll make it a foursome. Perhaps you'd better get in touch with the others, though. You won't forget to tell them about the evening wear?"

"I think we can manage without embarrassing you or Fantasy Floats, T. Stratton," she said tartly. "Shall we meet you there? I see the invitation says eight o'clock."

"I normally pick up my dates."

"Formal wear in your Wagoneer, T. Stratton? Mikki could probably get us a limo." She couldn't resist the little jab.

"Now who's needling? No Wagoneer, princess. And no limo. I figured you'd be wearing one of those slinky brocade numbers—like the red one you had on the first night I came to your house. I'll have a car.''

"What have you got against mandarin silk?" she asked. His faintly derisive tone irritated her.

"Not a thing," he answered smoothly. "Hey, this call is costing me an arm and a leg. Could we just nail down the particulars? Since I know where you live, how about if I pick you up first?"

Jade searched for a suitable reply. None were ladylike.

"Are you still there?" he said at last. "I didn't mean to offend you. I liked the dress. It was—" he paused "—you. Very proper. Correctly elegant. Very—"

"Fine, T. Stratton," she cut in. "I don't think I need any further fashion tips from you. I have work waiting. Unless you have more to say, I'll see you on Saturday."

It was T.J.'s turn to be silent. The conversation had gone downhill after he'd been forced to invite Mikki. But damn it, she deserved recognition, too. It was her design.

In the background Jade could hear hammering and the whir of some light engine. Just when she thought he was going to tell her to forget the whole thing, he muttered, "Nothing more," and quietly clicked off.

No "I'll see you Saturday," or "I'll be looking forward to seeing you." Just "Nothing more." Oooh, but sometimes he made her furious. Jade was still staring at the bleating receiver when Nell walked in.

"You and T.J. been on the phone all this time?" Nell asked. "I hope he doesn't forget this when the bill comes."

Jade returned the phone to its cradle with a bang. "I'd offer to pay for the call, but he'd only take my head off."

Nell grinned. "Had words again, did you? I'll grant you, T.J. has some funny quirks when it comes to money and women. It goes way back. He was a real wild one when he was younger. Then—as you know—Max took an interest in him, gave him a job and helped foot the bill for college. T.J. fell hard for one of the richest girls in school. He spared no expense showing her a good time. But nothing he did was good enough once her lawyer daddy found out about him. The girl had her orders and no one in her crowd ever spoke to T.J. again. Between that experience and never really having a name to call his own, I just imagine he's had to work through a lot of resentment."

"Cynthia has money, doesn't she?" Jade asked quietly.

Nell snorted. "That woman never had a dime until she married old man Osborn. And him old enough to be her grandfather. The airs she puts on now, you wouldn't know she came from the same background as T.J. But goodness, I shouldn't be gossiping like this."

"Nell, could I ask you something else?"

"Sure, anything." Nell threw her purse in the bottom drawer of her desk. "Well...almost anything."

Jade picked up the thick, gold-edged invitation from the Queen's Committee. "I think when T. Stratton looks at me, he sees Suzie Wong. I'd like to show him people don't always fit in his neat little pigeonholes. I was wondering, Nell...do you have any suggestions on how I could become a little more..."

"Hip, you mean?" Nell chuckled. "With it?"

IT WAS APPROACHING six forty-five on the night of the Coronation Ball and Jade was pacing in front of the full-length mirror set in the corner of her bedroom. Wrinks sat on the bed, tilting his head from side to side, not knowing what to make of her. Occasionally he'd growl low in his throat.

"I wish you'd stop that, mutt," Jade said after one such rumble. "I'm already beginning to wonder what possessed me to do this. Keep it up and see who takes you for your morning run." Crossing the room, she tugged distractedly at his soft ears while trying to gain a back view of herself in the mirror. In the distance, she heard the hollow echo of the door chime. She straightened and grew still. "Oh, no! He's here. Why did I listen to Nell?" she wailed.

Snatching up her wrap, Jade raced for the stairs. She wanted to miss her grandfather. Halfway down the long staircase, she paused, composed herself and took each step in a slow, dignified manner. The ruffled tiers on the black taffeta dress hit her midthigh and whispered against her black silk stockings. Grandfather was already at the door. Jade dawdled, attempting to put off the inevitable.

Still one step from the bottom, she watched T. Stratton's entrance. He'd had his hair cut for the occasion, but not too short. He looked wonderful—good enough to steal her breath away. She hid a smile when he offered Wrinks a rawhide bone. Her heart gave a funny twist as he made small talk with her grandfather. If only she could tell them both right now that she wasn't going to marry Mikki. But of course that was impossible.

Suddenly Trask stopped speaking and glanced up, causing Jade's grandfather to turn and look, too.

Jade tensed, wishing one of them would say something. Anything. Instead, T. Stratton's amber eyes swept her from head to toe and up again. He was well on his way through a third slow sweep of a dress that left her shoulders bare, except for thin spaghetti straps connecting the front of a form-fitting shirred bodice to a very low-cut back, when surprisingly Grandfather Han spoke in clear, concise English.

"Jade Han! What have you done with your beautiful hair? You've cut it off. You look like a boy. And that dress..." His English faltered, then gained magnitude. "You will not leave this house in that dress."

Trask took two steps forward. "No boy ever looked like this, Mr. Han. Hair will grow. The dress, ah...the dress is...well, it's in a different class from the red silk she wore to your Chinese New Year. That's a fact."

"Legs," the old man spat. "It is disgraceful. She is all legs."

"Mmm." Trask smiled a purely male smile.

"You think it's too...too—" Jade began, but his look cut her off. A steamy look, proclaiming she was all woman.

"No doubt about it." Trask's smile quickly switched to a scowl. "That dress is too, too everything." He studied her patent-strapped heels and a diamond studded ankle bracelet as she donned a wrap and preceded him to the door. Those ankles and similar strappy shoes were what had first caught his attention. His blood heated back then; it boiled now.

"Mikki will not be pleased with the changes you have made to yourself, Jade," warned her grandfather, hovering near the door. "You should have consulted him first." The last was said in Cantonese.

"Don't worry, Grandfather." Jade answered in English. "Mikki is much more progressive than you think."

"He won't understand," the old man called as she left the house.

"He sure won't," Trask muttered under his breath, handing Jade into the BMW he'd rented for the evening.

"Nonsense," she purred, lowering her lashes. "Of course he will."

Yet a scant half hour later, Jade was proved wrong. Not only in how Mikki viewed her transformation, but how Mei Li did, as well. Appalled would come closer to describing her friends' explosive reactions.

"I can't believe you cut your hair, Jade," Mikki complained after the initial shock wore off. "My family will be here in less than a month. They are expecting the young Chinese woman whose pictures they've seen." His lips thinned. "Furthermore, you are showing a total disrespect for me tonight. Those heels you have on make you a good three inches taller than me. It's humiliating."

"You did this on purpose, Jade," hissed Mei Li. "It'll ruin everything. Why, you don't even look Chinese anymore."

Trask's gaze shifted from one to another.

"Something you seem to forget," Jade reminded gently, "is that I'm only half Chinese. So tell me, what has changed?"

Trask stood aside and studied the two women. Jade was only pointing out the obvious. Mei Li wore a long straight dress of pale pink brocade with feminine cap sleeves and traditional frog closures. Her fine black hair was done up in a tight knot and circled by a spray of tiny white flowers. Compared to Jade, she looked very Chinese. Yet Trask was left with an uncomfortable feeling that he was missing something important in the conversation.

Touching Mikki's sleeve, Mei Li pleaded, "Let's not argue tonight, please. You heard Jade. Nothing's changed. Myself, I've never been to a queen's coronation. I'm so looking forward to seeing Jade's float all decked out. We should thank Mr. Jennings, Mikki."

Mikki's scowl faded as he turned to look at the smaller woman. "At least you have not taken leave of your senses, little sparrow," he said, adjusting the cutaway jacket he was wearing. Smoothing his hair, he turned to Trask. "Thank you, Jennings." He reached around Jade and pumped Trask's hand.

"I promise there will be no demonstration of wing chun tonight, eh?"

Trask touched a finger to his newly healed eye and grimaced. "Fine by me, Chan. Tonight we're going to pay tribute to a new tournament queen and to Jade's design. Shall we get on with it instead of quibbling over which of these ladies is more beautiful?" He whisked the back door open, expecting Mikki to assist Jade inside. To his surprise, Mikki handed Mei Li in, then climbed in himself, leaving Jade standing at the curb.

Trask shared her embarrassment as he watched uncertainty cloud her gray eyes. He tried to relieve her discomfort by joking, "I see how this chaperon business works. Separate seats definitely curtail a young man's fancy and his thoughts of..." Arching a brow, he left his sentence hanging.

Jade blushed. She took the front seat, acting as if it was the accepted arrangement all along. Any guilt she might have suffered from Mikki's snub fled quickly as her evening took on a whole new magic.

"Oh, have you ever seen anything this romantic?" squealed Mei Li, some minutes later as the four of them made their way into a cleverly made replica of a royal castle.

Trask waved a hand. "This is all in keeping with the larger theme of this year's parade which is Castles, Kings and Legendary Queens. It's impressive, but this event also brings home to me how close we are to the end of our season. Look, Jade—" he nudged her "—up on stage is your coach. Someone's done a superb job with the fresh flowers."

The lights dimmed and a single spotlight picked out prancing dappled horses and a pumpkin-shaped carriage sitting on a flat bed covered in greenery and dotted with willowy golden trees. The workmanship on the new foliage was exquisite.

There it was—her coach! Seeing it on stage, surrounded by the gorgeous members of the queen's court, brought tears to Jade's eye. "T. Stratton," she breathed, "without you, this would not have been possible."

Then all at once, the tears meant something different: she knew how close she was to leaving Fantasy Floats. The end of her apprenticeship. An end to seeing T. Stratton and his team. A good team. A happy year in spite of a few major pitfalls along the way. Jade hated seeing it end. She glanced at him through a curtain of tears. Tears of happiness, and of longing.

He stared at her with understanding and helplessness.

"Those horses look almost real enough to ride, don't they, Mikki," Mei Li whispered, her voice filled with awe. "Isn't Jade clever?"

Mikki grunted. "Shh," he hissed. "They are getting ready to introduce the princesses. Who do you think will win?"

Mikki was still in a snit because his plans had gone awry. She didn't envy her friend having to live with his petulance. Still, it was Mei Li's choice. And she was happy.

Trask reluctantly averted his gaze to scan the field of contestants. The tender moment passed with his saying, "How can they go wrong? The field is terrific. Did you know, Chan, that each area high school selects one princess? This process has been going on in the community for months now."

"All beautiful, athletic and blond, no doubt," said Mei Li, "like they're cut from an identical mold. At least, it was when I was in school."

Jade smiled. "Haven't you noticed all fairy-tale princesses look like Cinderella? T. Stratton is right. They couldn't go wrong in choosing one over another tonight. But Mei Li, where have you been? For the past several years they've had women of color in their court."

Trask tipped his head and studied her. "You're wrong in thinking all fairy-tale beauties are blond. If I recall, Snow White was a tall, willowy brunette. Rather like someone else we know."

Jade lowered her lashes and blushed.

"Snow White did not wear three-inch heels," Mikki pointed out. "I remember seeing the movie when it came to Hong Kong. She wore flat shoes out of deference to those little men who helped her. Quite unlike the someone we know, Jennings."

"Mikki, honestly, I never gave the heels a thought," Jade rallied. "I just grabbed a pair that matched the dress. Besides, we never dance together. You always dance with Mei Li."

He had the grace to flush, but before he could respond, Trask was summoned to the stage. He grasped Jade by the hand and tugged her along, insisting she accept her share of the glory.

On stage, she did little but hug the plaque they were given and gaze at him with her heart in her eyes.

He made his speech short and accepted on behalf of the whole Fantasy Floats team. Soon after the applause died out, a new tournament queen was crowned amid much hoopla; she was, as predicted, a pretty blonde. Immediately the band struck up a tune, and Jade and T. Stratton helped themselves from the long buffet tables groaning with food. She regretted that her parents weren't alive to share her success or to meet the one man who'd made it all possible.

"Would you do me the honor of a dance, Jade?" Trask whispered near her ear when things had settled down. He smiled, lifting her fingers to his lips. "I see Mikki has already claimed my date. If he chooses not to dance with the noted designer of the Cinderella coach, it's his loss."

"Noted designer," she scoffed. "I almost fell apart up on the stage. Is this sort of thing required often?"

He gathered her close to his tuxedoed shoulder and soothed away her nerves as he moved her out under a sparkling mirrored ball revolving slowly overhead. Silver lights flickered in and around the sphere, releasing pinpoints of light like a shower of moon dust.

Chuckling softly, Trask whirled her through the magical mist. "I've accepted a few awards in my time, but I've never had the pleasure of building a special queen's float. That honor, my lady, came to Fantasy Floats with you." His grin widened. "Truthfully, I can say I've never had the pleasure of dancing with my designer before, either." Their shared laughter died as they drifted past Mikki and Mei Li. "So, what's with him tonight?"

"I'm sorry about your date with Mei Li, T. Stratton," Jade apologized.

Trask rubbed his palm lightly over her bare back. "Did you ever consider that those two might be better suited?" he murmured, liking the feel of her in his arms. "Maybe you should suggest it."

Jade blinked. His sherry-colored eyes bathed her upturned face. Her knees wobbled and she missed a step. There it was again—the guilt attached to an intricate web of lies. "It must be Mei Li's traditional dress," she mumbled.

He stepped back, pretending to study her. "Hmm. If you say so." Then he laughed, a deep knowing laugh, and pulled her close.

She drank in his subtle scent of sand and sea, wanting to ask if he liked Mei Li's dress better—reluctant to impose her own interpretation on that drawn-out "hmm." But perhaps she was reading more into the magic of the night than was really there.

"I can't believe the holiday season is just around the corner, Jade." Trask's voice was a deep rumble near her ear. "Do you celebrate Christmas?"

The song ended and Jade slipped out of his arms. Before she escaped, the band struck up again, a slow dreamy waltz this time, and Trask reclaimed her. He moved sensuously against her body as they danced.

Jade's mind struggled to recall the conversation. "My grandparents are Buddhist," she murmured, "but my parents weren't. Sometimes I feel torn between two worlds. Oh, don't get me wrong, T. Stratton. I love my grandparents. And it's not so much the gifts I miss as the anticipation."

"I envy you having two cultures to draw from, Jade. Somehow, I didn't even manage one. I used to imagine what it would be like having grandparents."

As T. Stratton's chest rose and fell with the music, Jade tried to ignore the picture of a lonely little boy. She concentrated on how neatly her head nestled below his chin, how her short hair brushed his lips, three-inch heels and all.

"What do you do for Christmas, T. Stratton?" she asked brightly, giving herself a good hard shake.

He breathed in the tantalizing scent of her perfume and disregarded the sharp pain that her innocent remark had caused. It was silly, he knew, but suddenly the thought of spending another Christmas alone seemed bleak.

"Nothing," he muttered tightly. "I do nothing for the holidays."

His clipped response seemed to rip a jagged hole in Jade's tender heart. "Everyone does something on Christmas, T. Stratton." She tried making light of it. "Surely you visit friends?" She might have expanded her query to mention Max. Would have, if his face hadn't reflected his deep pain.

"It's a family holiday." His terse reminder was meant to turn their conversation in a different direction. No one could have been more surprised than Trask when his eyes locked with hers and he found himself begging, "Spend Christmas with me this year, Jade. I'll put up a tree. I'll even cook dinner. All you need to do is provide your company."

Jade felt as if she were tripping over her own feet. She had other considerations, she told herself. Mikki's family was arriving soon to prepare for a wedding—a wedding they assumed included her. It was unthinkable to promise T. Stratton a whole day. Any day.

Lifting a hand, she ran a finger gently over his cheek—a gesture meant to let him down easy. Yet something about the tense line of his jaw compelled her to murmur, "I'd like that very much, T. Stratton. Count on me for Christmas." It was difficult to tell which of them was more shocked.

CHAPTER TEN

DECEMBER DAWNED cold and clear. T.J. flipped the pages of his desk calendar, amazed at the speed with which November had hurtled past. He hadn't realized he'd been measuring everything in terms of the Coronation Ball until he caught himself circling December twenty-fifth with a red marking pen. Then he tilted back his chair and grinned. There was a change in the way he looked at Jade Han, too.

For one thing, he made excuses to be on hand during her morning t'ai chuan exercises with the crew. Not to the extent of joining them, even though Jade continued to invite him. But he'd definitely stopped resenting the time it took for her routine. Once or twice he actually found it hard not to smile.

Jade's hair had grown a bit and framed her face as she floated through the dance. Frequently, Trask daydreamed about how she'd look in the twinkling lights of his very first Christmas tree.

Nell shook him out of this morning's reverie with bad news. "T.J., this sudden cold snap is wreaking havoc with the flower growers again. Perkins just phoned. They can't fill our request for orange or yellow mums."

"Damn! Did they offer any alternatives?" His chair snapped down, and when she shook her head, he barked, "Have Jade bring in her mosaics. Maybe we can substitute marigolds or carnations. Carnations have a lot of petals."

"They're also more expensive, boss. What about the added cost?"

Trask scowled. "At this late date, do we have a choice?"

Jade saw them in a huddle as she stopped to switch off the tape player. "Is something wrong, T. Stratton?" she called.

"It's nothing." Trask shot Nell a warning look. "Could you bring me the charts for all the floats requiring gold or yellow

mums? I'm thinking of trying something a little different."
Before Jade could question him, he hurried off.

Shrugging, Nell followed. Jade stared after them.

"Trouble?" asked Joe pausing beside her.

She shook her head. "I don't know. T. Stratton says not. He mentioned making a switch in flowers. Isn't it late to do that?"

Joe rubbed the back of his neck. "I dunno. Reports are this is starting out the coldest December on record. T.J. contracted with one of our northern valley growers. I wouldn't worry until he says to. Can you possibly work late tonight? Dan's having trouble with that drawbridge again. We're nearing countdown, and I don't want to move any of the floats to the volunteer barn for the flower work until I know they're all shipshape."

"I'll check," she offered. "This will make the third night this week I've canceled out on my family." She bit her lip. "Mikki's parents arrived Monday. I hope we get some of these problems ironed out soon. And speaking of problems, did Greg tell you I thought we should add braces to a couple of our taller floats? They seem a little flimsy to me."

"Well, the structural design is Greg's forte. I'll talk to him about it."

"Jade!" Trask yelled from the doorway. "I don't have all day. Will you get me those drawings?"

"Uh-oh," Joe said under his breath. "You'd better go, Jade. The boss has that bent-on-hell look in his eye." He winked. "And don't worry so much. I know this is your first year in the business, but Fantasy Floats always comes through."

Jade grimaced as she hurried off. Technically it wasn't her first year. She had four years of working on college entries. But it was true that the Fantasy Floats crew had logged in many more hours than she. Maybe it was selfish, but she wanted the floats safely moved so T. Stratton would relax and they could enjoy Christmas together. "I'm coming," she called to him, shaking off an uneasy feeling.

As she hurried to find the drawings, her thoughts flitted ahead to the phone call home to make another round of apologies. Soon after, they leapt to the problems she'd been having with the waterfall on the Hawaiian float. Greg said the water was too heavy, and every time they moved the float, the weight in the tanks shifted. That was only one among many obstacles they seemed to be facing at the last minute. Perhaps it was normal in this crazy occupation, she thought, picking up the case with the detailed drawings.

Suddenly she was struck by what a tremendous burden T. Stratton carried. He was the one to guarantee his clients a perfect ending. And what was she doing? Fantasizing about enjoying a carefree holiday when she should be supporting him.

A week whizzed by. Flower growers installed smudge pots in their fields and saved some blooms. Still, the number that died meant ten percent added on the final bill. Then, in the midst of what Jade already thought was pandemonium, hoards of visitors began flocking to the warehouse for guided tours. It was a toss-up as to which was worse—the tourists or her endless sessions with Mikki's mother. Mei Li kept her evenings tied up, and Mikki's mother scheduled her lunches.

In trying to allay Mei Li's worries, Jade took to extending her lunch hour and slipping out on breaks to view wedding dresses. Nothing pleased Mrs. Chan and she hated Jade's hair. Among other things, Jade was forced to jump from English to Chinese at a moment's notice. The added stress of watching that she didn't let anything slip, coupled with a full week of pressure at work, soon took its toll. One day when Jade was pressed to the limit, Trask chanced to overhear her snap at one of the tourists.

Having put in a series of eighteen-hour days himself, he was less than tolerant when he took her aside. "I don't like hearing you speak to a guest that way, Jade. Tours are part of our business. You never know when one of these people will end up as next year's client. I suggest you find him and make amends."

Jade might have accepted his reprimand more readily if Cynthia had not arrived just then and quite brazenly listened in. But that was another development making Jade edgy. Cynthia had started spiriting T. Stratton away at lunchtime almost daily. Rationally, Jade knew she had no right to get angry; today she wasn't rational. "I'm not a robot, T. Stratton. When you went over my job description, you didn't mention answering stupid questions time and time again during our busiest weeks. Did you hear that man? He wanted to know why a 'cutie like me is working in a man's field.'"

"What?" Trask bellowed. "Why didn't you tell me? I would have set him straight. In fact, I will."

Cynthia curled her palm around Trask's upper arm. "It's like I said yesterday, sweetie," she purred. "You need a hostess to conduct your tours. If you recall, I volunteered." Her lips curved into a sultry pout. "I'm bored, Trask. I have no place at the bank now." Glancing at Jade, she lowered her voice. "The new president is edging me out. Let me help here, please."

"Maybe that wouldn't be a bad idea," he muttered. "Nell is cross. Jade's a zombie. And Greg's temper is on simmer."

Jade ground her back teeth. If T. Stratton had bothered to look, he'd see she was simmering, too. Maybe closer to boiling. She resented being sweaty and splotched with glue while Cynthia always seemed to breeze in looking like a page out of *Vogue*. Now this. And to make matters worse, Mikki's mother was getting to her. The woman never ceased comparing her blue jeans to Mei Li's dresses. Twice recently, she'd almost spilled the beans; each time Mei Li's pleading look had stopped her.

Luckily, nothing lasted forever. Two weeks and one day, to be exact, until dinner with T. Stratton. Also the day Roger was due home. Jade decided she could tough anything out for two weeks. She forced a smile.

"Well—" Trask turned to glance at Cynthia and rubbed a frown from his brow "—it can't hurt. Ask Nell for a badge after lunch." He snapped his fingers. "Oh, and Jade, remind Joe to post Keep Off signs along the upper catwalks. All I'd need about now is a lawsuit—one of those camera buffs landing in the middle of a float, for instance. If Joe asks, I'll be at lunch. By the way, will you stay tonight? I'm afraid we have more flower substitutions."

"Well," she hedged, "tonight they're doing Cinderella at the ballet. Mikki has tickets for the Mings, his family and mine. I thought it would be fun, considering the coach...." She sighed. "I'll call them."

"I did warn you this would happen when you started. I'm sorry if it's a family thing, but—" Nearing the exit, he stopped abruptly. "Hey, you wouldn't happen to know anything about a hefty donation sent to the youth center for my camp project, would you? It's enough to guarantee that we can meet the January dedication."

Jade lifted startled eyes.

"That's what I thought," he said, softening his tone. "Consider it a loan. I'll pay you back. Since you've helped make it possible, maybe you'd like to attend the grand opening."

"T.J.," Cynthia chided, "she'd be bored stiff. What does she care about abandoned kids? Don't forget, for her it's a healthy write-off."

Trask tore his gaze from Jade. "I just thought... Never mind. I'll see you get a tax slip from the foundation."

Jade wished she had the energy to protest. But what was the use with Cynthia hovering?

Nell leaned around the door. "Phone call, Jade. It's your friend, Mei Li."

Jade slipped past T. Stratton and Cynthia, just as the woman suggested they attend the dedication together. Jade's heart gave another of those funny little lurches. The two were spending a lot of time together lately. Was T. Stratton regretting that he'd invited her and not Cynthia for Christmas?

Mei Li canceled their noon shopping trip, for which Jade was grateful. It allowed her to submerge herself in work, to forget about personal problems. Yet her conversation with T. Stratton remained so much on her mind that she wondered, that evening, if her thoughts had transmitted themselves to him when they were the only two left and he brought up the subject of the holiday.

"I was going to fix a crown roast for Christmas, Jade. Hillary gave me her fail-safe recipe. But I keep seeing ads on TV for turkey with all the trimmings. I started thinking you might prefer that, or duck."

"I, ah, thought you might cancel our day," she said.

"Are you backing out?" Trask straightened away from the table in her workstation, where he'd been poring over one of her blueprints. "Joe mentioned Mikki's family has been demanding all your spare time."

"Ah, yes, they are. But not Christmas Day," she added quickly. "Crown roast will be just fine, T. Stratton. It's only that, well, I heard you talking with Cynthia before lunch." Her voice faltered. "I thought perhaps... you and she..."

Placing a finger beneath her chin, Trask forced Jade to meet his eyes. "Cynthia is going through a hard time right now. She's depressed. She doesn't want to go to Aspen alone over the holidays."

Jade swallowed the lump in her throat and nibbled at her bottom lip. Did he want release from an invitation he'd made on impulse? It hurt, but she'd be graceful about it. "You need to get away, I'm sure," she murmured.

Leaning forward, he let his gaze sweep her face. "I couldn't go, even if I wanted to—which I don't." His lips were only inches from hers, his eyes looking deep into her own. "We move floats to the sheds Christmas Eve and the volunteers pick up their assignments. I never take winter vacations."

"Oh," she said in a small voice. "Then does that mean—"

"Say again, please," he urged, tilting her chin higher.

Her lashes lifted a fraction. "Say what? All I said was 'Oh'—"

The minute her mouth formed the small circle, his lips closed over hers in a kiss that was soft, tender and seeking.

Jade swallowed the breath trapped in her throat, the "oh" automatically silenced.

He pulled back and smiled. "I've wanted to do that for weeks. It forces you to look at me. Do you know you have the most maddening way of avoiding eye contact?"

Jade had full eye contact now and her knees had gone rubbery from his kiss. Verbal response was impossible.

"I'm counting the days until Christmas, Jade." Trask ran his fingers through her hair and framed her upturned face with his hands. "Don't ask me to explain what's happening here, because I can't. Just promise me you'll spend the holiday with me. Come early. Dinner at one o'clock?"

She nodded mutely, guessing from the telltale darkening of his eyes that he was going to kiss her again. She moved to meet him. There were times when words were not required. However, she had barely begun sampling the dark, spicy flavor of his kiss when the back door to the warehouse crashed open and they sprang apart with a guilty start.

Outside Jade's cubicle, Dan's voice boomed. "Hey, you two, you want some company? I was driving by on my way home from racquetball and saw the lights. You sure know how to make a guy feel guilty.'' He arrived at the door and leaned one shoulder negligently against the frame. ''I had a thought on the waterfall.'' He glanced from one to the other. ''Say, you two been fighting again?''

Jade's head came up. She could feel her cheeks flame. She'd escaped T. Stratton's loose grasp, but she was so nervous Dan couldn't help seeing something was amiss. She busied herself at the back table and tried to act nonchalant.

T.J. stayed by the drawing board, glaring at his engineer. He felt like throttling him. He cleared his throat. ''Not exactly a fight, Dan.'' He shrugged. ''You know how tensions build this close to parade day. We have a lot of holes yet. Go ahead and do what you came to do. Jade and I are almost finished here. Don't forget, we all have to be back on these projects at the crack of dawn.''

''Right,'' drawled Dan. ''I can take a hint. So neither of you wants to tell me what the argument was about. Hey, that's cool. All the same, T.J., I wish you'd lay off Jade. She works as hard or harder than the rest of us. Sometime you might try telling her thanks.'' Not waiting for his boss's response, Dan whirled and stalked away.

Trask reached out an arm and pulled Jade up against his chest. Giving her a quick kiss on the nose, he said lightly, ''Consider yourself thanked.'' His eyes twinkled. ''I didn't think you'd want him to know precisely what we were doing.'' Then he kissed her again and this time it was no gentle kiss.

''T. Stratton,'' she whispered, wiggling out of his arms, trying in vain to collect her thoughts, ''you don't owe me thanks, or anything. We simply shouldn't...*I* shouldn't be kissing you, or letting you kiss me.'' She put a hand to her temple. ''I'm more tired tonight than I thought. Could we complete this run-through in the morning?''

He wouldn't pretend her denial didn't hurt, but on closer inspection, T.J. could tell she was near exhaustion. He wondered why he hadn't noticed the dark circles under her eyes before. ''Tomorrow it is,'' he agreed, trailing a finger down her cheek. ''I'll see if I can help Dan. Then I think I'll crash here tonight and get an early start. You drive carefully and take an extra hour in the morning, okay?''

"Uh...thank you, I will, T. Stratton," she said, unable to keep from remembering the last time he'd kissed her and told her to take an extra hour—the night the coach had disappeared. Quickly she gathered her jacket and handbag and slipped out, calling goodbye to Dan as she left.

She was in on time the next day. Pressure mounted and by week's end Jade wished she could take that extra hour and more. No small part of her wish was due to Cynthia's breezing in at nine every morning to take charge of the tours and anything else she deemed needed her attention. Nell threatened to quit at least twice a day.

"I tell you, Jade," the older woman said, just before noon on the fifth day of Cynthia's volunteer stint, "if T.J. doesn't keep that woman away from me, I'm going to throw a ledger at her. Go with me out to lunch, please, before I commit mayhem and murder."

"I shouldn't, Nell. But I will, because I feel the same way." Jade dug her bag out of her bottom drawer and led the way out. When they were in the car and safely out of earshot, she complained, "Can't T. Stratton see how uptight she's making everyone? Cynthia acts like Fantasy Floats is *her* company."

Nell shook her head. "I really don't think he sees it. He's going off in all directions at once. Besides, when Mrs. Snazzy Britches isn't busy with guests, she waits on him hand and foot. It's sickening to watch her in action."

"Mrs. Snazzy Britches..." Jade giggled. "How appropriate. Yesterday Cynthia wore white linen of all things, in the warehouse. Then she took poor Greg apart when he rolled out from under a float on the dolly and accidentally brushed up against her pants. He offered to pay for cleaning, but not even that appeased her."

"And did you hear the way she went on and on to the sponsor who dropped by this morning?" Nell demanded in a disgusted tone. "No? Well, let me tell you, she promised him the most expensive flowers. Much more help like that and T.J. will go bankrupt."

Jade stopped the car in front of the pizza parlor and tried to look unaffected even though a sudden chill shot through her and left her feeling ill. "Is he in danger of that?"

"I'm probably exaggerating," Nell admitted. "We're having a light year is all. Unusual since T.J. took over, but if nothing else goes wrong, we'll still make a profit. Those two extra floats will keep us in the black."

Frowning, Jade followed Nell into the dark interior of the restaurant. "Well, I can't think of much that could go wrong this close to completion."

Nell sank into an empty booth with a sigh. "Don't worry, Jade. I feel better already, just knowing I've got an hour away from that woman to relax."

Nell's candor made Jade smile. Still, she couldn't seem to shake a sense of foreboding. But maybe it was just because she was so tired and because so many things involving her personal life were still up in the air. Lately she had begun imagining what it would be like to stay at Fantasy Floats—what it would be like working year after year with T. Stratton. Maybe as his partner. The last time Hank had dropped in, he'd joked with Dan about changing careers. Jade forced her attention back to what Nell was saying, gave her order, then tuned out again.

Dreams—that's what everything was right now. However, she might mention the idea of a partnership to T. Stratton after they'd moved the floats. Once Mei Li and Mikki made their announcement, there would be nothing holding her back. This time, feeling much happier, Jade gave all her attention to Nell.

But her newfound sense of harmony lasted only until Mei Li phoned that night. The younger woman was excited about the brunch and festivities that her parents were planning for Christmas Day.

"Impossible, Mei Li," Jade said around a yawn. "Since when did your parents start celebrating Christmas?"

"Since I convinced them it would be the perfect day to entertain Mikki's parents. You have to come, Jade," she pleaded. "If you don't it will ruin everything. I'm nervous enough as it is. Roger is due in that morning, and of course my parents insisted on including his family. Mikki says it will be better to have everyone in one room when he makes the announcement. But I can't eat for worrying about it."

"If it was any other day..." Jade twisted the phone cord, hating to refuse her friend.

"Christmas is the perfect day," Mei Li argued. "Surely your boss doesn't expect you to work on the holiday."

Jade hadn't told Mei Li or Mikki about her invitation to dinner. She hadn't wanted a lecture on the impropriety of her spending the day alone with a man. "It's not work," she said sharply. "He's cooking dinner for me. He has no family to spend the holiday with—and I'm going, Mei Li."

"Oh," Mei Li said in a small voice, then she fell silent.

"I'm sorry to snap at you," Jade apologized, "but I'm growing tired of all this vacillation. Why not tell your family, Mikki's and my grandparents before Roger gets home? I mean, it's not as if you're going to change your mind. Ask your mother to make it dinner on Christmas Eve, instead."

"Have you forgotten we promised to take Mikki to Olvera Street for the breaking of the piñata on Christmas Eve? You're not backing out of that, too, are you?"

Jade stopped wiggling the sock she'd been using for a tug-of-war with Wrinks. She *had* forgotten. However, the old cobblestone street, lined with quaint Mexican shops decked out in bright holiday splendor, was one of her favorite treats. Every night for seven nights before Christmas, the merchants of Olvera Street provided a giant piñata in the courtyard. Children of all cultures took turns being blindfolded and having a whack at the papier-mâché creation. When each child had had a turn, the honor of breaking it went to an older boy or girl. Then they all scrambled for wrapped hard candy and small prizes. Jade found herself wishing she could share that experience with T. Stratton. But he hadn't said anything about Christmas Eve; perhaps he had other plans. Getting back to Mei Li's question, she murmured, "I'd love to join you and Mikki, if you aren't planning on leaving too early. We move floats all day. We'll be getting them set up and ready for the volunteers to come after Christmas and attach the flowers. Maybe you two would like to help."

"If we volunteer, will you come for brunch?" Mei Li quickly countered.

Jade wadded up the old wool sock and threw it for Wrinks to chase. "I swear, Mei Li, you're as tenacious as Wrinks when he's caught hold of T. Stratton's pant leg." She chuckled. "I told you about that, didn't I?"

Mei Li joined in the laughter. "Several times," she said dryly. "As much as you talk about that man, you'd think he was more to you than a boss."

Jade's spine stiffened and her laughter faded. Her old friend had hit a nerve. For weeks now, she'd successfully avoided examining her feelings for T. Stratton, feelings that went beyond those of designer for master builder. Suddenly she wanted to get off the telephone and consider them. "I'll give you until eleven-thirty at your brunch, but that's absolutely it," she said quickly.

"What?" Mei Li teased, her triumph audible in the happy lilt of her voice. "The creator of Cinderella's coach won't give me until the stroke of twelve?"

"Funny, Mei Li. Eleven-thirty and not one minute more. So you'd better practice talking fast—beginning now. Christmas Eve, I'll plan on meeting you at the candle shop on Olvera Street—say eight o'clock? See you then. 'Bye." She replaced the receiver and dropped heavily onto her bed, absently accepting the sock Wrinks had retrieved.

What would her grandparents say if they had any inkling that not only did she wish to continue designing floats for T. Stratton Jennings, but that somehow, somewhere along the way, she had also begun dreaming of a more personal kind of relationship?

Flopping back on the bed, Jade stared disconsolately at the ceiling. She could just imagine the number of impurities Grandmother Han would find in a blond, amber-eyed American who had not a single clue about his background. And Grandfather—he would shake his head and remind her that mere mortals shouldn't tamper with *shujing*. And for all she knew, maybe they shouldn't.

CHAPTER ELEVEN

THE NEXT DAY Jade was so quiet and subdued at work the crew asked if she was sick. Because her "no" held little conviction, they didn't believe her. The men, including T. Stratton, went out of their way to be kind.

Jade studied him with every opportunity that came her way. She needed to know exactly what she found to love about T. Stratton Jennings. By noon, she'd racked up a hundred little things, not including the way his kisses made her feel. His crooked smile, his capable hands, his willingness to work alongside his crew and his careful attention to detail were but a few. Not necessarily traits to please grandparents—especially grandparents offering a dowry for acceptable bloodlines.

Her despondence increased and Greg Sanders wasted time clowning in an effort to make her laugh. Not only wasn't Jade cheered, but it drew him censure from T.J. and also from the others, who by then were worried about dark clouds rolling in from the coast and a threat of rain.

Transporting the floats from the warehouse to the sheds turned out to be a monumental task. A cold wind accompanied the cloud front and the taller floats took a beating. Tempers were on short leashes all around. The only good thing about the day, Jade thought, was that Cynthia bowed out early, saying she had to pack for her trip.

"Actually, she just doesn't want to get her hands dirty," Greg confided to Jade when Nell remarked on Cynthia's abrupt departure.

"You'd think she'd wise up," snorted Dan. "Can't she see T.J. is only nice to her because he feels sorry for her? If Cynthia had her way, she'd have T.J. dump the business and go into banking. She's in a snit because he doesn't leave all the menial tasks to his lowly crew and hurry off to Aspen to spend the holidays with her.''

''Oh?'' Jade looked up from tying a red flag on the back of Snow White's float. ''Did he sound like he wanted to go?''

Greg shook his head. ''Nope. He's got plans. But he won't tell any of us what they are. Say, maybe he's taking a last run out to the boys' camp. You know how important Max's dedication is to him.''

''Mmm,'' Jade mumbled. Who was he trying to protect by not telling anyone he planned to spend the day with her? Himself or her? Perhaps he'd rather be going with Cynthia, after all. She found the thought sobering—enough to keep her from asking him to join the Olvera Street expedition. Enough so that her apprehension ruined an evening that should have been fun.

Jade made excuses to leave right after the breaking of the piñata. Expecting protests from Mikki and Mei Li, she was surprised when they waved her away. They were so wrapped up in each other and their wedding plans she doubted they even noticed her inattention.

It was only after she'd dragged herself home and snuggled deep into her pillow that Jade remembered wanting to pick up a Christmas gift for T. Stratton on Olvera Street. She fought being lulled to sleep by Wrinks's soft whuffles long enough to decide she'd get him a nice bottle of rice wine. To make it decorative, she would add a carved jade stopper that had been a favorite of her father. Somehow she thought T. Stratton would appreciate the gesture. And maybe, following the Mings' brunch, she'd finally be free to tell him the truth about Mikki and Mei Li. Maybe then he'd kiss her again. Jade drifted off to sleep, dreaming of amber eyes and tantalizing kisses. Beyond that were hidden fantasies about which she could only wonder.

Because she hadn't set her alarm, Jade slept late. Letting her body awaken naturally on Christmas morning was a luxury, she discovered.

Lying there, listening to the faint patter of rain on her windows, she felt the pleasure of her anticipation in sharing the holiday with T. Stratton seep through every pore. Her elation dimmed when Mei Li called and in hushed tones announced

Roger's plane had been delayed due to heavy snows on the East Coast.

"Then there's no reason for me to come, Mei Li," Jade stated, deciding to stand firm. "Roger or no Roger, this is the very last day I'm going along with your charade. Do you realize my grandparents talked with a realtor last week about selling the house? It's simply not right to let them make plans, thinking I'm going to marry Mikki. If you don't tell them today, I will."

"Will you hush and listen, Jade," Mei Li blurted out with a little determination of her own. "Roger is bringing a friend home for the holidays—a *woman*." She laughed. "Can you beat it? Roger's parents and mine are in shock. I'm calling to tell you Mikki and I will take care of our announcement and your grandparents. You enjoy your day."

Feeling freed from an enormous burden, Jade arrived at T. Stratton's condominium at least twenty minutes early. Not wanting to seem eager, she sat in the car, drumming her fingers on the steering wheel, staring through the windshield at a light rain.

Gathering the wine and her handbag and taking one last deep breath to settle the hummingbirds in her stomach, Jade dashed through raindrops that were pelting harder now.

She knocked several times and was about to turn away, certain he'd forgotten, after all, when flushed and out of breath, Trask jerked open the door. He stared at her for long moments without inviting her in.

"Ah...you were expecting me, right?" Jade could feel heat rising in her cheeks.

"Of course. I—I was cooking," he stammered. "And it's...well, the rain in your hair sparkles like diamonds. Mmm...and you smell of ripe peaches." He reached out and pulled her inside.

Jade laughed. "It's apricots. Mei Li gave me soap, powder and hand cream for my birthday. It's not too overpowering?" she asked anxiously.

"Never," he murmured. "In that pink coat, you look like cotton candy. You look...angelic." He paused. "Did I ever tell you, the first time we met I thought you were my personal angel?" His eyes slid over her and grew dark.

"No," she said, brushing the droplets of water from her short hair to ease her embarrassment. "Well, maybe I do recall you muttering something. But I thought you were a little, you know..." She blushed at his deep, delighted laughter. "Something smells yummy," she said, turning. "Is that dinner?"

"Yes, it's dinner." He helped her remove her coat. "Now that you've effectively evaded my compliment, what can I get you to drink?"

Jade quickly thrust a sack into his hands. "I brought you a gift of wine. It isn't wrapped. You can serve it now or put it under your tree. The decorative cork was my father's. I want you to have it."

He took it and studied the label. "Imported. Nice. I don't believe I've had rice wine before. The stopper looks antique. Your father's?" His touch lingered on the intricately carved jade. "No one's ever given me such a rare gift." His jaw worked. "I couldn't serve it. Please. Put it under the tree. I have a California wine already chilled."

Jade crossed the room to where he'd indicated, expecting to see a small tree. "T. Stratton!" she gasped. "Your tree almost touches the ceiling. It must have cost a fortune in decorations."

"Not so much. Nell brought me some she doesn't use anymore, and so did Joe." He grinned at her across a built-in bar. "Sometimes it pays to be a helpless bachelor."

"Helpless?" she teased. "You?"

She set her gift under the tree beside an intriguing small package with her name on it. She hadn't expected a gift. Should she refuse it and tell him to save his money? No. What she wanted to do was rattle the package with the big red bow and guess what was inside—the way she had when she was little. Resisting temptation, she rose and walked to the window overlooking his inner courtyard. Jade saw that it was raining harder now. The wind had picked up and was making ripples in the swimming pool.

She felt the heat of T. Stratton's body as he came up behind her. Whirling, she nearly upset the wine. "Oops! Sorry," she murmured. "I was just watching the storm. I think it's getting worse."

"I heard on the radio that it's only a squall. Relax, Jade." He handed her a frosty glass and clinked it lightly with his own. "Here's to Fantasy Floats' continued success. And here's to us. We're lucky we got the floats moved before this hit."

Jade turned back and looked at the darkening sky. She shivered. *Us.* It had a nice ring. But of course, he'd only meant "us" as in the team, the crew.

"Hey, are you cold?" Trask grabbed her hand and tugged her across the room. "I have a fire all laid in the fireplace. I'd planned it for after dinner, but there's no reason not to light it now."

She broke away and sank down on the couch. "How thoughtful of you, T. Stratton. But then, I'm sure you entertain a lot."

He lit the fire and watched the flame dance in the open grate before he turned and dusted his hands on charcoal-gray slacks. "Would you believe this is a first for me? Christmas has always been just another workday. Your coming today is special. I want it to be the same for you."

Jade held her breath, thinking he had a way of speaking frankly at times that was most unnerving. Idly she wiped condensation off the wineglass with one finger, wondering if he was going to kiss her—wishing he would. But when he placed a hand on the arm of the couch and leaned closer, a buzzer sounded in the next room and he pulled back with a sheepish grin.

"Dinner is ready," he announced. "It's a good thing you were early. I must have miscalculated the time."

Jade felt the tension ooze from her limbs. She shouldn't be soliciting his kisses. Mei Li would be thoroughly shocked if she knew. But soon, Mei Li would be in Hong Kong and wouldn't care what her friend did or didn't do. The moment passed and Jade forgot her anxiety enough to exclaim over the attractive table he'd set. "This is beautiful, T. Stratton. Candles and real linen. It's better than a restaurant."

"This is the best it gets," he teased, winking. "You're seeing the sum total of my culinary talent in this one meal." He placed a green salad in front of her with a flourish.

After that, they talked of general things. Then Jade asked about his plans for the dedication of the camp, and like a key, it opened up a whole gamut of nostalgic reminiscences on his part. When at last there was a lull in the conversation and he rose to replenish their wine, Jade felt as if she'd finally begun to understand him. Her heart wept for the lonely, abandoned child.

"Enough about me," he said, returning to the table. "I don't usually ramble on like this about myself. If you're finished eating, Jade, what do you say we go back in by the fire? I intended to save your present until it got dark outside, but I can't stand the suspense. I want you to open it now."

"Let me help with the dishes first."

"Absolutely not. This is Christmas. The good elves will come later and do them."

Jade saw excitement sparkle in his eyes. How she wished she'd bought him a real gift. Something new. Slanting him a shy smile, she gave in. "But I will help clean up later, T. Stratton. Give the good elves a holiday."

Trask led her into the living room, where he pointed her toward a fluffy white area rug near the tree. He added a log to the fire before joining her, then without ceremony, he took the foil-wrapped gift from beneath the tree and placed it in her hands.

Jade hesitated, loving all his fuss. Trask leapt to his feet. "Wait!" he said. "I believe, with the storm and all, it's dark enough outside to turn off the lamps and use the Christmas-tree lights. That's half the fun, don't you think?"

"Definitely." Jade nodded, although the whistle of the rising wind was adding to her sudden case of nerves.

They sat for a moment in companionable silence, watching the twinkling lights. After a bit, Trask scooted closer and murmured, "I've always envisioned my first tree with heaps of presents underneath." He touched the gift now lying idle in her lap. "This looked terribly lonely under such a big tree. Someday, I think I'll have a passel of kids to buy for."

She felt her excitement return and, giving in to her childish desire, shook the gift to see if it rattled. "I'd almost forgotten how my father used to tease me about the best things coming in small packages." Her eyes grew dewy with the memory. "He spoiled me."

"So quit stalling and open it." Trask's gaze slid to his wine. Potent stuff, he thought. He wanted to spoil her, too. How many times today had he pictured what it would be like coming home to her every night? Now, foolishly, he'd added children to the scene. "Hurry up," he urged, holding tight to his glass, knowing that without it he'd say to hell with the package and get down to kissing her.

Jade unwrapped the gift slowly to draw out the suspense, to make the moment last. She gasped when the first layer came off, revealing a box from a well-known jeweler. Her gaze widened and flew to meet his. "Oh," she said in a small voice, hesitating, her fingers curled around the lid. "T. Stratton, you shouldn't have." Yet before he could say anything, she lifted the lid and stared, transfixed by a sparkling glass slipper attached to a slender gold chain. "Oh," she whispered again. "It's beautiful." She touched a trembling finger to the crystal toe. "Since my parents died, no one has given me anything this lovely."

His heart twisted in his chest. Kneeling beside her and using great care, he lifted the charm gently and clasped it around her neck. Unable to stop himself, he placed a lingering kiss at the nape of her creamy neck where the clasp fell.

She shivered and turned to look at him, her eyes brimming with tears.

As their gazes met, he felt the faint tremor of her slender body. He heard the wind rattle the window and the rain beat on the glass, but he was certain the storm outside was no fiercer than the one raging inside him. Never had he wanted any woman the way he wanted her right now. And yet there was more—there was tenderness, trust and a need to protect her from the calamities of the world. New feelings for him.

Trask traced her lips with his finger. He wanted her to understand. He'd never ventured his love since Kitty. Today, he'd spell it out.

"It's a gift from my heart, Jade."

A tear slid down her cheek as she touched the cool crystal where it lay in the hollow of her throat against her heated skin. "And I thank you from the bottom of mine," she said, turning and throwing her arms around his neck. "I will treasure it always, even after I leave Fantasy Floats."

"Hush. Don't talk of leaving." He used both thumbs to wipe away her tears. All afternoon, he'd been wanting to kiss her.

Indulging that desire now, he placed a tiny kiss near her ear. Craving more, he moved the length of her chin in the same lazy manner.

She let out a silvery sigh, and it was enough to drive him wild. Tilting his head, he crushed her quivering lips beneath his own, even after telling himself to take it slow. Knowing they needed to talk first.

For just a moment, the hummingbirds in Jade's stomach took off in mad flight, then all at once they stilled. This was, after all, what she wanted.

Heat exploded suddenly between them and things moved far faster than Trask had intended.

When they broke apart, Jade was shocked to find she had slipped down on the rug and her skirt was askew. "T. Stratton," she gasped, tugging at her skirt. "What are you... what am I...?"

His smile slowly turned into a frown. "What's wrong? Surely you aren't going to tell me you still plan to marry Mikki Chan?"

"No, I'm not." Jade struggled to stand. "I'm not going to marry Mikki. I never have been and I wanted to tell you before, but I couldn't."

His frown deepened. "Never have been? You mean you've let me think... What kind of game is this?"

She looked puzzled. "No game. There was Mei Li's promise to Roger and my grandparents to consider. Family honor means everything to them—and to me." She fingered the glass slipper nervously. "Oh, dear. You don't understand."

Trask clenched his teeth. Kitty Ferris had talked about honor, too. Later he'd found out she really meant money. "I understand more than you give me credit for, Jade," he said in a cold voice. "On your side of town, blood and money are very thick."

"Please, T. Stratton." She spread her hands. "Money doesn't enter into this. It has to do with family and friends."

"I was a fool to think you'd be different," he raged. "How long did you plan to wait until you ripped out my heart and threw it back in my face? What a cheat you are, Jade Han. A fraud."

Outside, lightning cracked. The lights on the Christmas tree blinked and went out. Jade felt her joy in the day snuffed as surely as the tree lights. When thunder shook the window and raindrops beat the glass in renewed fury, she shook her head sadly and hurried to retrieve her coat and handbag.

"The storm is getting worse, T. Stratton. I think I'd better leave. Thank you for dinner and for the charm," she said stiffly. "Will I see you at the volunteer shed tomorrow morning—the way we planned?"

He stared at her, hating her proper little speech. Hating the fact that he'd been right about her all along. "You got your coach built—what more do you want from Fantasy Floats? From me?"

Jade opened her mouth to respond, but the telephone shrilled and cut her off. It hurt that he thought her so shallow. As he turned away to answer his call, she moved in a daze toward the front door. What had she done wrong?

"Wait," he instructed. "We're not finished." But as the phone rang for the third time, he snatched up the receiver and barked hello. "What do you mean, my floats are in danger?" he shouted. "Gusts up to ninety miles an hour? But our shed is holding, right?"

Jade paused with her hand on the doorknob and listened to the one-sided conversation.

"I'll be right there, Manny. We'll tie every one of them down if we have to until this storm blows over. It won't last long. That's the beauty of Southern California."

"Is everything okay?" Jade asked in a worried tone as he replaced the receiver.

"What? Oh, fine," he muttered. "That was Security. The storm has picked up over near the floats."

"I'll come, too."

"No. No need," he said sharply. "It's my worry."

He was hurt by her deception and Jade couldn't blame him. Maybe tomorrow he'd be more reasonable. Mumbling goodbye, she let herself out into the pouring rain. Very soon, driving became so treacherous that their argument slipped to the back of her mind. Never had Jade driven in such a storm. She bypassed the freeway, taking surface roads. Rivers of water obliterated the center line and the wind battered her small car from all sides. When she finally pulled into her own driveway, her knuckles were white from gripping the wheel and her knees quivered.

Surprised to see lights in the house, Jade ducked her head and made a run for it. She had hoped her grandparents would still be at the Mings'.

The old couple rushed to meet her as she stamped into the hall shaking water all over Wrinks. Worry haunted their eyes and etched deep lines around their mouths. "We've been alarmed for you, Jade," said her grandfather. "The television is filled with news about the destruction of your floats. Part of a roof has collapsed and it's been reported that your Mr. Jennings has been injured. Mei Li and Mikki have gone to find you."

Jade was shocked into stillness by the news. Her heart beat like a trip-hammer in her breast. Fear welled up, choking her.

CHAPTER TWELVE

JADE SPRINTED down the hall to the sitting room and the TV, a cry lodged in her throat. Dropping her handbag on the floor, she flipped through channels, irritated at finding nothing but meaningless programs. At last she hit on a broadcast showing the devastation wrought by the freak storm.

Making a quick assessment, Jade thought that Fantasy Floats had fared better than some. Those who had erected circus tents to shelter their floats suffered the worst damage. In T. Stratton's shed, the wind had blown away a portion of the roof; a corner lay atop Snow White. King Kamehameha, too, appeared in need of repairs. It was impossible to see what lay beyond. Tears sprang to Jade's eyes when the photographer panned the flower huts out behind the main structure. More than half were virtually leveled.

What she waited to hear was not immediately forthcoming—news of T. Stratton's injuries. Instead, the announcer gave estimates of overall losses. The dollar figures were staggering. Fear that it might ruin Fantasy Floats almost buckled Jade's knees. She pulled a chair close to the set and sat on the edge, hardly believing the cavalier manner in which the newscaster glossed over two injuries that had occurred—T. Stratton and a security guard from another camp. Several times the commentator said how fortunate it was that the storm had hit on a holiday rather than after the thousands of volunteers started work. Which was true of course, but even so...

It soon became apparent that if she wanted information on T. Stratton, she would have to go and see for herself.

"I'm going to change into work clothes and go help," she told her grandparents, who had come to stand quietly behind her.

"It is dangerous, Jade," cautioned her grandfather. "The storm is not yet over. And it isn't your problem. For this folly you have already lost Mikki. But there will be other opportunities in Hong Kong. Yesterday I sold the house. Now there is nothing to keep us here."

She blinked back tears. "I don't care about the house, but I never meant to hurt you. I love you both. However, I can't go to Hong Kong. I won't leave. Please understand, T. Stratton needs me."

"Then Mei Li was right," the old man said, switching to Chinese. "This is not about designing floats."

Jade shook her head. "It is and it isn't. My roots are in California, just as yours are in Hong Kong. And Mei Li relates only what is in *my* heart, Grandfather. T. Stratton has no such feelings for me. Still, I must go to him."

Grandfather Han's face gentled. "You lack patience, my child."

Jade's grandmother stepped around her husband and helped Jade to her feet. "Tsk," she said, "what do men know?"

Jade was pleasantly surprised by her grandmother's support, but worry for T. Stratton sapped most of her pleasure. At the door, she gave Wrinks one last hug and promised her grandfather she'd be careful.

She was backing down the long drive when she met Mikki and Mei Li driving in.

"Jade, we're so glad to see you. We've been concerned," scolded Mei Li. "We tried going to the shed, but the police have it cordoned off. Why didn't you call us?" she accused. "And why are you going out again in this downpour?"

"T. Stratton's been injured," Jade managed to stammer. "I'm going to do whatever I can to help."

Mikki pursed his lips. "I hope Jennings appreciates your loyalty, Jade."

Mei Li shushed him. "Jade's grandparents will soon forget being hurt, Mikki. Already, my parents have."

"Oh, please," begged Jade, extending a hand. "I must hurry. Did you mean what you said about volunteering? I'd welcome your help now."

"You lead and we'll follow. Our debt to you is great, Jade," Mikki said, changing tack and giving his support.

Jade fretted over delays caused by slow traffic and she worried constantly about T. Stratton's condition. The only positive thing she could see countering a whole list of negatives was that the winds had died down. The rain had begun to slacken as she approached Rosemont Street and turned toward the float barns. At the next intersection, she had to talk her way through a maze of police. Even two blocks from the sheds, streets were littered with overturned pots, bent and mutilated foliage and debris.

Jade pulled in beside Greg's pickup. Joe wheeled in right behind Mikki and jumped out of his truck almost before the engine shut off. His face was pasty white and his lips were set in a grim line.

"Yo, Jade," he called in a low voice. "Have you been inside yet? What do you estimate is the extent of our damage?"

She let her engine idle. "I haven't. I just arrived. What about T. Stratton? On the news they said he'd been hurt."

Joe massaged his neck. "I stopped by Desert Memorial. He's holding his own. So far they've turned up a compound fracture of his left leg and one or two broken ribs. He's anxious as hell about the financial setback. Cynthia heard the news. She's there and has promised to keep me informed. I decided T.J. would be happier if I zipped back here and got to work."

"Well, I'm going to the hospital. I want to make sure he's all right," Jade said, revving up her car.

Joe shook his head. "What will you do at the hospital? You're needed more here. We've got less than a week to get these floats put back together. The flower loss alone gives me shivers."

Her face fell. She wanted to see for herself how he was. Yet in a way the floats *were* T. Stratton. "He won't like it, Joe, but I know where we can get foliage," she said, biting her lip.

"Don't let being our Cinderella girl go to your head, Jade. It would take more than a fairy godmother to find foliage at this late date. We aren't talking a few daisies here. And it's not just us. Float-builders unite when disaster strikes. I'm willing to listen to any idea, but I can't chance a repeat of one other year, when a big freeze wiped out all the poinsettias. One of our more enterprising volunteers swore he could supply them. T.J. was so busy with last-minute problems, he gave the kid the keys to his Wagoneer and told him to get get 'em." Joe smiled. "Sure enough, this guy was as good as his word. He returned with a load of poinsettias. We no sooner glued down the last petal when the police arrived. Our volunteer had made a trip through Forest Lawn—you know, the cemetery?"

They all laughed as Joe helped Jade from her car. "I guess you know T.J. was livid. For a minute, I thought he was going to explode. Then he saw the humor. We settled on a public apology, a healthy fine and the parade went on as scheduled. Oh, the stories I could tell if we only had time."

Jade's smile faded. "I don't have anything that drastic in mind. Oh, but look!" she cried, dashing toward the damaged floats.

Greg Sanders walked out from behind one, carrying a ladder. His freckles stood out against his white face as he presented them with a detailed list of structural damage. His words sobered everyone.

Crew members drifted in one at a time and all worked side by side throughout the afternoon and evening. The biggest job was clearing roof debris and covering the hole enough to block out the rain. It was almost ten o'clock when Jade paused for a breather. She felt guilty because no one had checked on T. Stratton. Tired as she was, she volunteered to go to the nearest all-night market for coffee and promised to phone the hospital.

Mikki and Mei Li elected to go home. Both said they'd be back to help the next day. They walked out hand in hand and Jade felt a stab of envy.

Later, her fingers shook as she fed a quarter into the slot of the pay telephone and asked to be put through to T. Stratton's room. The rain had let up, but temperatures were dropping. She prayed it wouldn't freeze. Although Joe had mentioned leaving Trask in the care of Cynthia, who'd flown back from Aspen when she'd heard the news, Jade wasn't prepared to have the woman answer in his room at this late hour. "This is Jade Han," she murmured through icy lips. "We've just taken a break and Joe asked me to check on T. Stratton." Her breath curled into the night air as she spoke.

"Joe promised to call me earlier," Cynthia accused. "They've taken Trask to surgery for a collapsed lung. I won't know anything until he's out of recovery. Have Joe call back around midnight.''

"I'll come right over," Jade blurted.

"Why? So you can worry him to death with those stupid floats? He already gives eighteen to twenty hours a day, Miss Han. Must he give his last breath, too?"

Jade felt the ground shift beneath her feet. She squeezed her eyes shut and gripped the receiver so tightly her knuckles ached. "How bad is he?" she whispered.

"Oh, I'm sure he'll recover with rest," Cynthia ground out. "But you realize this wouldn't have happened if he'd gone with me to Aspen!"

Jade was overcome by a rush of guilt. If she hadn't gone to his place for Christmas... Maybe in spite of what he'd said, he would have gone to Aspen. Perhaps what Cynthia said was true.

On the other end of the line, Cynthia quickly cut into her thoughts. "Have Joe call." Then before Jade could respond, there was a click.

Hanging up, she stared at the telephone until some man asked if she was taking up residence in the booth. Even though her fingers were numb, she gathered up her stray coins and hurried into the store to pick up coffee. Driving back to the shed, Jade felt as if her world had lost all focus and she was spinning like a top. T. Stratton didn't need her. Not really. He had Cynthia. Over and over the terrible truth slammed into her heart. All her dreams for becoming his partner evaporated like her breath on the cold air.

Before Jade delivered coffee to the crew, she removed the Cinderella slipper from around her neck and carefully cushioned it in the box she'd left in the glove compartment of her car. The crystal charm had lost its sparkle, as had her dream.

Closing the velvet lid, Jade wished she could box up her pain as effectively. *Shujing*, harmony, would never come to her now. A tear slid down her cheek and splashed on the lid of the box. No one had ever warned her that it would hurt so much, this shattering of an illusion.

TRASK STIRRED RESTLESSLY in his hospital bed. For almost a week, he'd been confined. He was feeling well enough to resent the immobility and bad enough to curse anyone unfortunate enough to stand within earshot. "No newspapers, no television, no visitors," he railed at Cynthia. "Is this a conspiracy? I want to know what's happening to my floats. Where in hell is Joe? Why do I pay him to manage if he can't even bring me reports? Or Nell? She's the financial wizard. Why doesn't she bring me an update on what all this damage is costing? Did you call them like I asked?"

"Come on, sweetie, settle down. You're beginning to get feverish. I'm only following doctor's orders." Cynthia patted his hand. "He doesn't want you getting upset over something you can't control. You spend entirely too much time walking a tightrope in this business. I've told you before, I know where you can get a job with better hours, less frustration and more money."

"Forget it, Cyn. I'm not cut out to be a banker and you know it." He shifted, attempting to turn onto his side. Failing, he gave up with a groan. "Damn it, where is Jade?" His eyes glittered with fever.

Cynthia spun away from the window and picked up her tote from the chair. "I'm tired of hearing you ask about your little designer. The doctor said not to bother you with float news, but I found this amusing." Pulling the entertainment section of the newspaper from her bag, she walked over and tossed it in his lap.

The headlines leaped out at Trask. "Visiting TV Star to Wed Sweetheart's Best Friend." The article told how Mikki Chan, grand master of wing chun and heartthrob of half of Asia, would marry not the woman selected for him by his family but Mei Li Ming, best friend of the chosen bride. It went on to mention that the newlyweds would make their home in Hong Kong following a lavish ceremony written into the script of Mr. Chan's series.

Letting the page slip from his fingers, Trask stared at the wall. He tried to remember what Jade had said about Mikki on Christmas Day. He should have listened. Had she, in fact, been humiliated? The way he'd left things between them had haunted him day and night.

Wadding up the newspaper, Trask flung it across the room. "No wonder the men haven't come to see me." They were probably furious with him for hurting Jade. He closed his eyes, needing to block out visions.

"So," he snarled, "how are they managing? What's happening? Get Joe down here on the double. Tell him I won't take no for an answer."

"Now, Trask—" Cynthia reached out a hand and smoothed his forehead "—you've got to relax. The doctor says you shouldn't fret about business. Pneumonia's a real danger." She straightened his covers. "You'd recover faster if you had some sun. Cozumel is nice, or Hawaii. What do you say? Give yourself an early vacation and I'll make reservations? We could call it a honeymoon," she said casually.

Trask's stormy gaze skipped over hers, then skidded back. "Honeymoon?" His mouth dropped open. "Cyn. We're friends. I've more or less considered you a sister. But marriage—no." He shook his head doggedly.

"I don't want you for a brother, T.J. Are you so buried in that company you can't see? Things were progressing between us until you started mooning over Jade Han. Have you forgotten Kitty? What would happen when the Hans shake your family tree?"

"Unlike you, I don't whitewash what I've been. Just leave it, Cynthia. You have no idea what I felt for Jade, what I'm feeling now. And it doesn't alter our situation. We're not suited. Someday you'll thank me."

"Fine. You don't have to hit me over the head. So who needs a workaholic husband?" Spinning on her heel, Cynthia slammed out of his room.

IT WAS NEW YEAR'S EVE and Jade slipped quietly into a broom closet at the drafty barn where they'd set up a makeshift office during the first phase of the crisis. She sank gratefully into the room's lone chair and felt the crinkle of paper in her jacket pocket. Pulling out the offending item, she struck her head with the palm of her hand. A week gone by, and she hadn't yet taken time to mail the get-well card to T. Stratton.

She'd been on her way to post it when she overheard Nell and Joe talking about the company's finances. Joe agreed that two bad years, coupled with T.J.'s having borrowed against their buildings, as well as an expensive hospital stay, might be enough to tip the scales irrevocably into the red. She had taken it upon herself to order in the flowers and redouble her work efforts. But T. Stratton was never far from her thoughts.

"Ah, Jade. I figured I might find you here." Joe Forrester stuck his head around the door.

She quickly stuffed the card back into her pocket and nervously brushed a lock of hair from her smudged forehead. "I thought if I didn't sit down a minute, Joe, I'd fall down. But I'm ready to help wherever I'm needed. Sorry I hid out. I know we only have one day left to accomplish miracles."

"No, no!" He held up a hand. "Sit back down. You've already accomplished miracles. All the float-company owners are indebted to you for helping with the flowers. It hasn't been easy keeping the truth from T.J., but I haven't said a word, as you requested. I can't believe he refused the discount the first time. No, I take that back." Joe chuckled. "No prouder or more stubborn man exists than our boss. Yet if you needed it, he'd give you the last dime he had, no questions asked."

Jade looked thoughtful. "He'll be furious when he finds out what I've done, Joe. But it's almost over. Tonight we'll be up all night feathering the birds on the Hawaiian float. Greg's gone now to meet a late shipment of Dutch iris." She sighed. "With the new snowfall in the mountains, we lost half our high school volunteers. But never mind that now. I'm sure you had other reasons for tracking me down. Is T. Stratton okay?"

"I guess. It's been three days since anyone's been to see him. I swear you've lost twenty pounds and you've got none to spare, Jade. If T.J. doesn't thank you when all is said and done, he's not the man I think he is. Outside of the few hours you took off for Mikki and Mei Li's wedding, you've been here around the clock. Not that I begrudge anyone a honeymoon, but we're going to feel the pinch of their defection, too."

"I'll tell Mikki you said that. He actually had so much fun he wanted to stay. And you're a fine one to talk. Hillary dropped by this morning just so your kids could recall what their dad looks like."

Joe rubbed the back of his neck. "Hillary planned to visit T.J., but our youngest started throwing up. Flu, I guess. I called to check with Cynthia and got transferred to the nursing station. The boss is running a fever. They've begun treatment for some secondary infection. The nurse said it'll be a few days before he can have visitors." Joe grinned. "Knowing T.J., he'd get out of a deathbed to watch the parade on TV."

Jade glanced away. "Can you believe another new year starts the day after tomorrow? A whole float season gone and it seems like only yesterday I met the crew," she said wistfully. "Has anyone told T. Stratton you're all dashing out of here after the parade for vacations?"

"It's the same every year." Joe snapped his fingers. "That reminds me. Hank called to say he's taken a job designing sets for one of the major movie studios. This opens up a permanent job at Fantasy Floats. I haven't talked to T.J., but I'm sure it's yours if you want it."

Tears filled Jade's eyes. A week ago she'd have jumped at the chance. But things were different now. What if T. Stratton and Cynthia...? She didn't complete the thought. Instead she shrugged. "Let's see if we win any awards, shall we? T. Stratton sets great store by awards." Rising, she walked to the door, needing to get away before her tears fell.

"I'm betting we'll take at least three," Joe predicted, following her. "The Humor award, the Animation, and very possibly the Theme trophy." He yanked a lock of hair falling over her eyes. "Not bad for a beginner," he teased. "Why so glum?"

"It's partly that I miss my grandparents, I guess." Her voice cracked. "Don't forget we promised the volunteers a special party at the end of all this. They deserve it, as hard as both shifts have worked. Hasn't the response by the community been heartwarming? I only hope I can hold up to the end. I've never torn apart so many flowers or glued so much pampas grass and eucalyptus bark as this week. Look—my fingers may never be the same." She managed to force a laugh.

THE PARADE WAS a success. Except for the mechanical failure of a competitor's float heading north on Orange Grove, which Jade and Greg worked feverishly to get running and back on the route, things went without a hitch. She helped the Rasmussen brothers, too. Remembering the trouble they'd caused when they stole the coach, Jade thought about making them grovel. But she didn't, of course. The loss of Charlie's float with the flying magic carpet would have disappointed the many viewers who'd braved the cold weather.

Ready to drop, Jade heaved a sigh of relief as the last float rolled into Victory Park, where they would be left on display for leisurely viewing. It was there she learned that Fantasy Floats had garnered a total of four awards. In addition to the ones Joe had mentioned, her favorite float had taken the Sweepstake trophy. Everywhere Jade turned, someone hurried to congratulate her. It should have been the happiest day of her life. So what was wrong?

Feeling a terrible letdown following the last burst of adrenaline, Jade grew melancholy. It could be as simple as missing Mei Li and her grandparents. Until her family left, she hadn't realized the narrowness of her world. After today, it would be smaller still. The way her heart sped up each time she heard someone mention T. Stratton's name, Jade knew she had only one choice. She must end all contact with float-building.

Slipping away, unable to face telling the crew members goodbye, Jade climbed into her car and resolutely made her way to the warehouse. As she stepped through the door for what would be the last time, Jade refused to think about how much she'd miss working here. Cleaning out her personal effects didn't take long. What took time was writing a farewell note to T. Stratton.

After much consideration and a few salty tears, Jade settled on saying he'd been right all along—she wasn't cut out for the work. She left the flower stock certificates as her parting gift to the crew. He could hardly refuse something meant for them. More difficult to leave behind was the glass slipper. Jade tried three times to say what was in her heart. Each time some memory rose up to intrude. At last she ripped all her attempts to shreds and stuffed the brief note along with the mangled get-well card into a manila envelope and put T. Stratton's name on the front.

She was tempted to call the hospital one last time to check on his condition. But feeling too fragile to deal with Cynthia's shrewish tongue and seeing no point in prolonging any anguish to herself, Jade left the building, acknowledging she was a jellyfish where T. Stratton Jennings was concerned.

As SOON AS HE WAS pronounced recovered from his bout with a bacterial infection, Trask badgered the doctor into releasing him. Parade day had passed, and for the first time since starting this crazy business, he'd been too sick to care. Now his entire crew was off, gone on their respective vacations. The nurses had relayed their messages. There was none from Jade, but then, he hadn't really expected one. Joe listed the awards they'd collected and had tacked on a postscript about Hank's taking a new job. Somehow, Trask couldn't bear the thought of looking for a designer.

Moments after he convinced the doctor he'd mastered crutches, Trask called for a cab. His first stop was the warehouse, but he was ill-prepared for the wave of nostalgia that struck him when he stepped inside.

The sights, the smells, even the drawings hanging along the walls reminded him of Jade. Only now did he realize how very much he'd miss her smile, her enthusiasm and her diligence. Damn, but it wasn't fair. Just when he'd begun to count on her for his sense of well-being, she'd vanished like smoke. It shocked him to find he wanted her back. He'd even miss watching her lead those damned enchanting exercises.

Angry, Trask thrust the image away and hobbled into the office to check the stack of mail Nell had left. Another disappointment was the camp dedication. It had been postponed until mid-January. Max was undergoing chemotherapy. Trask blinked. Something must have flown into his eye.

The first page in his stack was Nell's neat profit-and-loss statement. Fantasy Floats was running in the black even after all the bills were paid. Trask studied each column. Nell must be a magician.

There were a number of letters from competitors thanking him for the outstanding help his crew had given after the storm. He smiled. His team always went the extra distance. First chance, he'd tell them how proud he was. Puzzled by the mention of his generosity in terms of flowers, Trask set a few notes aside to check with Joe.

The next item was a large manila envelope. He opened it and out fell the jeweler's box he'd given Jade and a bent, stamped envelope. Grimacing, he ripped it open—it was a get-well card. So she hadn't forgotten. And there were certificates in a Netherlands flower company, too, along with an impersonal note written in Jade's flowery scrawl.

Hesitating, Trask rechecked each item. It took several minutes for the truth to hit him. Jade had saved Fantasy Floats from ruin. His and several others, too, from the looks of it.

With his heart racing, he reached for the phone. He owed her a big apology. A recording informed him that number was no longer in service. Slamming the instrument back in its cradle, Trask decided he'd take a run over to Beverly Hills. The drive would do him good; he'd been cooped up too long. Snatching up the charm, which he was determined she keep, he propelled himself slowly to his Wagoneer.

Trask managed to reach Jade's house just as the sun was beginning its descent. As he made his way to her front door, he couldn't help wondering how Wrinks would react to his cast. Never once had he come to visit that the dog hadn't attacked his pant leg. He grinned. If it was a case of "love me, love my dog," he was prepared to bribe the ferocious mop of fur with a juicy steak.

The doorbell echoed hollowly inside the house. After three attempts, Trask reluctantly admitted that no one was home. He was standing in the driveway, fighting disappointment, when a neighbor called, "Are you looking for the new owners or the old?"

New owners! Trask felt a chill run down his spine. "I'm looking for Jade Han," he called back.

"Oh." The neighbor nodded. "Her grandparents moved to Hong Kong. Jade stayed in the area, I believe. Someone said she moved to Redondo Beach."

The knot in Trask's stomach unraveled. "I've been laid up a while." He tapped the cast. "Do you happen to know where she went?"

"It was a house she's had her eye on. There was a deal pending, but it fell through and she snapped the place up. Sorry I can't be of more help."

It was a long shot, Trask knew, but just possibly it was the house she'd admired the day they'd argued about the flowers. He wasn't even sure he could find the street again, especially now in the waning light.

Struggling to get himself and his crutches back in the Wagoneer, Trask felt a ripple of fear. What if she hadn't bought that house? He'd feel pretty stupid hammering on some stranger's door after dark. But the need to find her was overwhelming.

It wasn't quite dark when he spotted the house on the knoll. A thick mist was beginning to roll in off the ocean. If this wasn't the most impulsive thing he'd ever done, it ranked right up there, Trask thought, stopping and swearing to himself as his crutches sank into the soft, damp sand.

Suddenly he saw her walking toward him out of the fog, and all his discomfort dissipated like heat curling up through a chimney. She had her head bent and appeared to be talking to the stubby-legged dog trotting briskly at her side.

Her cap of midnight-black hair—a modern cut he'd come to love—was gilded in mist and tangled by the wind. He remembered how she'd looked the very first time he'd seen her. His angel come to life. Trask thought now, as he had then, that she'd been sent for his salvation.

Jade looked up, sensing someone approach. She thought the shrouded figure was a figment of her imagination. The smile she'd had for Wrinks's antics died on her lips. "T. Stratton?" His name came out huskily.

He hobbled toward her.

"It is you," she gasped. "Should you be walking on that leg?"

Wrinks bounded across the sand. He ran right up to Trask, then stopped and sniffed at the open-toed cast. When the dog started to lick his toes, Trask laughed with relief. "Look. Fudog welcomes me. It's a good sign. I don't work these crutches well enough yet to do a fifty-yard dash."

"Quit clowning, T. Stratton. Can you manage the stairs? It's getting cold out here." She rushed to his side and let him lean on her. As his arm slipped around her shoulders, the ice that had been forming around her heart began to melt. Still, she lacked the courage to ask him why he'd come.

The trip up the steps to the house took some doing. Both were winded by the time Jade unlocked the door and ushered him inside.

For long moments, Trask stood there and let the warmth of her new home seep into his tired limbs. Even with boxes sitting around, it spoke to him of comfort—of permanence and family.

"I came to apologize, Jade," he said quietly, while she bustled around turning up the heat. "Will you forgive me?"

She turned, her eyes registering surprise. "Me? Forgive you?" She bent to remove Wrinks's collar. "You wouldn't have been hurt if it hadn't been for me. Do you forgive *me?*"

"How do you figure that?" He looked genuinely perplexed.

"If not for me, you'd have gone to Aspen with Cynthia."

He shook his head. "You mean you didn't believe me when I said I'd never do that?"

"No." She glanced over her shoulder with a sober look. "Does Cynthia?"

"She does now," he said. "Say, I read about the wedding. And your neighbor said your grandparents have moved to Hong Kong. I'm not sorry you didn't marry Mikki, but I'm sorry if your working caused trouble."

"It's been Mikki and Mei Li almost from the start," she said and related the full story at last. She ended by saying, "I'm delighted they fell in love." Drifting over to the mantel, she lightly touched a replica of her Cinderella coach. "Are you saying you and Cynthia ... ?"

"Never," he repeated, reaching out to touch her cheek.

She wheeled away. "I'm confused, T. Stratton."

He joined her in front of the fireplace. "Cynthia has never been the problem between us, Jade. A long time ago, I was jilted by a girl who thought more of family money than she did of me. And ever since then ... Well, false pride is tough to shake."

She turned, letting her gaze scan his face. The golden eyes she'd once thought dangerous showered her in a hail of sparks that set her heart ablaze. "So you cast me in the same mold?" She held her breath.

He looked steadily into her eyes. "Not really. Underneath, I always wanted to slay dragons for you, Jade. My own ambivalence is what made believing in you so difficult."

"And now?" She tilted her head to one side and smiled.

"Now—this minute?" He shook his head regretfully. "The most I could slay is small spiders, I'm afraid." He tapped a crutch to his thigh-high cast.

Her grin erupted in laughter. "It'd serve you right if I accepted your offer! There's one on the ceiling in my spare bedroom. So far it's a standoff."

"Now if it was *your* bedroom..." He winked. "When are your grandparents due back?"

"They aren't coming back." She chewed her lip, frowning. "Why do you ask?"

"You said they were traditional. I plan to ask for your hand in marriage." Lifting her fingers to his lips, he kissed them. "None of this dowry stuff, though," he growled.

She swallowed a quick intake of breath and her hand flew to her breast. "You want to marry me?"

"I don't have a ring," he said, catching her fingers. "But wait." Dropping her hand, he fumbled in his pocket until he found the box holding the glass slipper. "Would you accept this as a token of my intentions—until I can do better?" He dropped his crutches and drew her into the circle of his arms. "I'm trying to say I love, you, Jade."

Her heart skipped a beat. "I love you too, T. Stratton." She touched a hand wonderingly to his face. "The glass slipper is better than a ring. Before I rushed off to see how badly you were hurt, Grandmother gave me some advice. Should my prince come bearing a glass slipper, she said, I needn't think twice—just prove it's mine." Jade laughed. "Grandfather Han always maintained that if I waited, *shujing*—which means perfect harmony—would come into my life of its own accord. Grandmother told me to give *shujing* a nudge. Would you believe she admitted doing the same to win my grandfather? Her solution was quite modern."

Trask placed the chain around her neck and fastened it. "Oh? How modern?" he asked, bending to kiss the smooth skin between her breasts where the crystal gleamed brightly.

Her laugh was like a rich melody. "Not *that* modern. The old method of courtship is part of the mystique," she teased, leaning back enough to sneak her arms around his neck. "But I accept your proposal, T. Stratton," she breathed, reaching up to seal their bargain with an old-fashioned yet thoroughly modern kiss.

"You rode out a tough year," he said, nibbling at her neck. "It's an unpredictable business, Jade, but it's in my blood."

"Mine, too," she murmured. "Won't you please let me help? Financially, I mean?"

"No, keep your money."

"I've been thinking—why couldn't I be a partner? Like Max was." At his frown, she added quickly, "Don't you want to build a legacy for our children?" She pulled his face back for a kiss.

He pressed closer. "You want children? You never said. All you've talked about is a design career."

"I could design floats at home." She ran her hands lazily beneath his shirt. "Upstairs in the third bedroom."

He bit back a groan. "Okay...partner." He smiled. "Mmm, I could get used to the sound of that. Partners... Well, partner, we have three weeks before the season starts again. If you don't object to marrying a man in a cast, we could honeymoon in Hong Kong and ask for your grandparents' blessing after the fact."

"Oh, could we?" she breathed. "I'd like to see them settled."

Wrinks barked excitedly and bathed Trask's bare toes with a wet, sloppy kiss. Trask teetered, a little off balance. "Sorry, Fudog. We'll find you a sitter, okay? Maybe Nell?" Jade nodded. "We'll need to be back in time for the camp dedication," he went on. "I want you to meet Max."

Jade smiled and glanced down, thinking to scold Wrinks away, but the strangest thing happened. For just a moment, she could have sworn she was wearing a long gown of the finest blue satin, with a full skirt standing out against the white of T. Stratton's cast. All around them, strange wild music seemed to fill the air, and deep inside, the two halves of her heart, American and Chinese, clicked together in one final perfect match. *Shujing*. How wise a man, her grandfather. How diplomatic a woman, her grandmother.

my VALENTINE 1992

Celebrate the most romantic day of the year with
MY VALENTINE 1992—a sexy new collection of four
romantic stories written by our famous Temptation
authors:

> GINA WILKENS
> KRISTINE ROLOFSON
> JOANN ROSS
> VICKI LEWIS THOMPSON

My Valentine 1992—an exquisite escape into a romantic
and sensuous world.

 Harlequin Books®

VAL-92

HARLEQUIN
PROUDLY PRESENTS
A DAZZLING NEW CONCEPT IN ROMANCE FICTION

One small town—twelve terrific love stories

Welcome to Tyler, Wisconsin—a town full of people
you'll enjoy getting to know, memorable friends and
unforgettable lovers, and a long-buried secret that
lurks beneath its serene surface....

JOIN US FOR A YEAR IN THE LIFE OF TYLER

Each book set in Tyler is a self-contained love story;
together, the twelve novels stitch the fabric of a
community.

LOSE YOUR HEART TO TYLER!

The excitement begins in March 1992, with
WHIRLWIND, by Nancy Martin. When lively, brash
Liza Baron arrives home unexpectedly, she moves
into the old family lodge, where the silent and
mysterious Cliff Forrester has been living in seclusion
for years....

WATCH FOR ALL TWELVE BOOKS
OF THE TYLER SERIES
Available wherever Harlequin books are sold

Back by Popular Demand

Janet Dailey
Americana

A romantic tour of America through fifty favorite
Harlequin Presents, each set in a different state
researched by Janet and her husband, Bill. A journey
of a lifetime in one cherished collection.

In January, don't miss the exciting states featured in:

Title #23 **MINNESOTA**
Giant of Mesabi

#24 **MISSISSIPPI**
A Tradition of Pride

Available wherever
Harlequin books are sold.

Harlequin Superromance®
Family ties...

SEVENTH HEAVEN

In the introduction to the Osborne family trilogy,
Kate Osborne finds her destiny with Police
Commissioner Donovan Cade.

Available in December

ON CLOUD NINE

Kate's second daughter, Juliet, has old-fashioned
values like her mother's. But those values are tested
when she meets Ross Stafford, a jazz musician,
sometime actor and teaching assistant . . . and the
object of her younger sister's affections. Can Juliet
only achieve her heart's desire at the cost of her
integrity?

Coming in January

SWINGING ON A STAR

Meridee is Kate's oldest daughter, but very much her
own person. Determined to climb the corporate
ladder, she has never had time for love. But her life is
turned upside down when Zeb Farrell storms into
town determined to eliminate jobs in her company—
her sister's among them! Meridee is prepared to do
battle, but for once she's met her match.

Coming in February

Rebels & Rogues

All men are not created equal. Some are rough around the edges. Tough-minded but tenderhearted. Incredibly sexy. The tempting fulfillment of every woman's fantasy.

When it's time to fight for what they believe in, to win that special woman, our Rebels and Rogues are heroes at heart.

Josh: He swore never to play the hero . . . unless the price was right.

THE PRIVATE EYE by Jayne Ann Krentz.
Temptation #377, January 1992.

Matt: A hard man to forget . . . and an even harder man not to love.

THE HOOD by Carin Rafferty.
Temptation #381, February 1992.

At Temptation, 1992 is the Year of Rebels and Rogues. Look for twelve exciting stories about bold and courageous men, one each month. Don't miss upcoming books from your favorite authors, including Candace Schuler, JoAnn Ross and Janice Kaiser.

Available wherever Harlequin books are sold.   RR-1

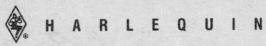

HARLEQUIN

A Calendar of Romance

Be a part of American Romance's year-long celebration of love and the holidays of 1992. Experience all the passion of falling in love during the excitement of each month's holiday. Some of your favorite authors will help you celebrate those special times of the year, like the revelry of New Year's Eve, the romance of Valentine's Day, the magic of St. Patrick's Day.

Start counting down to the new year with

#421 HAPPY NEW YEAR, DARLING
by Margaret St. George

Read all the books in *A Calendar of Romance*, coming to you one each month, all year, from Harlequin American Romance.

American Romance®